MW00748397

Sheila
Baby's First Zombie Apocalypse

Brian Malbon

Copyright © 2014 Brian Malbon
All rights reserved.

ISBN-10: 1-62827-962-1
ISBN-13: 978-1-62827-962-7

Without limiting the rights under copyright reserved above, no part
of this publication may be reproduced, stored, or transmitted in
any form or by any means, without prior written permission of the
publisher of this book.

This book is a work of fiction. Names, characters, places, and
incidents are products of this author's imagination or are used
fictitiously. Any resemblance to actual events or locales or persons
living or dead is entirely coincidental.

Published by Bad Day Books, an imprint of
Assent Publishing

To my children, for giving me a reason to write,
and to Jennifer, for giving me someone to write for.

PROLOGUE

Nine o'clock in the morning and the day was already warm—too warm in fact and shaping up to be a scorcher. Carrie shielded her eyes against the glare of sun on the water and wished she'd thought to bring sunglasses. Behind and beside her, two tiny sets of hands tugged on her clothes, two tiny mouths shrieked at her and at each other. Carrie heard their shrieks and whines as if from another reality. She felt the cold stares of the people around her, a mixture of pity and revulsion. Poor lazy irresponsible woman cannot even reign in her own children.

Joke's on you people, she thought, *these kids aren't mine.* Carrie sighed and wished for the thousandth time that she'd thought this plan through a little more.

Forgetting her sunglasses was just a symptom, an early indicator that today was going to go badly and fast. It had seemed like such a great plan in the cool of the evening, watching the Wonder Twins compete for the attention of their busy parents. What a simple, wonderful idea to take advantage of the warm September weather and get the kids out of the house. Centreville would only be open for one

1

more week this season and the girls had never been to the place. They could spend the day there, eat lunch on the grass, ride the rides before the twins grew too large for them, build some real memories. Carrie could actually see them all having fun for a change, and maybe the twins would finally warm up to her.

Who knew, maybe she would even warm up to them.

Everything seems perfect in the idea stage. Reality often steps in and works hard to give you the exact opposite experience from the one you intended. She hadn't counted on Indian Summer crossing into a full-bore heat wave with the humidity up in the thirties and not even a light breeze coming off the lake. She hadn't counted on every other parent and caregiver in the city having precisely the same idea as her—and to judge from the crowd cramming the ferry like sardines, that was almost exactly what was happening—and she especially hadn't counted on the Wonder Twins. For some reason, in her mind she'd imagined the girls would be somehow transformed by the potential of the day into perfect little angels. Instead, they were just as petulant and demanding as always.

A sailboat cruised by on her left, creating a gentle wake and looking more peaceful than Carrie had felt in a long time. She could barely see the captain, a bronzed blip on the white deck, steering with both hands on the comically oversized tiller. She pictured the wind in his hair as he pushed ahead, running the motor in the dead calm, sail hanging limp in front of him but free. For about a thousand times since the semester started without her, she questioned her life choices, and wasn't sure she liked where they were leading her.

She'd always believed in the honor and dignity of hard work, and in the importance of the work she was studying for. Teaching children wasn't a choice, she felt it was a calling. It was what she was meant to do. On the other hand, the path she was on left absolutely zero chance of ever affording her the luxury of cruising idly around the harbor on a yacht on a weekday. She wondered if—

"Look, a sailboat!" shouted Maddy.

"I wanna go on a sailboat!" chimed in Addy. "Carrie, take us on a sailboat!"

Carrie knelt down to the level of the girls' little faces. "We can't go on a sailboat today," she said in her most pleasant voice. "Remember, we're going to go ride on a Ferris wheel, and a train, and eat cotton candy, and—"

"But I wanna go on a *sail*boat!" Maddy screamed, stamping her tiny foot and bursting into loud false tears. Her sister, deciding she wasn't going to let Maddy have all the fun, launched into her own tantrum. Now all eyes on the ferry were on her and the two screaming four-year-olds. Carrie sighed and took a page out of their mother's own parenting handbook; she ignored them both, staring instead out over the lake as she watched the yacht sail out of sight on sun-dappled water.

In the excitement of docking at Ward's Island and the chance to run around on endless green grass, the girls forgot to be miserable for a bit. They ran shrieking with delight, wild smiles on their chubby cheeks and endless wonder in their big blue eyes. The sun on their hair turned their curls to gold. Carrie was beginning to think she hated them.

It had made sense to take a summer job in the same field she was studying. Mrs. Abernathy was a power-suit-wearing, Bluetooth-type success story whose nanny had quit without notice that spring. Carrie was the perfect choice for a temporary replacement, and having a place to stay rent-free for the summer meant that all of the money she made could go toward her tuition. The girls seemed sweet enough, and anyway, it was only until September.

Then it was July, and Mrs. Abernathy hadn't found anybody to replace her yet.

Somehow, she found herself agreeing to take a semester off. The money was ridiculous; not only could she pay off her loans from the past year but even have a good chunk left over for next year. She might not even *need* a loan when she went back. The offer was too good to be true, and she hadn't really had time to become frustrated by Mrs. Abernathy's professional disdain, her keep-those-kids-away-from-me-at-all-times attitude except when she wanted to look like a mother in front of somebody. She hadn't yet had time to discover Addison and Madison's—yes, those were their names; how they would grow to hate their parents—screechy entitlement.

The girls were already getting tired by the time they arrived at the park. A wide footbridge bordered by gorgeous willow trees welcomed any and all to Centreville Amusement Park, the Toronto Islands' first and foremost tourist attraction. On the other side of the bridge, wonders awaited anyone under the age of six: swan-shaped pedal boats, a bright blue child-sized train that circled the park, rides and toys and candy, oh my! But Carrie was beginning to doubt they would ever enjoy any of it. With the heat bearing down even in the cool shade of the willows and the twins' energy spent on the grass before they even went in, it would be a wonder if they even made it over the bridge.

"Come on, girls," she said, taking their hands, "We're

going to have some fun today if it kills us."

Their tiredness forgotten as soon as they crossed the bridge, Addy and Maddy were soon pulling Carrie in two directions at once. Addy wanted a balloon from a man who was walking by with a dozen floating SpongeBobs tied to his belt. Maddy wanted to ride on the train, never mind that they hadn't gotten tickets yet. When Carrie saw the line for the ticket booth, her heart sank.

"Okay, we just have to wait for a little bit in this line-up, and then we can go do whatever you want, okay?"

"But I want a balloon NOW!" screamed Addy, wrenching her hand away from Carrie's. Carrie snatched it back and held on, screaming or no.

The line was interminable. How much time did it take to buy a roll of tickets? They shuffled forward, a half step each time, until Carrie felt she was either going to have to go home or kill the kids—maybe both. Addison never stopped shrieking about the stupid balloon until finally she whirled on them, looked both girls dead in the eye at once—a trick that would no doubt save her ass in the classroom, she thought—and said, "Look. We are going to get balloons. And hot dogs and cotton candy and we are going to ride on lots of rides and have lots of fun. But if I hear even one more peep from either of you while we're in this line, we are going to turn around and walk away from this park, get back on the ferry, and go home. Then there will be no balloons and no rides. Do you understand me?" Too stunned to speak, the girls just nodded, their eyes wide as dinner plates. Nobody had ever spoken to them like that before. Carrie stood up again and faced forward. "Not one peep," she repeated.

When her turn at the counter came, she suddenly

understood why the line was so slow. There were too many choices. Did she want a Family Bundle of forty tickets or a single strip of ten? Or a ride-all-day wristband? She didn't even know how many tickets a single ride took.

"What should I get?" she asked the bored-looking teenager. "We're here all day, but I don't know how many rides they can go on."

The kid looked down at the twins through waves of gelled black hair that hung in spikes in front of his eyes and shrugged. "Get the wristband," he said. "It's thirty bucks and you don't have to come back."

She could see in his eyes that neither one of them wanted her to come back here. Besides, it was Mrs. Abernathy's money she was spending, not hers. "Three wristbands, please."

She had to drop the kids' hands to reach into her purse for the debit card. Just like that, ninety dollars gone and they hadn't done anything yet. "Come here, girls, the man has to put these bracelets on us." She looked down. Madison stared silently up at her. Her hands were stuffed in the pockets of her overalls and her eyes were scared but defiant. Addison was gone.

They hadn't made a peep.

Nobody ever told the Abernathy twins *no*. They always got what they wanted. Their mother made sure that they never lacked for anything their little hearts desired, except perhaps attention. Addison wanted a balloon, and so she would get one; that was how it *worked*, and Carrie was nothing but a mean old lady who didn't understand.

Addy wove through a thick forest of bare legs and strollers, keeping one eye on the floating cloud of grinning

SpongeBobs bobbing above the crowd. It didn't occur to her that he might not let her have one without money; the world didn't work that way for her.

The cloud of bug-eyed yellow balloons tied to the man's belt wove this way and that, past the train, down by the swans, up by the bridge. In the heat and the chaos and the teeming of the crowd, no one looked twice at the four-year-old girl moving with deadly purpose in hot pursuit.

Until someone did.

He didn't know how long he'd stood there in the shade with his shoes soaked in water and his shirt soaked with blood. How long he'd wandered since he'd risen or how many people he'd encountered, he could not have said. He lived in a world of white. His empty eyes stared out at nothing and his jaws worked rhythmically up and down, anticipating chewing, keeping in practice.

He saw shapes but they made no sense. He heard sounds but they came in too many directions to focus on one. Occasionally, some bright color would splash across his fractured vision and he would move to it, but always some other noise or movement would draw him another way.

In an ideal world, he would have stood there, paralyzed by choices he had no ability to make. In an ideal world, someone would have looked beneath the bridge and seen his tattered clothes, his ruined face, and called the police.

Instead, a splash of bright yellow passed right in front of him, drawing his eyes. Instead, he took a step forward, then another, because something small and fast was running straight toward him, a small blur of pulsing life that shrieked "Ballooooooon!!!" at the top of its high-pitched voice.

Base instinct took over. The world of white turned red.

She wanted a goddamn balloon, thought Carrie, *Jesus Christ, she'd better be all right or I'll kill her.*

She shoved her way through the crowd, holding Madison's arm in an iron grip and dragging her behind. She kept her eyes on the balloons waving above the crowd. Madison was crying, and the eyes of a thousand judgmental people were on her. *Where were you two minutes ago,* she thought.

"Addy!" she called, more for their benefit than hers. She knew where Addy was going, but maybe people would get out of the goddamn way and *help* her if they understood. "Addison!"

She rounded the bend and was crossing the tiny train tracks when she heard the scream and doubled her pace.

Addison stood on a wide, grassy bank, frozen in terror. Looming above her was a face that would haunt Carrie the rest of her short life. Grinning through a torn cheek, blood dribbling from his gashed lips and down his chin, eyes like white embers in hollow dark sockets. Someone was screaming, but no one was moving. Addy herself was rigid, too frightened to run or scream or even move.

Carrie didn't think. She raced down the bank and her fingers closed on the back of Addy's overalls. She yanked her back and thrust her up the hill toward her sister. It was all she had time to do. The monster leaped with astounding speed, and then he was on top of her, hands and arms and teeth.

She had time to think a comforting thought: *I don't hate them. I'm not a monster.* Then she could only scream.

...listening to Talk News 1080, on this beautiful September day. And here's the weather!

Oh, it's gonna be another scorcher today, Bob. Temperatures in the mid-thirties and no relief in sight. We should see a break in the pressure by the weekend, but I wouldn't be making any barbecue plans, because...

...*zzt...zzt...*

...the victim of a savage drug-related attack at Centre Island this morning. Twenty-two year old Carrie Daniels was airlifted to Toronto General Hospital in critical condition, and authorities are saying that...

...*zzt...zzt...*

...the two children were returned to their parents and said to be doing fine, under the circumstances. The girls' mother, Linda Abernathy, is...

...*zzt...zzt...*

...rolling in from the south. We should expect some heavy rains by as early as next week, and I can guarantee you that, folks, or I'm not...

...*zzt...zzt...*

...calling Carrie Daniels a hero today, says an eyewitness on the scene. Carol Stephenson, who was visiting the park with her six-year old daughter, witnessed the attack. "It was horrible. He was like some kind of a... of a..."

...*zzt...zzt...*

...Zombie this morning? Then you need to stop in at King Street Coffee, where our fresh, delicious brew can even wake up the...

...*zzt...zzt...*

...dead. Doctors say they did everything they could, but the injuries sustained were too great. Carrie Daniels was a third-year education major at the University of Toronto, where a memorial is being held tonight at seven. Chief of Police Gord Roberts has vowed, "We will not rest until we have apprehended the perpetrator of this horrendous..."

...*zzt...zzt...*

...attacks reported all over the Toronto Islands this afternoon, all bearing a frightening resemblance to the savage mutilation of Carrie Daniels yesterday morning. Authorities are not saying if these are related *attacks or the work of a copycat, however eyewitness reports describe multiple assailants, with dozens of...*

...zzt...zzt...

...Kids! Yes, I'm talking to you, kids! Is school getting you down already? Do you need to take a break from all that homework? Then come on down to Crunch, the hottest new all-ages club in town! This Friday night, we're having a...

...zzt...zzt...

...party at an all-ages nightclub downtown quickly turned into what some authorities are calling a massacre, with over fifteen dead and more than two hundred injured, when several unidentified assailants wearing glow-in-the-dark contact lenses began attacking, and some say biting, the teenaged club goers. More on these...

...zzt...zzt...

...violent incidents at Toronto General Hospital as police and firefighters were called to the scene. No word on what occurred inside, but city officials have imposed a...

...zzt...zzt...

...quarantine of the entire...

...zzt...zzt...

...city as army units are...

...zzt...zzt...

...required to stay in your homes and lock all...

...zzt...zzt...

"-doors open at seven for the new...

...zzt...zzt...

...state of chaos and terror that has...

...zzt...zzt...

...overcome. Police forces in the downtown area have been overcome by what some are calling the most violent...

...zzzzz...

...night...

…zzt…zzt…
…of the…
…living…
…zzt…zzt…
…dead. I repeat, the dead are walking. They aren't staying dead. They're getting up and they're…they're fucking eating people! Goddammit, it's not a hoax, it's real! We need to get out of…
…zzt…zzt…
…
…

PART ONE
AFTER THE RAINS

CHAPTER ONE

The phone was sleek. Jet black and shiny, it was an object of beauty. It was the newest, the best, the most perfect merging of aesthetics and technology. It could surf the net, pick up Wi-Fi, and receive an IM seconds after it was sent from half a world away. In an instant, it could look up Thai restaurants in the area, link you to the best peer review pages, and give you turn-by-turn directions to get there from the exact spot you were standing in. The phone could see you from space. Oh, and it could also receive phone calls.

Its battery life was incredible. Days after its last charge, but the screen still lit up with an incoming call. An HD photo of the caller shone brightly from its flawless screen while the speaker belted out "Party Rockers" in 5-channel Dolby sound. It rang for about thirty seconds, then went dark again.

A pair of expensive but scuffed and filthy shoes turned toward it when it lit up. They began to move in the direction of the phone, the feet inside constantly in danger of pulling right out of its broken laces. Their pace began to quicken as they neared the sound and the light, always almost stumbling over each other. Then the ringing stopped, the phone went dead. The shoes stopped, too, stood in place for a few seconds looking as confused as shoes can, then turned and began slowly walking away down the cracked pavement.

The phone lay forgotten on a sidewalk on a deserted street in a rundown part of town. It lay next to an overturned garbage can, a smashed newspaper box, and a dried pool of brownish blood. Somehow, alone in the chaos of litter and carnage, the phone was unmarked. Not a scratch marred its perfect screen. Not a drop of blood touched its streamlined body.

The phone rang again. The owner of the shoes squatted by the remains of a car that had careened, crashed, and then exploded days ago, poking idly at bits of melted foam. Its head snapped up with a hunter's wary alertness, empty white eyes gleaming in the near-dark, lipless mouth drawn open in anticipation to bite. "Party Rockers" again urged the world to party, and possibly to rock. The man in the street stood up, turned, and began to stumble toward the sound. When he rounded the newspaper box and saw the brilliant, beautiful light shining from the sidewalk in oh so many colors, he quickened his stride. When he was about four feet away, the music stopped. The light shut off as fast as it had come on.

The man stopped, waiting alone in the wind and the twilight, his face forlorn and the tie of his expensive suit comically askew; he looked like a man who'd gone into the kitchen and then forgotten what he was doing there. Had the mere sight of his destroyed face not inspired a grisly horror, the tableau would look heartbreakingly sad. He stood still a moment more, then turned and walked away, just as he had every time the phone had rung in the last two days.

Directly above his head, from the safety of one of the last wrought-iron fire escapes in Toronto, Wendell Jenkins watched with revolted fascination. He'd been observing Phone Man for the past two hours, working his way through a warm six-pack of beer for lack of anything better to do. Watching the dead man enact his endless pattern, one that would no doubt continue forever unless the phone's battery died or the man's body rotted from under him, Wendell could only wonder, *how did they beat us?*

The phone probably wasn't going to ring again right away and the last thick drops of beer were sitting heavily in Wendell's stomach, so he stood up and brushed the rust from the seat of his pants. It would be full dark soon. It would be time to move.

Wendell had spent most of the past few days waiting and watching. Patience was his gift, and it had so far kept him alive much longer than he had expected. Longer than many others, he knew.

The third evening, after taking an electric saw to both of the building's stairwells, he'd retired to the fire escape to cool off. Down the street, just past where he could see, was an outdoor sports outfitter that did decent business before the outbreak. This wasn't the movies, and Ontario's gun control laws were strict, so Wendell had no illusions that the store offered a mecca of unclaimed firearms ripe for the plucking by stern-faced zombie hunters. The store might not have carried any guns, but apparently it was well stocked, because Wendell saw three men go racing down the street that night, whooping and hollering, armed with bows and bristling with arrows. They disappeared beyond the next building over from his, but Wendell could hear their hooting and calls to one another for some time after.

The next morning, he saw one of them slouching back the way he had come, eyes blank, his bow with its ruptured string dragging by its carry strap from one sliding boot.

Lesson One, thought Wendell. *Weapons aren't everything.* Wendell had learned a number of things from his observations. Tonight, he planned to put them to the test.

It was dark enough now that it was difficult to see Phone Man. A few more minutes, and it would be time. As quietly as he could, he slid the ladder off its hook and lowered it slowly to the ground.

The ladder met the pavement with a teeth-grinding *SCREEE* of rusted metal. Directly below him, a pair of white eyes swiveled around, locked on the sound and slicing the dusk with an unearthly glow. Wendell froze, staring down at those eyes unmoving. His right hand twitched toward the hatchet that hung from his belt. He forced himself to keep still. If it followed the noise, if it found the ladder, if it called its friends…

Somewhere in the bowels of an automated system, a timer clicked over, bathing the street, the building, and the zombie in bright yellow-orange light. Phone Man jerked, his head swinging around in a mad attempt to process every new stimulus at once, and fell on his side. After flailing on the ground roach-like for a bit he clambered to his feet and began wandering in the general direction of one of the streetlights. *Lesson two,* thought Wendell, *the dead have severe ADD.*

He gritted his teeth when his foot on the top rung made the ladder creak, but nothing moved on the street except Phone Man, and his attention was elsewhere. As quick and quiet as he could manage, he shimmied down to the ground. Seeing the street from this angle gave him a giddy feeling, a mingling of fear and relief. It had been days since he'd been outside the building.

Almost immediately, he felt a panicked urge to look every

direction at once, to spin his head around like the Phone Man to try to see who might be behind him now, or now, or... *now!* But he ignored the impulse. Panic would kill him. That was the first lesson. So would speed, so he forced down his second impulse, which was to *run*, run as fast as humanly possible and get this over with *now*, goddammit!

Instead, he walked with slow, measured steps. He kept his eyes moving and stayed in the light. If he was right, the light was where he was safest. His right hand gripped his hatchet. On his belt, dangling from a small carabiner, hung a small lump of plastic with a button. He carried the latter with all the care of a live grenade. It could either save or destroy him just as fast as one.

Phone Man was on his left now, completely entranced by something down the street. Wendell didn't bother to find out what. The street ahead of him was clear but for a pair of smashed up cars and one dead cat in the gutter. He stayed in the middle, right on the dotted white line.

The distance from his building to the co-op was maybe two city blocks, but it was the longest walk of Wendell's life. Nothing moved, in the shadow or the light, yet Wendell kept jumping at half-seen shadows and imagined movement. A darkened doorway hid unspeakable horrors. A stalled car— *was that a hand reaching out of the open door, or just a strap of seatbelt?* His every step was the beat of a bass drum on the pavement—BOOM! *Over here!* BOOM! *Over heeere! Come on out and play! Tear me to shreds and feast! Feast!* BOOM!

The silence unnerved him most of all. It was violent, it screamed. King Street was usually all noise: cars honking, engines revving, and people holding a thousand conversations at once as they moved through their day. Even at night, the city street was alive. There was a kind of music to it. Now there was nothing. Not even the wailing of a stray cat. Only the sound of death approaching on silent, padding feet, drawing ever closer behind him, coiling for the strike, a bare whisper of a hiss escaping its lips as Wendell whirled around. Nothing was there. All the way back to his building, the street was empty. Far away, Phone Man stared at the ground, looking lost.

Lesson One, he thought. *Quit imagining things.*

Vast and looming after block upon block of square brick apartment buildings and tiny storefront businesses, the co-op building was an imposing wall of darkness. The modern, glass-and-steel construction squatted beyond a parking lot of nearly two-dozen spaces, easily one of the bigger lots in this part of Toronto. Wendell's skin prickled when he looked at its front door, and it took him a moment to realize why; while the streetlights and most of the signs, billboards, and even windows in the area were lit right up in silent tribute to Ontario Hydro's commitment to the blackout-proof failsafe, the co-op was dark. Not one light shone from its windows, not even the federally mandated emergency lights. Wendell suppressed a sudden shudder.

Movement on his left made him turn. There was the first of them, coming up the sidewalk. Its face was in shadow; it could have been a man or a woman. It could have been still alive, for all Wendell could see, but for its gait. It walked with a rolling swagger, one leg taking too large a step for the other to catch up to, one arm hanging too low to be entirely comfortable. It was dead, and it was only the first of many. *Where one zombie was seen, a dozen more lurked nearby. That* was *Lesson One.*

Now or never. Go for the co-op or turn around and

hightail it back to the safety of the building. The moment of choice was now.

But Wendell knew there was no going back.

As quickly and silently as he knew how, Wendell loped across the parking lot to the blacked-out store. A muffled groan told him he'd been spotted. Abandoning all pretence to silence, he ran.

The large glass windows at the front presented an inviting target, but would only announce his presence even more and invite entrapment in the store in the dark as more and more mangled figures slipped in through the glass behind him. Some extra care was needed. He ducked around the side of the building, hugging the shadow. Just in time, he turned around to see a young man in ripped jeans and a green T-shirt come stumbling into the lot. He stopped short, his searchlight eyes glowing slightly in the dark. After a minute or two, he moved on up the street. He had forgotten all about Wendell Jenkins.

Wendell breathed a silent sigh of relief and turned toward the darkness of the alley. A pair of glowing white eyes floated in the dark directly in front of him.

"AAH!" blurted Wendell, the scream startled out of him.

"Uuh," said the zombie and leaped.

THUNK! went the hatchet into the zombie's skull.

To Wendell's utter shock and against the rules of every movie ever made on the subject, the zombie didn't drop from the first blow. It staggered and fell on its face as the momentum of its one burst of energy carried it downward instead of forward, but its hands scrabbled at the pavement and it rose to its knees. Its eyes turned upwards to regard Wendell with a pale white flame.

With mounting terror, Wendell gripped the axe handle and

yanked upwards. The axe didn't budge, lodged in the thing's skull like a knotty log. He jammed one heavy work boot on the zombie's neck, forcing it back to the pavement. Tough they might be, but long on endurance they weren't. Having spent its stored energy in its one failed pounce, the zombie lacked the strength to force its weight up. Getting leverage behind its head, Wendell worked the handle back and forth. The axe creaked as it slowly came loose, and Wendell had to fight down a wave of nausea. Finally, with a last pull that sent him staggering backwards, the handle came free. Wendell got to his feet, said a prayer, and buried the axe head into the back of its neck.

This time, the zombie dropped, stone still, to the ground. The glow faded from its eyes and one young man was at peace.

He had to hurry now. More would be coming, and soon.

He had to find a door.

At the back of the store was a loading dock, a concrete slab five feet high. Someone had cleverly stacked a dozen empty wooden skids against the steps leading up to the top, so Wendell jumped and hoisted himself up over the edge. He was breathing heavily now. The exertion let him know, in case he ever forgot, that he wasn't a young man anymore. Here beneath the building's overhang, the darkness was complete. Wendell didn't dare go for the tiny Maglite in his pocket. Instead, he fumbled at the walls looking for a handle.

When his hand closed on it, he was surprised to feel the latch move freely. A door opened to even greater blackness. He shut the door behind him and risked a light.

He stood at the edge of a storeroom. Dozens of corrugated-steel shelves marched off into the darkness in an orderly line. On the upper tiers, he could make out the shape of packing crates, but he had neither the time nor the means to discover whatever was in them. His best bet would be on the main sales floor, so he doused the light and followed one line of shelves with his hand. If he was not alone, he would see their eyes before they saw him.

After feeling onward only a few yards in complete darkness, a square of yellow light became visible to his left. Sure enough, a swinging door led out to the showroom floor, dimly lit from the streetlights out front. He caught the glint of knives in a display case and was making for it when the slide of a boot sliced through the silence. He froze.

Slowly, he turned toward the sound. Whoever it was stayed in the shadows. Now he heard others, quietly but purposefully moving into place to surround him.

"I'm not looking for trouble," he said, keeping his voice as calm as he could manage. "I came looking for supplies. I thought there was nobody here."

A low voice from somewhere to his right spoke. "You thought wrong."

Shit, thought Wendell. "I have nothing you need, and I don't want anything of yours. Let me leave in peace and I won't bother you again."

A figure rose up from behind the knife case Wendell had been heading for. It was a tall man, silhouetted by the streetlights, his face a shadow. The silhouette of the rifle in his hands spoke volumes, but the man made no sound.

"Why should we let you go?" said the voice from his right. "What happens when all your friends come back with you to steal what we've got?"

Was there even a point to reasoning with them? If they wanted to kill him, they could have already. But they wanted him to know who was in charge of the situation. They wanted him to humiliate himself, to beg for his life.

"Obviously, if I was coming with an army, we'd be here already," he said. "I told you before, I don't want trouble. I'm going to leave now, back the way I came. I won't bother you or your people again."

"You'll leave when we say you will!" shouted one of the shadows. His voice was the wobbly half-squeak of a teenager trying to impress the big kids, and in his excitement, he'd forgotten *Lesson One*—

"Fucking be quiet!" hissed the shadow nearest him.

"Sorry!" shouted the teenager, even louder this time.

"Enough!" barked the man with the rifle, so quiet he was barely heard, but with enough power in his voice that they fell silent. He turned and pointed the barrel at Wendell's chest.

"Leave your weapon," he said. Wendell stared at him in horror.

"But I—"

"Drop. The axe." The slide cocked back on the rifle with a distinctive *CHIKK*. Wendell let the bloody hatchet fall from his hand. "What's on your belt?" Wendell showed him. Wendell couldn't see his face, but did it seem as if he smiled? It did. He nodded. "Go. No one will harm you. Don't come back here again."

Wendell nodded, unwilling to let relief show on his face just yet. He turned to go back through the storeroom.

"No," said the rifleman. "The front door." Seeing the look on his face, the shadow seemed to smile again. To his surprise, there was no malice in his voice. "I said you will not be harmed. We'll draw the dead around back. You'll be safe enough until you reach the next block. You've got wits. Use them."

Wendell nodded and turned away. The man who held the rifle called back as he neared the door. "Go home. Find someplace to wait out the storm, like we have. Just don't come back here."

Wendell Jenkins pushed open the front door and stepped out onto the street.

CHAPTER TWO

Wendell pushed open the door marked *EXIT* and stepped outside. Sure enough, there was a sizable crowd in the parking lot. They stood in a ring around the co-op doors, ripped and tattered and bloody, all of them swaying like drunks at the end of the night, disconcertingly all of them swaying in unison. He might be able to dodge through them to the other side, but it wouldn't be easy. And there would always be more. It was one of the lessons he'd learned.

The dead would wander on their own and be very much interested in their own activities as long as nothing was going on, but as soon as one of them rang the dinner bell, a silent signal seemed to pass through all of the zombies nearby and they would come, whether they were in hearing range or not. The effect seemed to expand in effectiveness as more bodies were involved, and if they didn't either find something to eat or lose their quarry and eventually their interest, they would just keep coming and coming.

The zombie he had killed in the alleyway had called them to the hunt. Now it wouldn't end until he was safely hidden—or dead.

He had to run, and he had to run now. And he very likely would die in pain anyway.

Just as he was steadying himself for the last desperate dash of his life, a noise split the night and every head including his turned to look up the street. On instinct, he froze.

Somewhere up the street, he knew, was a branch of the Toronto Dominion Bank. He couldn't see it from here, but its bright green sign no doubt lit up the nearby intersection with a haunting light. Somehow, someway, the bank's security alarm had gone off; a blaring, jangling sound could be heard for blocks.

Almost as one, the crowd of zombies took a step to the left and swayed up the street toward the sound.

Surprised and annoyed, not sure how the rednecks inside the co-op had managed it, not sure whether to feel outraged at their treatment of him or grateful for the elaborate and clever way the shadows had saved his life, Wendell ran in the opposite direction, not toward safety but away from danger. Some zombies, arriving late to the feast, were still ambling up the street, but without a weapon, Wendell could only dodge and run.

He passed his building without looking. There was nothing left there for him. His liquor was there, but he'd sworn off the stuff. His bed was there, but a woman lay dead across his wife's favorite duvet. Safety was there, but he would never see it again. Instead, he ran on, with his legs feeling like lead, with his side cramping up from the exertion, with the blood pounding in his head. He stumbled, and a pair of filth-blackened hands brushed his jacket. He looked up into the glowing eyes of Phone Man. A scream forced its way out of his throat. He drove a fist into Phone Man's stomach. The zombie didn't double over in pain or even slow, but a single hiss, like air from a punctured tire, wheezed from its drooling mouth. Wendell's own forward momentum carried them both into a roll, and Wendell found himself lying on top of Phone Man, scrambling to his feet even as Phone Man continued to grasp at him, mouth full of gnashing teeth. He fought his way free and dug a heavy work boot into the dead man's mouth as he fled.

He was gulping for air, his heart hammered in his chest. He was forty-two and out of shape. The mad dash from the co-op was the longest he'd run since high school. He needed to get under cover fast, before his vision turned to spots and he ran headlong into another zombie. Up ahead, he saw the lights of a convenience store and ran for it.

He threw open the door and dashed inside. The bell jangled *DING-ling*, announcing his presence to anything near enough to hear. Forcing the door shut against its slow-close safety spring, he threw the lock just as a blackened hand slapped the glass.

Wendell looked up. Like all convenience stores, this one had a set of pull-down security bars. Like all consumers, he had often wondered why a twenty-four-hour convenience store would bother with a security grate when they never closed, but now he breathed a prayer of thanks and yanked it down. He couldn't lock it without a key, but it was better than the wall of endless glass the store presented when it was open. He leaned back against the grate and looked around.

The counter, the drink coolers, the cash register were all patterned with rust-brown splashes of drying blood. Someone had fought for his life here, and lost, but the silence and the absence of shadows eased his mind. A quick glance behind the counter and down each short aisle made sure he was alone in the store. Just to be safe, he piled two cases of pop against the storeroom door. If anybody came in from the back, he would hear it in time to get away.

He drank endlessly from the water bottles in the cooler as he tried to get his breath back. When he felt almost like himself again, he made himself a supper of a can of microwave soup and a bag of chips. He found a set of keys in the drawer beneath the till and locked up the security gate, even dared to venture into the storeroom to make sure that it was empty and the back entry was locked.

He was safe and secure. He had food, water, and a locked door. There was no liquor, but there were endless cartons of cigarettes if he wanted to trade one awful habit for another. He could wait out the crisis here if he wanted, or even die here if he felt like it. There was enough poison locked in the cleaning-supply cupboard to make it quick, if not painless.

But Wendell wasn't ready to die. He had something to do first.

Two things made him finally decide to leave the safety of the apartment building. Well, Gracie of course, and the way she had smiled at him as she left for the streetcar. But besides Gracie, there had been two things that pushed him over the edge. Two things that made him decide enough was enough.

Ellie was one. The family in Apartment 2F was the other.

It was only a day after he'd finally given up and destroyed the stairs. As superintendent of Viscount Suites, he had felt it was his duty to keep the building safe for its tenants, should they ever return home. How awful would it be to fight your way home through desperation and horror only to find yourself trapped on the sidewalk, surrounded and unable to get in? He waited three days, sitting in the stairwell with his axe and jumping with fright every time one of the dead rattled the locked door to the lobby, fingering the cross around his neck and praying they would move along without testing the very breakable glass surrounding the lock. Finally, he decided that no one was coming back. They'd all stayed in the office, made their own fortifications, and hunkered down—he hoped—or were wandering around downtown themselves with glowing eyes and endless hunger.

He hardly ever needed to use the SkilSaw. Half of the tools at his disposal were unnecessary to the jobs at hand of fixing loose baseboards and loosening stuck locks. A hammer and a can of WD-40 were the only tools in his belt that saw much use, but the day he pulled out the heavy saw, it felt right in his hand.

The saw made a ridiculous racket. Before he was halfway done with the job, it had drawn a crowd. He knelt on the third step up, glancing up at his slack-jawed audience more and more often and willing the saw to hurry. The staircase was harder to wreck than he'd ever thought possible. Beneath the tile and metal there was plywood, and beneath that, a sturdier construction of joists and buttresses than he had ever believed while walking up and down them every day for so many years. When at last one whole step gave way, toppling down to the basement beneath, he hopped up a step and began again.

The crowd never stopped growing. He would later look out the window and see dozens of them surrounding the building, pushing their way toward the door as if they were groupies and he was the only rock show in town. When he was on the fourth step, either one of them got smart or the press of bodies was just too much, and he watched in horror as a hard, wide forehead smashed through the glass, shattering the window and leaving its face a bloody mess.

Then the rest of them were through. The Beatles had left the building, and the girls were going wild.

Wendell thumbed the deadman switch and threw the saw. It caused carnage among the mob, but not enough, as he leapt up the stairs to the first floor. Some of them toppled through the hole he'd already made to fall broken on the concrete floor below, but more made the leap and landed on the stairwell.

This is it, thought Wendell. His only hope now was to barricade himself in his own apartment and wait for the scratching of a thousand fingers to tell him his time was up. Still he stood at the top of the stairs and watched with sick fascination, his hatchet held ready in his hand. He'd already decided to bury it in the first head to top the stairs, when he heard a groan from beneath. A groan not of the ravenous dead but of stressed wood. All at once the weakened staircase collapsed, sending the writhing mass of zombies plummeting. Wendell stood dumbfounded at the edge of a suddenly open pit, while below him dead arms reached plaintively up at him from a broken puddle of bodies.

The next morning he took the back basement stairs down and began to cart the bodies one by one to the dumpster. When it was full, he wheeled it out into the parking lot and took the saw to the basement stairs. Heavy work, that, and both mentally and physically draining, but nothing he'd seen came even close to preparing him for the horror of Apartment 2F.

As the superintendent—and sole remaining tenant—of Viscount Suites, he decided that the other apartments were fair game. He would need supplies if he were going to last this out until the end, and surely no one would begrudge him some canned soup and candles, especially if they were in no position to use them themselves. His system was simple. First, he would knock politely to ensure no one was home. He was certain no one else was alive in the building—their paths would have crossed in the past four days—but that no longer meant that the building was empty. A polite knock would set off a spate of groans and scratches inside, and he would mark that door with a magic marker Z and move on. His system was put to the test and almost failed right at the start when he knocked on the door next to his and it swung open, only to come to a slamming halt when it reached the end of the security chain. Four grey, groping fingers slid through the six-inch opening, and Wendell backed away in horror as the tenant within snarled and slavered.

If his knock went unanswered from within he would use his master keys to open the door and set about exploring the apartment. Aside from a decent stockpile of canned goods and almost-but-not-yet spoiled fruit, he acquired a bowl of strawberry Jell-O, several bottles of whiskey, and more beer than he could drink, provided the crisis only lasted a week. Then he came on his whistling way to 2F.

Only silence answered his knock. He eased the door open slowly and looked around. All of the apartments in the Viscount Suites had the exact same layout, so Wendell knew his way around. He stood in the tiny entranceway, with both the kitchen and living areas in full view. Around the dividing wall, he knew he'd find the TV in the exact same spot as in every other apartment, and then a small dining nook beyond that. Behind the living room to the left, would be the bedrooms and the one tiny bathroom. It was only in the incidentals that each home differed from the others.

This one was primarily given over to the endless stuff of children. From stuffed animals and toy trucks scattered across the living room carpet, to colorful plastic sippy cups and Dora the Explorer bowls in the kitchen sink, to stacks and stacks of DVDs featuring giant costumed characters and animated cutesy bears on top of the TV. He knew most of the people who had lived in the building by sight at least, but the family in 2F had only recently moved in. He hadn't seen much of any of them, aside from an occasional friendly hello from Mr. 2F from time to time. Of Mrs. 2F or the smaller 2Fs he'd seen no sign. He'd actually pegged Mr. as a bachelor or a divorcee. He had the sad careworn look of someone who had been through a lot and was doing his best with what was left.

There were lots of goodies in the kitchen, as was the wont with a small child or two, but what Wendell was really in need of was something to do. Like the famous *Twilight Zone* character, Wendell planned on spending the end of the world catching up on his reading, and he at least didn't need to worry about breaking his glasses; his vision, unlike the rest of him, was perfect. What he lacked was a good book he hadn't read over and over again. Selection in the Viscount Suites was thin on that ground.

There were no bookshelves in the main area. They must not have much room for adult entertainments with all the kiddie stuff all over. Wendell figured he'd find a bookshelf in one of the bedrooms.

If he had known, he would have just stolen a *Reader's Digest* from the coffee table in 3G.

The first bedroom was obviously the children's. A set of bunk beds sat off to one side, matching Elmo sheets on top and bottom. More toys spilled out of the toy box and onto the floor, and there were some books, but all of the *Paper Bag Princess* variety. He gently closed the door again and crossed the hall to the other room.

If Norman Rockwell had been commissioned by the *Saturday Evening Post* to create a series of touching yet horrifying depictions of the zombie apocalypse, he could not have done better than the quaint family get-together in 2F's master bedroom.

The first thing he saw was Momma, and now Wendell knew why he'd never seen her around the building. Her wasted figure lay on what was obviously a hospital bed, wheeled up to be side-by-side to the double marital bed. Tubes went from now-empty bags of fluid into her arms and a portable heart monitor next to her droned out a continuous flatline that Wendell must either have tuned out or failed to hear through the heavy door. Her face was shrunken to the skull, but her eyes were alive with pale fire as her head rolled weakly from side to side and she reached for him with what remained of her left arm. Mr. 2F stood beside her, and it could have been a moving testament to love lingering through illness if he didn't have her blood staining his chin, or didn't seem to be still chewing on something.

Wendell recoiled in mute horror and vomited strawberry Jell-O all over the burgundy carpet. And that was when the two children charged him from the other side of the bed.

Wendell added four more bodies to the dumpster out back. Then he drank until he couldn't see their faces. It took two days...and two bottles. He still cried out in his sleep.

With his head pounding from a raging hangover and nothing better to do, Wendell went outside and sat on the fire escape to watch the storm.

It had been blowing in all day, and as it strengthened over

Lake Ontario, the oppressive heat in the city only grew worse. The winds picked up, beating against the buildings and scattering the worse-than-usual litter, but it didn't offer any relief from the heat. Finally came the moment when the wind stopped altogether, when the mid-afternoon light changed the very air to that particular shade of dull orange that only comes before a heavy summer storm, and the city seemed to hush. No birds sang. No insects buzzed. Somewhere a screen door banged open and closed over and over again, in counterpoint to the low hum—almost felt rather than heard—of the power lines that inexplicably continued to buzz with electricity.

After all that he'd been through, Gracie and the streetcar, the stairwell, and Apartment 2F's family dinner, Wendell had decided that the best way to keep his sanity was to try to take joy from the tiny things in life. The taste of coffee. The smell of good food—no more Jell-O, he would never eat Jell-O again for the rest of his life. The silent stillness before a storm, and the cacophonic crash as it washed away everything before it. He stationed a lawn chair on the grating and poured himself a fresh coffee. He was going to sit here and enjoy the storm, and if he got drenched, well, he'd enjoy that, too.

Ahead up the street he could just make out the figure of Phone Man, right in the middle of his sad little ritual, his head hanging as if in dismay that he could not find what it was that drew him so obsessively. Wendell wondered if the phone would survive the storm. If it did, he would not be surprised. They make things to last these days.

He felt the first fat drop on the back of his hand. Down below, Phone Man started, whirled and glared at the sky, at this new intruder on his private misery. Here it comes, thought Wendell with grim satisfaction, and settled in to enjoy the show.

That was when he heard her.

"Helloo," came a voice from below. Wendell's head snapped up, startled. Down in the street, Phone Man did the same.

"HELLOOO! Is anybody home?"

At first, he thought it was Grace, returned home against all hope. But of course, that was impossible. He peered over the railing and was immediately soaked as the downpour began in earnest. Below him stood a large blob of a raincoat, a large paisley umbrella unable to block her from view entirely. A face wide, earnest, and devoid of rational thought smiled up at him from above the one and below the other.

"I knew I'd find you here!" she shouted over the torrent. "Are you going to let me up, or am I to be soaked?"

Her name was Ellie, and from the moment she climbed up the ladder, they were off on the wrong foot. She bothered him just by existing in that alleyway with no concern for her own safety. She irritated him by insisting on fumbling up the ladder with that hideous umbrella, even with curious Phone Man right on her heels. She annoyed him by carrying on a continuous prattle as she climbed. "I've seen you around the building before! I live just next door! There's no one left at my building either, so I thought you'd like some company! Oh this is *hard!* Why did you have to go and ruin a perfectly good staircase?"

She was a kind-looking woman of about forty, with features that could best be described as pillowy. She had a soft, white, *pillowy* face and big, *pillowy* breasts that could barely be contained by a straining bra. Her thick, *pillowy* arms wrapped around both ladder and umbrella with a determined grip. She reached the top and her wide, gormless smile took on a sardonic tilt.

"Well, aren't you going to help a lady over?" she asked.

"Hurry up," he yelled. "Before that thing figures out how to climb!" A part of him was surprised at how short he sounded. He was normally very friendly. Another part of him said, *Too bad. I've got a splitting headache and who the hell does she think she is?* Never mind that she was the first living soul he'd spoken to in a week.

Once she was over and the ladder was raised—Phone Man still standing at the bottom in total confusion over the strange things to appear in his life—she introduced herself and began her life story, though Wendell had hardly asked and was hardly listening. At some point in the chatter, he must have grunted out his own name.

"Why so glum then, Wendell Jenkins? You seem positively vexed!"

"I don't know," he snapped. "I'm soaking wet, for one thing, and do you have any idea how close you came to getting yourself killed?"

"Oh, pshaw," she poofed. "I didn't, though, did I? Can't live in the past, Mr. Jenkins. That's what I always tell my Michael. You'd like him, I think. He's a very good boy. Always respectful to his elders, and always treats a lady with dignity." She looked pointedly at Wendell, her eyebrows arched and a small smile playing across her lips. She obviously felt she'd made a very important point and Wendell should be grateful for it. He had so many available responses to Ellie, but some sense of good manners prevailed and all he did was roll his eyes and duck through the window to his apartment.

"You coming?"

It was obvious that Ellie was born to be a mother. She was kind, in a patronizing, down-talking way, and encouraging in the same backhanded manner. She had the kind of disposition that all small children seem to gravitate to—in fact, she reminded Wendell of his own kindergarten teacher—but was off-putting to everyone else. His opinion of her didn't improve, but on the other hand, she was alive and that was a rare quality in this day and age.

"Oh," she said, her eyes rolling up a little at his offer of a can of beer. "Well, I don't usually drink the cheap stuff, but I guess beggars can't be choosers." She popped the tab and took a hearty swig. Wendell, with his head still pounding from the night before, was sticking to his coffee.

They talked idly of this and that. She told him all about *her Michael* and what a wonderful little boy he was. "So clever. He's just started grade two, and Ms. Rinehart wishes she had a dozen more just like him. Thank goodness he went to visit his aunt in Orillia, he'll be perfectly safe from danger there!" Somehow Wendell found himself talking about Grace. Her small smile, like she was always in on a joke nobody else was smart enough to get, the way she always seemed to float above the things that weighed everybody else down, the sparkle in her eyes.

"We've been married for ten years," he said with a grin, raising his coffee cup to his lips and finding a can of beer in his hand instead, "And sometimes I still get clumsy around her. You know, like a nervous kid trying to talk to a girl for the first time. She knows it, too, and it always makes her laugh." He was surprised to find two empty cans beside him in addition to the one he held in his hand. His old kitchen had taken on a hazy glow.

"She sounds like a hell of a woman," said Ellie with a smile. "Where is she now?"

Wendell's glow vanished immediately and his stomach began to churn instead—the unpleasant side effects of drinking. Ellie had a silver cigarette case and every few minutes she pulled out a long white cigarette and lit it with a match. Wendell's empty coffee cup had long since begun to overflow with filter butts and bent matches.

"On Friday," he began. "Grace had to go to...an appointment. I usually went with her, but I had a lot to do here. Grace said not to worry. She would be fine. She kissed me goodbye and told me, 'Don't take any shit from the landlord,' and then she walked out the door."

"And then all hell broke loose," said Ellie with a smile Wendell didn't like. He nodded, cracked a fourth can.

"First the fire trucks went by," said Wendell. "A few minutes later, a whole troop of cop cars went the other way. I thought I heard screaming up the street, but I figured it was just kids at the park. You know how it is with kids, the more they're having fun, the more it sounds like they're being murdered.

"But then I saw a guy being hauled out of his car right outside the building while I was vacuuming the foyer. Two girls walked right up to him and hauled him out through the window. He was screaming, and I saw blood. I started over there, I think I was yelling something, but then one of the girls turned to look at me and I stopped dead. There was something about her that scared me, even from across the street. Her eyes. She dropped the guy's arm and started walking toward me, with her hair hanging over her face like the girl in that horrible movie, and I..."

"You ran," said Ellie.

"I ran. I left him to them. I left the vacuum on the front step and went inside and locked my door. I stayed there the rest of the day. I watched from the fire escape while the street turned to Hell."

"And Grace? Your lovely wife?"

"She never came back. I have to hope that she got away somehow, that she's somewhere safe and has no way to reach me."

Ellie nodded, stubbed out her cigarette in Wendell's favorite coffee cup, and turned to regard him with an expression of what he could only describe as malignant glee. "But you know that isn't true," she said. The corners of her lips turned up into a cruel smile. "You know she's dead, Wendell. Dead and walking around, staring at the pretty lights, and eating people, don't you?"

Wendell was taken aback. In a small hurt voice he said, "What's the matter with you?"

"I'm just the voice of unpleasant truth, dearie. If she's alive, after all these days, why hasn't she tried to find you? Is it because she knows you're a coward who hides in his house while people die?"

The slap came out of a part of Wendell that he did not know he possessed. He was more surprised than she was when his arm flew through the air and collided with her snide, grinning cheek with a crack that cut through the room. It sent her sideways off the chair, but it didn't break her grin. If anything, she smiled wider. She bored into his face with her hideous glee. She grinned from the floor, picked herself up, and came at him again.

"If you think she's alive, why haven't you gone looking for her, instead of hiding like a dog in this shitbox you call a home? Does she think she's better off without you? Did she take advantage of the end of the world to get the hell away from the sad, cowardly drunk she's been saddled with?"

He wanted to slap her again. Somehow he didn't. The world had turned red, pulsing, confused. His tongue gummed up, stuck to the roof of his mouth, and when he opened it, nothing came out but a meaningless stammer. He tried to turn away, but there was nowhere else to go.

"Why hasn't she called, Mr. Wendell Jenkins? Hmm? The power is still on, why not the phones? Have you tried? Have you?" She crossed to where his old, 1990s landline sat in its cradle on the kitchen counter, picked it up. It had never occurred to him that the phones might still work. To his surprise, even from across the room he could hear a dial tone as she held it out to him. Ellie turned around, glanced at the flier for Grace's favorite pizza place tacked above the phone, and punched in the number.

It rang.

It rang seven times. Then there was a click, and the hum of an open line, and Wendell heard wheezing, thumping, and from a distance, a haunting moan. A zombie, perhaps the same man who used to run DiNapoli's Pizza with a wide smile and a corny joke, had followed the sound and picked up the offending phone.

Wendell's world collapsed.

"I tried it," said Ellie. "I tried it for hours on the first day. I called Mikey's friends, my neighbors, even my mother. Even my sister in Orillia. Women turn first to the phone, Wendell. It might not have occurred to you, but it most definitely would have occurred to your wife.

"She's dead, Wendell," Ellie's hate-filled eyes locked on Wendell's. They filled with tears that spilled down her pillowy cheeks, but she didn't blink. "Your wife is dead, walking around, eating people. Just like my son."

She began to weep.

Then she started to take off her clothes.

By the time Wendell finished securing his temporary hideout, a light blue tinge had begun to kiss the air outside, and the tiny elm tree out front began to wave in an early morning breeze. With all the day left to him before he could move safely again, Wendell made himself a makeshift bed behind the counter out of piles of newspapers, and lay down. Before he closed his eyes, he reviewed his lessons.

Lesson One: Zombies are slow, until they decide to be fast.

Lesson One: Zombies only have the energy for one quick pounce; after that, they slow right down.

Lesson One: If you are bitten by a zombie, you have between four and six hours.

Thunder crashed outside and the rain came down in torrents. Ellie pulled her arms out of her sleeves and let her blue-flowered dress drop to her waist. Her large breasts were barely held in by a thick bra that was obviously purchased more for utility than titillation. Wendell stood stunned, utterly baffled by this woman who had first insulted, then berated him, called him a coward, and was now, for inexplicable reasons, weeping and stripping at the same time. Then he saw the blood.

Her enormous, vintage-looking bra was stained with splotches of red, vibrant blood, the mark of a wound that wouldn't close. With trembling hands, she undid the hooks and removed it, revealing a horror that sobered him instantly, and at the same time nearly choked him with alcohol-fuelled nausea. Her left breast was a mangled ruin. Only the sturdiness of the garment holding it in had allowed it to keep its shape. She'd been with him for nearly two hours, and yet it still bled freely, and when she reopened it, she gasped with pain, her face went white, and she collapsed to the kitchen floor, all her fire and rage gone out of her.

Wendell's own anger evaporated in an instant, and he found himself down on the floor, cradling her head in his hands as blood pooled on the tiles. Her face was full of pain, but her eyes were full of grief.

"My boy," she said. "My poor boy."

"What happened, Ellie?" he asked.

"He wanted to go to the park with his friends. My sister was coming to pick him up for a visit, but she wouldn't be there for another hour, so I let him. I let him go. He never came back.

"I looked for him. Even after the dead people started coming around, I kept looking, hoping my little Mikey would be okay somehow. I knew it was foolish, but it's a mother's prerogative to be foolish. I was always careful. It didn't take me long to learn to go in the evening, when they're distracted.

"I found him tonight, just before the storm started. He was walking with a group of dead people, and his eyes...he just looked so scared! So sad and scared. I just had to hold him, to pick him up and hold him to me and tell him that everything would be okay, just like I used to."

Wendell had nothing to say. He held her, and he stroked her cheek, and he watched the blood flow from her ruined chest.

"I knew," she said. "I knew it wasn't him, even before he bit me. That was the worst part. Knowing my little boy was gone and he wasn't coming back. I cried and I held him and I told him it would be okay, even though he was dead, even though I was going to die soon. I told him I loved him and I hit him with a hammer and I went home and cleaned myself up.

"I'm sorry. I had no right to come in here and bother you with any of this. I just…he died alone, and afraid, and then he came back, and I can't imagine what that would be like.

"Maybe I'm the coward," she continued. "I just couldn't bear the thought of it. I didn't want to die alone. I didn't want to come back, with no one there to…with no one there to…"

"Shhh," said Wendell. "It's okay."

There was nothing more to say. There was nothing more to do but wait. He held her and he waited, and when she stopped breathing, he went to the window and got his hatchet, and then he waited some more.

He waited until he saw the whites of her eyes.

Lesson One, thought Wendell as day came full and bright through the window, and he fell into a restless sleep. *Stay away from other people.*

CHAPTER THREE

Wendell lay on the floor below the cash register, and knew he was going to die. Black spots exploded behind his eyes, and behind those, fireworks and bolts of lightning. He was coughing hard enough to make his head explode, almost hard enough to vomit up the Spam he'd eaten for breakfast.

With heavy effort, he got his breath back, wiped his streaming eyes, and stabbed the cigarette violently out on the floor. It had taken him forty-two years to yield to teenage peer pressure to try that first cigarette. Maybe if he was still alive when he was eighty-four he'd try a second one.

Wendell rinsed the ash taste from his mouth with a gulp of instant coffee and looked at the ruin of a mess he'd made. Sleep had left him early, jolting him awake at only a little after noon, leaving him alone and trapped in the store with hours to kill before nightfall. He had a pile of newspapers from two weeks ago scattered on the floor—*Island Attacks Escalate*, screamed the headline—in which he'd done the crossword, tried and given up on the Sudoku, and read and failed to laugh at all the comics. He'd grown bored with drawing moustaches on the airbrushed celebrities on the covers of the tabloid magazines. He'd begun a game of solitaire, given up and begun a house of cards, then given up on that, too. He'd eaten snack cakes and mini donuts and pinged elastic bands at the walls. Eventually, for a lark, he'd decided to light a cigarette.

"Well, that's it," he told the walls, "There is absolutely nothing left to do but wait." Waiting was the worst part. Waiting involved thinking. Thinking led to thoughts he would rather avoid. Sitting still on the floor made him restless, and standing up to pace again around the little store only let him see outside. Wendell stood up.

Were there more of them or was he only imagining it? They stood utterly motionless, gazing in through the barred windows at him. Their eyes didn't blink, their hands didn't twitch. There were four of them—no, five now. The nearest was a woman in her thirties wearing a professional looking pantsuit. Something black and stringy was stuck in her front teeth. But the one that held his gaze—and his creeping horror—the most, was the little boy.

He was seven, maybe, or ten. Wendell realized he hadn't spent very much of his life in the company of children—not enough to accurately guess their ages, anyway. He stared in at Wendell with a disconcerting lack of any kind of curiosity or spark. His dead eyes, more than all the others, filled him with fear and grief. He was wearing a red backpack with cars on it, somehow still intact and in place on his back. It was probably still filled with his favorite sandwich and juice box, put there by a mother who smiled and tousled his hair and made him put on that blue jacket even though it wasn't cold—because it might be later, right?—and kissed him goodbye one fateful morning, never knowing that before the end of the day he would be dead, and maybe on his way back to her, empty eyes seeking a warm place to lay one last kiss.

He shook his head. He had to stop looking at them. He couldn't look at anything else. For all they moved, they might have been mannequins placed there by some sadistic joker. But Wendell knew full well that if he unlatched the grate they would move fast enough, working together to corner him in the tiny space and tear him to pieces, each of them getting a bit of Wendell to snack on, probably even while he was still alive.

Stop it! They were out there and he was in here. He didn't know for a fact that they knew he was here. They never tracked his movements, even when he walked right by the grate. For all he knew, they might see their own reflections or the sunlight in the glass or something. He would have to go among them eventually, but sunset was still a good ways off, and before then he would need a plan.

Lesson One, every single movie on the subject taught to *Never, never go outside*, and if you have to go outside, *Never go out without a weapon*. He didn't have a weapon. Again, that unreliable source, the movies, had let him hope for the hidden shotgun-under-the-counter of the inner-city convenience store, but the only thing he found hidden under the counter was the silver button for the silent alarm. Civilized times. Wendell took a deep breath and went through the door at the back of the store.

The storeroom was nothing but a long hallway with a toilet and sink. Bundles of paper towel rolls and toilet paper were stacked up along one wall, against which also leaned a desultory mop and broom. At the far end of the narrow corridor, across from a yellowing toilet and underneath a clipping of the December, 2011 *SunShine Girl*, was a low wooden cupboard, warped with moisture and speckled with grime. Wendell reached for the handle.

Toilet Duck and a disgusting grey-green toilet brush. Wendell sighed and sat down on the toilet, cradling his head in his hands.

It's amazing sometimes, how important things can be easily forgotten, but small details that hardly matter can be written in indelible ink. Wendell remembered the hum of the vacuum on the stairs, the detail in the thirty-year-old carpet he fought with every week in the foyer, but he couldn't remember what she'd been wearing when she left. He'd been standing in his ratty brown corduroys, pants so well worn-in that they felt like a second skin, the same pants he was wearing now, in fact, vacuuming the hall when she came down the stairs. What had she been wearing? He wanted to say it was her yellow jacket and favorite black pants. That was her favorite outfit to wear out because no matter that it was an ensemble put together at Value Village for eleven dollars, it looked like it cost a lot of money, and she said it made her look like she was worth more. "Impossible," he'd argue. "You're priceless already," and she'd give him that smile.

But no, the yellow jacket lost a button, and hadn't she been mad about that? It seemed there wasn't a sewing store anywhere in the Greater Toronto Area that sold buttons that size or particular shade of yellow. And the pants, her favorite black pants that made her ass look terrific, they were folded up in the closet because they didn't fit right anymore.

But he could remember the carpet, by God.

The landlord liked to say that the carpet was salmon because it sounded better than faded to pink. The carpet of the front foyer used to be a deep burnished red, as befitting a residence named Viscount Suites, but a Southwestern exposure meant it had faced the sun at its brightest for twenty-five years, and also the Viscount Suites was a dump with cheap rent and a cheaper landlord. The carpet had long since lost any of its elegant sheen, and to make matters worse, it was filthy in a way that showed up so strikingly in pink.

Vacuuming accomplished nothing, but Wendell did it often. It made his presence known in the building, and if he did nothing else all day, if the tenants saw him in the foyer with the Bissell in the morning, everyone would assume he was working just as hard later when they didn't see him. It was also, though he would never admit it, something he enjoyed. The whisper of the wheels across the carpet, the satisfying clitter-clatter when he sucked up something big and it went crackling down the hose, the pure Zen thanklessness of it. The foyer got cleaned a lot, because Wendell cleaned it every time he was angry or irritated. Which, lately, was often enough.

This time of course it was Stan who set him off. Stan didn't own the building any more than Wendell did. The owner owned the building. The owner never came near it, hired a property management company to collect the checks and handle the maintenance. Stan Alban was hired by them to oversee the buildings that they managed, and Wendell was hired by him. It was a long trickle of something rolling downhill, and it all rolled onto Wendell.

"There's a showing tomorrow," Stan's first words over the phone were never polite. He dove straight in, preferring to get off on the wrong foot right away.

"Okay," Wendell said. "Which apartment?" Knowing full well which one, of course, but not wanting to hear the answer.

"3G."

Wendell suppressed a groan. "Did we know about this before now?"

"Doesn't matter." Which meant, of course, that Stan had known well in advance, and forgotten. "We know now. It has to be done."

"Okay, except it can't," said Wendell. "It needs to be cleaned top to bottom, Stan. A woman died in there less than a week ago."

"Well then I suppose somebody should have been cleaning in the meantime."

"The relatives just came yesterday. The old lady's things were moved out yesterday afternoon. You were there, as I recall." He could feel a vein pulsing behind his forehead. Right at the edge of his vision, the room got a little cloudy. Wendell had to clench his fist hard; an impulse came to slam the phone against the tabletop, hard. He didn't.

"Look, it doesn't matter now," said Stan, dancing around the accusation. "It needs to be done. I'm in meetings all day, Wendell. I need to know that you can take care of this."

The magic words. You can take care of this. Wendell clenched his teeth. Somewhere behind him, Grace was watching him. He couldn't see her, but he knew her eyebrows were raised, widening her brown eyes. She could see the frustration in his back and arms, making him vibrate like a tuning fork. He knew she was worried, not just for him, but for what he might do.

"Fine," Wendell managed. "I'll get it done."

"Thanks a heap, Wendell. I knew I could count on you!"

Wendell was almost too polite to hang up without saying goodbye. Almost.

So there he stood in the lobby, vacuum in hand. It

wouldn't get the vacant apartment cleaned up any faster, but it was helping him feel better. Grace came down the stairs, tucking her keys into her huge black purse. He remembered the purse, of course. Seeing her there brought his anger back hot. She smiled at him, not *that* smile, but another one, this one tight against her lips, a thin pale line under raised eyebrows. *I know how disappointed you are,* that smile said, *and nothing I can do will cheer you up.* It didn't help Wendell at all.

"Good luck," he snarled at her, and instantly regretted it. Rather than apologize he turned on his vacuum cleaner and began to clean away from her. He wasn't even trying, just running the beater bar back and forth over the same spot while a red cloud tried to settle behind his eyes.

Her slim brown hand slid over his knuckles and her thumb found the OFF switch. She was small but inexorable as she turned him to face her. She was locked onto him, eye to eye, and only inches away. The warmth of her so close to him always seemed to drain everything else away. She kissed him lightly, and when she pulled away, the red cloud evaporated.

She said, "Wendell, honey, I know how important it was for you to come today. And that means the world to me. But it just wasn't in the cards, sweetie!" He opened his mouth, but she shushed him. "Now, you know I can take care of myself. Everything is going to be just fine."

He still wanted to be mad, but it just wasn't there anymore. He sighed. "You will get copies?"

"Sweetie, I'll be makin' copies for everybody I know, but I promise you that *you* are gonna see it first."

"Promise?"

"Promise. I'll pick up a bottle of something on the way home and you and I can curl up on the couch and watch our baby kick me in the gallbladder as soon as you're finished with Stan."

"Shit," said Wendell. "I'd like to finish with him. Fat bald prick."

"Now now," chided Grace. "There's no need for language, Wen. You'll need your nicest smile on when you tell him about the extra helpers you had to hire to get the place cleaned up on time."

"What extra—oh!" He grinned. "How many people do you figure I'll have to hire, anyway?"

"Oh, just one. I'll be happy to help when I get back. Just as long as Stan knows it's going to take us all night to finish the job."

Wendell's bad mood was completely vanished now. Of course he would be done by evening, but bilking Stan out of a night of double overtime almost made up for missing out on Grace's ultrasound.

He kissed her, then gave her a playful push. "Go on, get out of here," She went with a self-assured little sashay that always drove him wild, even with her widening figure. When she reached the doors, he yelled out.

"If you find out the sex, don't tell me!"

She turned back, gave him *that* smile. "Don't worry," she said, which of course made him worry. Then she was gone to catch the streetcar to take her to the subway to take her to the hospital to get the first pictures of their baby. He thumbed the little switch over, and the vacuum whirred back to life. With a much lighter heart, he contemplated the ugly, faded carpet. He even hummed a little tune.

That was the last time he'd been happy, the very last time he'd had any hope for the future. A million years or just over a week later, he sat on a dirty toilet in a two-bit convenience store with his head in his hands, trapped and despondent. There was nothing left to do.

Correction, he thought. There was one thing left to do, and he had to do it or die trying. Even if he had to go out into the street defenseless again.

He took his hands away from his face, and that was when he noticed the little grey box. Tucked in the back of the cupboard, deep under the sink and almost buried by old rags and Pine-Sol. It just might be what would save him.

The twilight deepened to dark and the streetlights came on. A half million twitching corpses tuned in to the Electric Light Show, and Wendell slipped silently out onto the street, holding in his right hand the hefty claw hammer he'd pulled from the bathroom tool box, and set off into the arc-sodium haze.

CHAPTER FOUR

"**R**ob, something has to be done," said David.

Rob sighed, put down his game, and heaved himself to his feet. When David thought something needed to be done, that meant it was Rob who would be doing the doing.

David Archibald was a good hotel manager. That meant he was kind, gentle, and caring to his guests and a miserable tyrant to his staff. Working for David had never been Rob's favorite part of the job, but it was getting worse. As David's staff had dwindled to just Rob and Yvonne, and his guest list went from the Who's Who of the city to a cluster of dead-eyed monsters, he seemed to actually get worse, not better. To Rob's eyes, the worst part was David's new attitude of we're-all-in-this-together camaraderie that put a sickly sweet edge on what were increasingly petulant demands. "Just call me David," he'd told Rob after they'd been trapped in the office together for two days. Before that, and even as the zombies raged through the hotel, it had been "Mr. Archibald."

In another corner of the small room, Yvonne stood

wiping down the filing cabinets with a rag that was now tattered and brown and a spray bottle he could not believe was not empty yet. Yvonne had cleaned the office at least twenty times by now and seemed not to know what to do with herself in between. She never spoke above a whisper, did everything David told her to do, and would not leave the office for anything.

David motioned Rob to the door. He opened it just a crack and the two men peered out. Beyond the office door in the spacious lobby, about twenty people milled about—what remained of the staff and guests of the Downtown Sheraton. They walked with their heads up and their mouths slack. Their empty eyes gleamed with a soft white light.

"We need to do something about them," said David. His immaculate, starched white shirt was yellow from days of wearing the same clothes, yet he still kept it buttoned all the way to the top, black tie cinched in a stuffy full-Windsor. Rob had a sudden urge to grab it and pull. "If we could clear out the lobby, we'd be able to move around in the building again."

"Yeah," said Rob. "But how do you plan on doing that?" He lit a cigarette and blew a jet of smoke through the door. David had shown remarkable courage in making his way to the bar one night and returning with a massive bottle of scotch and exactly one glass. It was the only time he'd left the office since the crisis began. The glass was always full. He'd never once offered either of the others a drink.

To annoy him, Rob had located a carton of cigarettes and chain-smoked them in the office in flagrant violation of workplace health codes and federal law. He was sick to his stomach of cigarettes, never wanted to see another one as long as he lived, but the look of disgust on David's face every time he lit one made it worth it every time.

Of course, it was only and entirely thanks to Rob that anybody was able to move around the building at all, even with extreme caution and risk. Rob had been responsible for keeping the hotel's free-roaming zombie population under thirty bodies. Rob had been the one to discover the magic of television.

On their second day of hiding, the need for food had become something desperate. Rob had figured out that by crouching beneath the admissions desk and throwing a stapler in the opposite direction, he could hurl himself across the lobby to the relative shelter of a Ficus plant while the zombies were looking the other way. After that, he could make it down the corridor to the restaurant kitchen unnoticed. He'd thrown together some sandwiches and was sneaking back through the bar when he chanced to look up and see what everyone was staring at.

Eight zombies, four of them waitresses he'd thought he might have had a chance with before they came over all dead and whatnot, stood frozen in the middle of the MacDonnell Lounge with their softly glowing eyes locked on one of the six TVs that dotted the bar. Most of the local channels had been showing twenty-four-hour coverage of the ongoing crisis, but were now black, the stations having all gone off the air. The TV above the bar, somehow, was still piped into the satellite and picking up a *Game of Thrones* marathon. The flickering screens so held the zombies' attention that he could almost have stood up and strolled back out to the lobby, stopping for a beer on the way. He did no such thing of course, but it had given him an idea.

After lunch and a cigarette—blowing foul blue smoke over David's sandwich with great delight—Rob had snuck into a stairwell and gone to work.

Starting at the top floor and working his way down, armed only with a master keycard and a mop, he'd burst into every suite, fended off whatever lurked there with the long mop, and turned on the TV. Instantly the hotel directory channel would pop up, a calm soothing voice would explain over and over how to operate the parental controls and what sights to see in downtown Toronto. After that, it was simply a matter of shutting the door quietly behind him and drawing a large Z on the door in Sharpie for future reference. Any zombies he found wandering the halls could be easily lured into a room and shut away with a flickering television for company.

The crowd in the lobby was a different story. Too many to be safely shut away or kept happy by a single television, they were nonetheless a much more real and immediate danger. So Rob, Yvonne, and David stayed in the office drinking water from the dispenser and relieving themselves as best they could in a bucket in the file room, and generally driving each other crazy. Rob slept on the floor with his back against the door, and David usually passed out at his desk after one last finger of scotch. Yvonne never slept, as far as Rob could tell. She was cleaning when he drifted off, and when he woke up she was either still cleaning or cleaning again. She had a hunted, hollow-eyed look and he wondered if she thought she'd be deported if she fell asleep at work.

David's point, that if they could clear out the lobby they would have the run of the hotel, was an attractive one. They could each take a suite upstairs, on separate floors and separate sides of the hotel, ride out this crisis in style, and never have to look at one another again. David, it seemed, had a plan. As a good manager, he had opted to delegate the enacting of his plan to Rob. To Rob's genuine surprise, it was a really good plan.

He crept out of the office one last time. He slunk over to the desk and yanked the mouse out from the computer terminal. He was running out of things to throw. The mouse flew across the lobby and clunked against the far wall, landing in a pile with the rest. As one, twenty heads swiveled away from him and forty feet set to shuffling in the direction of the sound. Phase One complete.

Rob pulled out his beloved Game Boy from his pocket. A vintage treasure, he had discovered it in pristine shape in a dusty box in Kensington Market. It had kept him from going completely insane over the last four days, and he desperately hoped he could get it back when this was all over.

He flicked the ON switch and dialed the volume all the way to high, then set it on the floor in the middle of the lobby before running full-tilt for the Ficus. After a few seconds, the familiar Tetris theme began to play from the tinny speakers.

Dun

Duh-na-na

Duh-na-na

Duh-na-na

Duh-na-nun

Da-Dun

Dun-dun-dun-dun

Like a flock of very stupid pigeons the crowd of zombies wheeled back to the center of the room and gathered around the singing Game Boy. Rob stood up again and ran around to the other end of the lobby.

Around a corner from the office was a spacious locked room, wide and empty and lined with shelves on three walls. Here, guests who had arrived early could stow their luggage in a secure space and head out for a drink or a meal while they waited for their room to be ready. Rob unlocked the door and swung it wide. With a claw hammer from the maintenance tool kit, he pried, whacked, and pounded on the inner doorknob until it snapped off. Now, according to every sitcom ever, the door could not be opened from inside once it was closed. That was Phase Two. Phase Three would be the riskiest thing he had ever attempted in his life, but if he could pull it off, it would be legendary.

Rob started to run. He raced easily past the lobby crowd gathered in the middle of the lobby. A few heads snapped up to follow his passage, but the rest stayed fixed on the tiny black-and-white screen of the Game Boy. Rob ran on into the bar. This time, rather than hiding behind the door and sneaking in at a crouch, he burst through the double doors so that they smashed into the walls and knocked over a hanging print.

"Hey!" he shouted at the waitresses and patron who swiveled hungry eyes to face him. "Hey, fuckers!" They began to shuffle toward him. The waitress nearest to him, a cute girl named Aimee that he'd been working up the balls to ask out when she was still alive, raised her arms to him, inviting an embrace.

"Yeah, baby, now you want me, don't you?" he said, then bolted back down the hall just as Aimee reached kissing distance.

His breath was short and the blood was pounding in his head by the time he reached the lobby. *Have to quit smoking.* Holy shit, he felt fifty.

"Come on, you assholes!" he gasped at the lobby crowd. One of them was holding his Game Boy like it might turn out to be a spider, he noticed. He dashed past, avoiding their outstretched arms, and with spots dancing in front of his eyes, raced for the luggage room.

A quick glance behind showed they were following much closer than he had expected. He rounded the corner, flung himself through the door and leapt at the shelves at the back.

They followed him through the door. He felt hands brush the hem of his hotel regulation black slacks as he climbed. He made it to the top shelf and looked down. They were packing in, filling the room with arms raised high like the world's smallest, deadest rave. He would have to scramble along the shelves to get back to the door, and hope his weight wasn't enough to topple them. He saw David standing at the threshold with a wide push broom, ready to shove back anyone who tried to leave the room. Good, thought Rob, about time he helped me out around here.

Rob gripped at the shelving and edged his way along the top. He was almost to the doorway. The entire crowd was now packed in, and only Aimee stood between Rob and freedom. If he could land a solid-enough kick he could force her back long enough to jump clear, and was just getting ready to launch himself off the shelf when the door swung shut and latched with a deadly, final *click*.

"Hey!" he cried. "Hey! No, you son of a bitch, open the door!" He leaned out at a dangerous angle and kicked at the door, a weak blow because of his precarious position, robbed of its justified vehemence.

There was no answer. No one was there to hear. He was alone with the dead.

David Archibald let go of the door, dropped the broom, and straightened his tie. Movement in the corner of his eye made him whirl, wide-eyed. But it was only Yvonne, staring at him from the office door.

"What?!" he barked, but she shook her head and disappeared from the doorway.

David was no fool. You didn't get to his position by being sentimental. A good manager had to make sacrifices for the good of the hotel. He knew that the infected would never stand still and allow him to shut them in without something to hold their attention, something a little more interesting than a Game Boy. The entire mob might have pushed their way back out. Even if one or two escaped, it would have meant killing them or being killed himself, and David Archibald was not going to be held responsible for the murder of a guest, not when a cure might yet be found. It was too bad for Rob, but the boy was a dead weight, on his last legs at this job even before the infection. At the least, thought David, he would never have to hear that incessant video game again, or smell one of those disgusting cigarettes.

The screams continued a lot longer than he would have thought. He paced around. The hotel was open to him, all fourteen floors of suites, the gym, the pool. The bar. He couldn't think of anywhere to go, so he went back to his office and poured another drink. Yvonne was gone. Fine, let her clean up some other room. She was driving him crazy with her incessant scrubbing. She was on her last legs in this job, too.

He paced around some more. He kicked something, looked down and saw it was Rob's half-empty pack of cigarettes. Out of curiosity, he lit one. Disgusting, he thought. He smoked it right to the filter. He got some cleaning supplies out of the maid's closet. He poured another drink.

Outside, it began to rain. The dead took no notice.

CHAPTER FIVE

An empty building sat on the corner, brooding squat and grey as it loomed over the tracks Wendell was following. It had been abandoned for as long as he could remember, and now nothing remained but a concrete shell, huge empty squares devoid of glass staring like dead eyes over the bridge that unofficially divided the shitty part of Eastern Toronto from the shitty part of Central Toronto. Under the bridge ran a tendril of the filthy Don River. Over it ran two matched sets of streetcar tracks, and at one end of it Wendell stopped and hid behind a van while he scoped out the area.

All along King Street so far, he'd been able to mostly walk in the open. The wide, well-lit street was open enough for him to see, if he was alert enough, anyone approaching long before they arrived, and provided enough cover in the form of an endless line of stalled and abandoned vehicles that he could hide more than he needed to fight. It being night and power in the city still running strong on its failsafes, there weren't many wanderers about. Those he did see eventually found somewhere new to wander without ever coming close to endangering him.

But now, he crouched across the bridge from the black gaping mouth of the empty shell of the abandoned building, and he questioned his chances. There were no doors or windows, and the interior could hide any number of surprises, he well knew. Once, as a teenager, he'd been walking home after leaving his friends, tipsy from a night of underage drinking, when from out of its dark recesses he'd been accosted by an emaciated prostitute with no teeth—a sickly, wasted creature who had asked in a gummy lisp if he wanted some company. Her denim shirt was held shut by only a single button, an attempt at alluring sexiness that only made the horror of her more profound. Utterly unsure how to react, the teenaged Wendell had politely stammered out a "no thank you" and fled as fast as he could down the dark street. The memory of that empty mouth and single button still haunted his nightmares.

He was afraid of that building, and he knew for a fact that what it was hiding now was a thousand times worse than any hooker. The first wisps of dawn were edging in and he needed to find shelter fast, but wasn't sure if his nerves could handle it. Not tonight.

He'd found himself involved in a brief short scrap that had his pulse still racing now, hours later. He'd been moving swiftly west on King, following the streetcar tracks that were the only clue he had to which way Grace had gone, when he heard the sound. A rhythmic, pulsing sound, somewhere between the whir of machinery and the scrape of a dragging foot. Approaching up a side street. And coming fast.

He'd thrown himself behind the open door of the nearest abandoned car and crouched, huddled and shaking, and praying that he hadn't been seen. The sound came closer and closer, passed him close on the other side of the car, and zoomed past at a speed much too fast for a zombie.

Ever so carefully, he'd eased his head up above the car's rear bumper in time to see, of all things, a girl. Strangely dressed, in some weird combination of a sexy schoolgirl and a well-padded rugby player, she went whipping down the street in the opposite direction from where he was going. As she sped between two cars, he'd seen the streetlights shine on a pair of bright green roller skates. He'd watched in stunned disbelief until she disappeared from view, and that was when a hand brushed the back of his neck.

With a scream that he was more than a little ashamed of, Wendell had whirled around to see a man leaning out of the front seat of the car, reaching for him with claw-like hands and glaring with what was left of his face.

Without even realizing he'd moved, Wendell was suddenly swinging his hammer up and down, smashing it repeatedly into the dead man's face until his arm was aching. He hadn't even realized he was screaming until he'd stopped and the silence came rushing back in to fill the void. Then, as he'd stood there panting, his arm burning with exertion and soaked in gore, he'd begun to hear the sliding footsteps on the street behind him, and knew it was time to start running. Just before he fled, he'd allowed himself one time to look at his handiwork.

There was nothing left of the zombie's face but mush, its nose caved in a cascade of shattered bone and cartilage, leaving a black hole that vomited blood and teeth. Yet, to his everlasting horror, the thing still held its head up, lurching blind and drunkenly from side to side looking for him. Wendell had nearly dropped his hammer, holding onto its gore-soaked handle only through sheer will. Leaving the faceless abomination writhing in the drivers' seat, he had turned and fled, stopping only once to vomit his disgust on the pavement of King Street East.

Even now, he couldn't understand it. Between the bodies he'd cleared out of the apartment building and the ones he'd encountered since leaving it, he'd killed his fair share of zombies. All of them had reacted exactly the way he'd been led to expect. All the movies, and common zombie lore by extension, said that a zombie could be killed by removing the head or destroying the brain. And sure enough, he'd had enough of them fall to his hatchet to prove the remove-the-head adage—back when he had a hatchet. But he'd done enough damage to the car zombie to have wrecked huge tracts of brain. By accepted logic, the car zombie should have been rightfully at peace now. Then he remembered the young man that attacked him outside the co-op. He'd driven his hatchet into its skull so hard he'd had trouble getting it back out again. That had thrown him for a curve, but he'd eventually been able to put the zombie down. How? He couldn't remember. The answer niggled at him, dancing tantalizingly close to the edge of his thoughts, but he just couldn't grasp it. It didn't matter now, anyway. He had a building to get past. He had to find safety before daylight hit. He could puzzle out the answer once he was locked up somewhere safe.

He could go around the building by taking a side street, circle around and find another bridge, but he knew the next nearest bridge was a long way away, and would mean leaving the streetcar tracks. He couldn't do that, not if it meant risking losing Grace. He had only one trick up his sleeve. It was desperate, and could be even worse than doing nothing. Clipped to his belt was the only thing he had left of his apartment, the only thing he'd been permitted to keep by the shadows at the sporting goods store. If there were zombies hiding in the recesses of the derelict building, it would certainly clear them out. The trouble was that it might also put more zombies in his path beyond the building than he could handle.

Grimly, he unhooked the carabiner that held Grace's old alarm clock to his belt. He set the alarm for five minutes from now and wound it up. Then he set the clock in the middle of the bridge and slunk away.

He was under the bridge, standing hip-deep in the murk of the Don River, when it went off with a high-pitched trilling that would ring and ring forever, or until it ran down, because nobody would ever be there to hit the snooze button. He used the noise to cover him as he splashed across the shallow channel, and poked his head up the other side to risk a peek.

A full half dozen shambling forms emerged from the recesses of the concrete husk. One by one, they all stumbled over the curb and onto the bridge. One of them passed within a foot of where Wendell's head poked up over the embankment, and he ducked down rapidly. None of them paid him any attention. But from behind them, just as he'd feared, came dozens, if not hundreds. The surrounding streets were emptying out, and the King Street Bridge was filling up.

He watched for longer than was really safe. He was searching the crowd for a yellow coat, half-hoping he'd spot it, half praying he wouldn't.

The bridge was one packed dance club, two dozen people swaying without rhythm around the toneless music of the shrill alarm. Wendell crouched in the water, wondering how long to wait, how far he could make it. No one was on the near street just then. A pair of stragglers shuffled along by the water, late to the party. With any luck, they wouldn't notice him. At any rate, they were the least of his worries. He put both hands into the mud of the embankment and heaved himself up over the edge.

Then he ran, not daring to look back, feeling ghostly fingers on his neck the whole way, and the distance seemed like miles, though it was only a few steps, and then he was in the pitch-dark shelter of the derelict building. He pressed his back to a concrete wall and risked a glance outside. The bridge was still packed. One of them was holding Grace's alarm clock, and the gathered crowd was staring at it like thirteen-year-olds who'd gotten hold of a *Playboy*. Nobody was looking his way. He'd made it.

He stood panting in an endless, inky blackness, which was both good and bad—good because he saw no eyes gleaming out at him, and bad because he imagined all sorts of worse horrors instead. He saw in his mind the man from the car, inching closer with his head held at a tilt, listening for Wendell's shallow breathing, faceless and awful.

Wendell held his breath. For an instant he thought he heard something squelching ever closer and was about to let out a fatal scream when he realized it was his own muddy boots on the floor.

Breathe, Wen, he heard Grace's voice in his head. *Breathe.* He breathed. He stepped out from the wall, inching his way in terror and silence through the darkness to the other door he knew had to be somewhere near. His fingers brushed hard stone, and he followed it along, until there was an opening and he went through into even deeper dark. He kept his hand on the wall and remembered, across a distance of years, the voice of the old firefighter.

"Always keep your left hand on the wall when searching a room. If you lose the wall, you'll get turned around in the smoke and wind up lost. You stay where you're supposed to be, you might save someone's life. You get lost, and then I have to save yours, and then I won't be happy."

He kept his hand on the wall and followed the room in a circle. It wasn't so bad. He imagined he was back in the smoke house, weighted down with heavy gear and an air tank that felt like it weighed more than he did, that first week, breathing through a mask that kept fogging up around his eyes. He'd wanted to be a firefighter, way back when. He'd wanted to be a hero. It turned out he'd wanted to want to be a firefighter more than he actually wanted to be one, and he hadn't stuck. But the training had, to his surprise, and he felt it coming back now. Stay calm. Stay low. Keep your eye on what's right ahead of you. Clear the room before going on to the next. *Lesson One.*

His hand brushed something sticky and wet and he gasped and choked back vomit, but he didn't lose the wall. He felt another doorway, and went through. On and on he went, how long he didn't know, hours maybe, maybe only minutes. Suddenly he was aware that he could see his fingertips against the black wall, then his feet.

Ahead of him was a window, a square glassless hole, and outside the night was as bright as day.

In the middle of King Street sat a corpse.

It wasn't quite dead, but unlike the others, it would not be rising again. Its wheels had come off the tracks, and now it lay sideways across the street at a dangerous tilt. Somehow, the tall radial still hooked to the cable above, feeding it from the city's seemingly endless power, and so its two headlights shone toward the doors of the coffee shop it had died in front of, gleaming like the eyes of its driver, still belted to his seat.

The Number Two streetcar.

Wendell wasn't prepared for it yet. On the pretence of scoping out the area, he let his eyes wander into the coffee shop, well lit by the headlights. It was a place he knew well. He'd been here on the happiest moment of his life.

She'd been sitting at the chipped Formica table in front of him, toying with a coffee spoon and smiling a winsome little smile.

"So," she said. "Do you want to find out?" They had just come from the doctor.

He sipped at his black coffee, strong and vile. The point of Nora's coffee shop wasn't actually the enjoyment of the coffee. "Actually, no, not really," he said.

"Why not, Wen? Aren't you excited?"

"Of course I'm excited," he said. "I just think that it would...I don't know, spoil the surprise, I guess."

This was his and Grace's favorite place to come and stare at one another. The coffee was terrible, the menu spare and bland, but the service was excellent, and after an evening walk, it was the best place nearby to stop and talk before turning back for home.

Grace shrugged. "Surprise me now or surprise me later, I'm still going to be surprised. Besides, how will we know what color to paint the room?"

"I don't really see how that's a problem. People have been getting by just fine not knowing for centuries."

"But the room..." she pouted.

"Can be white, or green, or whatever color we want it to be. Once you find out, you're kind of stuck with one or the other. I don't see how cutting out options is better." He lifted his giant chipped mug and drained the last dregs. One for me.

"More coffee, hon?"

Nora never failed to astound him. His mug hadn't even had time to make the trip back to the table, but Nora, a great vast woman who moved like a ninja despite her size, had slipped over so fast she might have been standing behind him. Just to be sure, he looked behind him anyway, satisfied that there really was a wall there.

"Now come on, Nora, you know you never need to ask that," laughed Grace as Nora's steady hand poured scalding hot tar into his mug.

"Well, how else is a woman supposed to get any attention around here? Good looking man like this walks into my shop and I can't even get him to look at me, he's so busy drowning in your eyes." Nora flirted with Wendell shamelessly every time they came in. It was a game between them.

"What can I say?" asked Wendell, "There's worse places to drown."

"Ha! One of these days you'll get so lost in them brown eyes you'll step off a curb and get run over by a bus, and then where will I be? Sitting here, consoling your poor widow. And meanwhile everyone will say, well, he was a hell of a handsome man, but boy was he dumb."

He looked at his wife for some assistance, but she was no help—holding her hand over her mouth and rocking with silent laughter. She pretended to be offended by Nora's flirting just as Wendell pretended to be flattered. In reality, he was on his own.

"You're always looking out for me, Nora."

Afterwards, when the coffee was drained, he would throw his money on the table, take Grace's hand and pull her close, and smile at Nora.

"Say goodnight, Gracie," he would say.

To which she always replied, her favorite joke and who cared who she stole it from, "Goodnight, Gracie."

The glass was smashed in now. All the tables were upended and pushed around. At the counter, staring at the streetcar's headlights like they held some secret was the enormous frame of a woman, her apron bloodied and her eyes glowing softly. It horrified him to think Nora and Grace may have died in sight of each other, but of course, he could never know that. He couldn't even tell which way the streetcar had been going—east to Yonge Street and the subway Grace would ride to the hospital, or west back to Wendell. He shouldered his grief and turned his eyes to the car.

The doors stood forced open. The interior was dark. Probably there hadn't been any lights on inside at ten in the morning. Other than the ghostly eyes of the driver, who stared at Wendell with an expression both hungry and pleading, the car was empty. The driver reached for him as he stepped aboard, but trapped by his shoulder belt he was as helpless as a baby. Wendell had an idea to put him out of his misery, but his failure with the man in the car held him up. He had no desire to repeat that horror.

Blood glistened on some of the seats as he walked up the aisle. He passed abandoned purses and forgotten newspapers, and one blue stroller that he steadfastly refused to look at.

The absence of people made it worse. Was the carnage total, or had some made it away? Did the attack come from outside after the streetcar ran aground, or was it the cause of the crash? Did they all flee in terror or die screaming and trapped when somebody woke up in the back?

His hand reached out of its own accord and closed on a thick piece of cloth. In the darkness, he couldn't make out the color, but he knew in his heart what he would see. A yellow coat, eleven dollars at Value Village but looking far more expensive, missing one button of a size and color that just couldn't be found anywhere in the city.

Puddles on the pavement shone with the reflected light of the streetlights. Above him, the sky was clear, though he could see no stars. From end to end, the street was silent. The flames spreading from Nora's kitchen were peaceful, almost pleasant as they lapped at the counter, the chairs, the owner. Wendell held his wife's coat and sobbed, gripped with a despair so total it seemed to fill every crack and radiate out of every fold. Not for the first time, he thought about killing himself. Just fall into the fire. Heat, and then pain, and then nothing. He willed the thought away.

He couldn't give up. Not yet.

Somewhere in the city, his wife was dead. She was walking around, trapped in a living hell, with glowing eyes and a hunger for flesh.

He had to find her, somehow. Find her and free her.

Only then could he let himself die.

PART TWO
SHEILA

CHAPTER SIX

She sat on the windowsill with her back to the night air, and lit another cigarette. The sidewalk below her was probably filled with spent butts, but it didn't matter anymore. The tremors began again, and she hugged her arms tight to herself until they passed. They were coming more frequently now. She didn't have much longer.

She leaned out of the window a little further and craned her neck to stare down a street as desolate as despair. Every time she saw a figure moving she dared to hope, but it would always turn out to be another shambling husk, one of the infected. Her people, soon enough. She wondered if Mark was one of them, and quickly shied away from that line of thought. She had to hope that someone would come, and soon. She hadn't much time left.

When the news reports started getting bad, she was alone, cuddled up with Sheila on the couch. The baby's colic had finally gone down a little bit, and she was enjoying a welcome break from the endless crying jags when the TV was interrupted for the first time. Mob attacks on Toronto General Hospital, was the first report. By the time Mark called from work, there were rumors of army units arriving to deal with what was then still described as civil unrest. She knew better, as did most people by that time.

"Don't go outside," Mark had said to her. "Lock the doors and wait. I'm on my way, Christine. I'll be home soon." That was eight days ago. Mark never arrived home.

Instead came the ravenous dead. So clumsy and stupid, almost comical the way they stumbled around on the street below, mindlessly bumping into lamp posts, cars, each other. To look at them, you would think they posed no reasonable threat. Christine knew different, though. She'd seen it on the third day. A man, probably just barely out of his teens, had come running down the street from who knew where, his eyes wild and his breath labored. She watched him from her third floor window and almost called out, though what she'd hoped to do for him she never could say. He slowed for only a moment, to catch his hiccupping breath.

The woman meandering around the parking meters must have been in her seventies when she died. She could barely stand on one rickety leg and one flayed piece of meat with a shoe on it. Christine had seen her topple down when faced with only a short curb to step over, but she caught sight of the fleeing young man and came around beside him. In a foot race, even barely breathing, he should have been able to outrun her, but then she leaped.

She pounced with staggering speed, her movements wild and uncontrolled and her aim a little off from her decimated leg, yet she closed the three feet between them in a single airborne hurtle. She hit him spread-eagle, a tangle of arms and legs, and the young man toppled. She heard him scream and turned away. As she closed the window on his cries, she saw a gaggle of them coming from all over the street, closing in.

The young man never got up. When the streetlights came on and the crowd dispersed, there wasn't enough left of him to animate.

Christine looked once more up the street with fading hope and shuddered as another tremor came on. Her vision grayed and the next thing she knew, she was on the living room floor. She didn't have much longer. The bandage around her arm was soaked red. The wound wouldn't close.

She stood up and stumbled to the bedroom. Sheila was asleep, thank God. Whatever happens, let her sleep through this, she prayed. She had filled every bottle in the apartment and left them piled on one side of the crib, so that if the baby awoke alone, she would eventually find them. She had no idea how much time it would buy. As Mark used to say, you never have all the answers. All you can do is do your best, and pray. She prayed now, though she was beginning to doubt anyone was listening. She shut the door softly and went back to the window, almost tripping over the dead man on the carpet. Her vision was beginning to fog, so she lit another cigarette to stay awake.

They had come to the sound of crying. Sheila's colic had returned and she was belting her loudest, her tiny hands screwed up tight and her face a red ball of scrunched-up pain and confusion. Christine heard the pounding on the door, the moans and grunts, but nothing she could do would quiet the noise. She held a meat cleaver in her hand, ready to swing it with all her force at the first thing that came through the door.

She got him in the back of the neck, a good hard swing with a satisfying thump. He dropped to the floor, but not without taking a piece of her, too.

The note was in her hand, clenched tight. No matter what,

she had to hold on to it. It said everything she needed to say. Now all there was to do was to lean back, so she would fall out, not in, and wait for the darkness to come.

A wave of dizziness. A lurching nausea. Did she imagine she saw someone on the sidewalk? Just a false hope, most likely.

She was floating, light as a feather.

Please, she thought, and that was all.

Wendell screamed. There might have been words in it somewhere, maybe a curse or two, but mostly it was just a mindless scream of horror as the body fell with a wet thud directly in front of him. He ducked back against the wall and looked around, waiting to see whose attention his cry had aroused. From far away he thought he heard an answering groan, but the street was mercifully silent.

He turned back to look at the body on the sidewalk. It was a shapeless lump in a terrycloth robe. Two bare feet splayed at odd angles underneath. He moved closer. The woman's neck was broken; her eyes were closed.

Run away, his mind screamed, but he couldn't leave. Not just yet. It was a mystery he had to understand. Of all the broken down tenements in the city, of all the empty, desolate streets he'd walked on, how did a woman come to almost fall on him right here and now?

There was blood everywhere, soaking her robe and the street below. Her left arm lay on top of her, wrapped with a crude cloth bandage. A bite.

A story unfolded in his mind: a young woman all alone, attacked and bitten by one of the dead. She keeps her cool somehow, realizes the worst thing would be to come back to life, and takes appropriate steps. Guns are hard to come by, he knew for a fact. There are many ways to kill yourself, but all of them mean a quick resurrection as a flesh eater. The only way she can think of—the only way it could be done, he realized—is to fall from a height. Destroy the brain, the movies all said. He reached down with trembling fingers and lifted her eyelid. A pale white orb stared back at him, but the eye was dark. There was no telltale glow. She had succeeded.

It was sad, he thought, but somehow triumphant. This woman had taken her death into her own hands and decreed that it be on her own terms. He stood up and brushed his hands on the legs of his pants, leaving twin smears of blood down his knees. That was when he saw the note.

She had it clutched tightly in her left hand with a deadly grip, but he saw the edge of the paper fluttering in the wind. The same voice demanded he ignore it and leave, leave now, leave before they came to feast. Instead, he knelt again in the blood and pried the note from her hands. It was what Grace would have done.

Third Floor, Apartment 305.
Down the hall, second bedroom.
Her name is Sheila.

Wendell's hands shook as he read the words. Suddenly he wished he had walked down a different street.

There was a body on the stairs. Wendell poked it with his boot to see if it would move. It didn't.

The third floor hallway was a wreck. Most of the doors bore scratches and splinters, smeared with black blood where they had torn their own flesh trying to enter. The lights were out halfway down, their fixtures smashed, plunging most of the hall into a flickering half-light that was worse than darkness. Here and there, he could see bodies; whether they were the attackers or the victims he couldn't tell. None of their eyes were open; none of them moved.

Apartment 305 was at the end of the long hallway. Its door hung ajar—his old boss Stan Alban may have been a cheap bastard, but even he would have looked at the ancient, rotted wood of the door and lintel and been horrified. The door didn't even have a deadbolt, just a poor lock on the doorknob and a safety chain, both of which had snapped off when the brittle wood was forced. He eased it open and peered into the apartment—hammer in hand.

A dead man lay on the floor facedown, a meat cleaver sticking out of the back of his neck. Toys and colorful picture books lay scattered amid the chaos of broken furniture and blood.

Her name is Sheila.

Who was Sheila? Did he honestly want to know? A part of Wendell was full of fear and wanted to run. Why was Sheila his problem? There were other survivors around, some with much more to live for and no dead wife to kill. He hadn't wanted to save anyone, only to find Grace and die with her. That was his mission. Now there was Sheila. A child? An infirm mother-in-law with dementia? Whose life had fate put in his hands and why, why now? It was…it was inconvenient. This Sheila was going to get him killed, and then where would he be?

Instead, he moved further into the apartment. A window hung open at the far end of the living room, an empty pack of cigarettes on the sill. Was that where the nameless woman sat and waited for death? It was clever, he thought, more clever than he would have been capable of, in the same situation. Sit on the sill, backwards so that the night lay at your back and you didn't have to look at the sidewalk and the long drop. Lean back and wait for the inevitable. A fall from three stories would kill you a second time, guarantee you wouldn't get up again. A high, keening cry pierced the silence, and he moved down the hall.

Second bedroom.

Her name is Sheila.

It was a small, neat room, its walls painted a warm, inviting peach. Somebody had painted an assortment of colorful smiling characters along one wall: a girl all in stripes with white flowers in her wild hair, and a creature that resembled a blue Gumby, holding up a red blanket in salute. Three smaller children in polka dot pants rounded out the group, bordered on one side by a green blimp and on the other by an odd red train. Wendell took all of this in as an aside; his eyes drawn inexorably to the crib from which the trilling cries came.

From the doorway, he could see a wide assortment of full bottles scattered at intervals around the rails. They held milk or formula, and had been left there in case the baby awoke before someone found her mother's body and the note. The baby hadn't discovered them yet. The cries were loud, dangerously loud, and tiny, balled fists no larger than a peach pit shook the air in helpless frustration. Two tiny feet encased in white footy pajamas kicked angrily. Wendell walked into the room.

Making strange was an expression he'd heard associated with infants, who might fuss and bawl in the presence of an unfamiliar person until returned to the comfort of their parents' arms. He entered slowly, sure the crying would get louder when the infant saw his strange face. Already they seemed loud enough to attract anything milling around out in the street. Half of him was still ready to leave, to run at the first sign of danger, run until his breath was gone and he'd left his conscience far behind. Instead, he came to stand above the crib, and looked down.

Her name is Sheila, the note said, and Sheila did not make strange. The minute he stepped into view, her crying stopped. Enormous dark eyes stared into his and she broke into a wide toothless smile.

Wendell picked up one of the bottles and placed it in her small clutching hands. Within moments, she was gulping greedily at the formula. He knew very little about babies, a subject he'd been looking forward to becoming expert on over the coming months, and had no way of guessing the age of the infant. She was past the squalling, red-faced newborn stage but not even close to taking her first steps. He seemed to remember that holding their own bottle was a milestone in itself, and so he put her age at somewhere between three and six months.

As she drank, her large eyes roamed around the room, pausing now and then to rest on Wendell's face. When their eyes met, he felt a tightening in his chest, an unfamiliar sensation that was part fear, part wonder, and he questioned that he had ever even entertained the notion of turning around and running. He found himself smiling back down at her.

A soft footfall on the carpet behind made him turn, and suddenly he was looking into an altogether different pair of wide eyes, burning with an altogether more vicious hunger.

Someone *had* come to investigate the noise.

She stood barely five feet tall, short silver curls matted with grime against her skull. Her face was lined with age, her mouth ringed with a lipstick of dried blood. Beneath her filthy brown skirt stood one bare leg, rotted and chewed, with tendrils of sinew dangling from the wound like tattered cloth. But when she charged it was with a savage growl and no trace of infirmity.

Wendell took the blow and rolled with it, allowing their combined weight to send them both crashing to the floor, then pushing up with his knees until they rolled together and she was under him. He held her at bay with both arms as she snapped her jaws in his face with inhuman strength, chomping at air just inches from his nose. It took all his strength just to keep her pinned. Above him, Sheila began to cry again.

His hammer lay on the beige carpet right next to him, but with both hands locked onto the woman's shoulders to hold her down, it might have been in another room. Besides, he had no wish to repeat the horror of his failed and grotesque beating of the night before, especially next to the crib where the baby lay helpless.

Still, he had to end this quickly. Whether by the old woman's ringing of the dinner bell or the baby's terrified cries, company would be coming soon. He expected to hear the pounding of feet on the floor outside and to be overwhelmed at any moment. If that happened, he had no doubt that both he and Sheila would die.

He shoved back and rolled away, catching the old woman with a heavy work boot to the jaw as she tried to rise. Something black shot out of her mouth and landed with a heavy wet thump on the floor beneath the crib. Then he was on his feet, hammer in his hand.

The old woman spun nimbly around and came to her feet. She stood swaying, her eyes unfocused. Her mouth hung open, but there was something wrong with the shape of it. It seemed too loose to Wendell, as if the skin around it drooped where a moment ago it had been tight around her teeth, locked in a ferocious grin and gnashing.

Her jaws opened wide and snapped shut on nothing. Empty grey gums bit vicious but pointlessly at the air, and Wendell realized suddenly that he'd kicked out the woman's teeth. He glanced down and saw a pair of slimy dentures lying under the baby's crib, dripping ooze all over the carpet. How she'd managed without will or wit to keep them in her mouth all these days he could never know, but the old woman was effectively neutered now. He came forward and shoved her with the hammer, driving her out through the bedroom door and away from the terrified Sheila.

Zombie or not, Wendell had no desire to beat someone's grandmother to death with a hammer, especially now that she posed no physical threat to him. She attacked him three times, charging forward, and he shoved her back into the living room. The third time she closed her toothless jaws over his sleeve, and when he pushed her back, tripping her over the body of the man with the meat cleaver in his neck, she left a trail of viscous black slime across his shirt.

She looked genuinely pathetic lying sprawled on the living room floor, jaws clenching in helpless rage with a mournful blank stare. Wendell regarded her with a mixture of revulsion and grief until his gaze fell on the dead man over whom she had tripped. The old woman's gnawed leg lay across the man's back. Next to it, the handle of the meat cleaver gleamed, heavy and black, its blade buried deep in the gristle ben~ ʰ the skull. Wendell had never yet felled a zombie with blow, but the unnamed woman who lay dead on the had managed it. How?

He thought about the man behind the sporting goods store. A blow to the head, just like in the movies. Nothing.

He thought about the family gathered around their dying mother's sickbed. Decapitated, all.

He thought about the baby's mother, lying face up beneath her living room window, staring at the streetlights' glow.

He looked again at the handle of the cleaver.

The sound of boots thumping on the landing outside snapped him back. He spun around and ran to brace the door just as it flew open and slammed into the door of the coat closet behind it. In stepped a corpse, drool flying from his lips.

Wendell didn't stop, but drove forward with his hammer swinging. Blow by blow, he pushed the zombie back, back, back until it was out of the apartment and back onto the landing. When he was clear of the splintered doorframe, Wendell reached out, grabbed his arm and spun him around.

They wound up pressed together like a cop and a perp in a primetime crime show. The zombie's arm was pinned behind his back and Wendell stood safely behind him, close enough to smell the fetid gas that escaped its putrefying lungs through its wildly champing teeth. Next, the cop would grab the other hand and cuff him while reading him his rights, but instead Wendell drew back with the hammer and hit him as hard as he could in the back of the neck, at the base of his skull.

Its body went limp and it dropped to the floor like a marionette with its strings cut.

He stared down at the corpse, adrenalin making his whole body tremble. He'd done it. He figured out the secret. In hindsight, it made perfect sense.

Wendell turned away from the body and went back inside the apartment. He shut the door, but it swung back open again with no latch to keep it shut.

He felt something soft close around his ankle and stumbled, nearly falling into the coat closet. The old woman held his leg in a viselike grip, still trying to gum him to death. Her toothless mouth morphed into a grotesque shape as she tried to gnaw on the leg of his jeans. Revolted, he kicked out reflexively and she staggered backwards over the sill and out the open window.

Later that night, when he looked out the window he saw that the old woman's body was gone from the sidewalk, but Sheila's mother glared up at him still.

CHAPTER SEVEN

W endell grabbed a heavy armchair from the living room
and dragged it across the small apartment and in front
of the door, then went back into the room where Sheila still
lay in her crib.

The baby was no longer crying, but a low, miserable
keening came from the crib. He reached down ever so gently
and picked her up.

Any last reservations he might have had disappeared the
moment he held her in his arms. Her tiny body teemed with
life. He could feel her rapid heartbeat through his palms. One
of her hands reached out and grabbed his sleeve. She had a
strong grip. Her eyes were wide and dark.

Even as he picked her up, he could smell what was making
her so miserable. Looking around the room, he found a table
with a padded mat on top. He laid her down on the mat and
realized he'd made a mistake—with one hand he had to hold
her to the padding so she wouldn't roll off while he fumbled
blindly with the other through a confusing assortment of
cubbies and baskets to find a diaper.

Changing a baby was another skill he'd hoped to learn

somewhere down the line, ideally with Grace standing beside him and showing him what to do. Instead, Wendell was about to have a crash course on diaper studies, with no qualified instructor in sight.

He tugged on the feet of her pajamas. The damn thing was all one form-fitting piece. "How the hell do you get this off?" He couldn't find a zipper, a button, an instruction manual. "How the—" He tugged again, and with a muted pop, a seam opened up beside her foot. Further investigation revealed a row of tiny snaps on the inside of the pajama legs running in a U-shape all the way up to the diaper area and back down again. "Gotcha," he whispered. Sheila stared up at him in silence. She seemed to recognize that whatever was wrong was being fixed, and she watched him curiously, as if she hoped to learn the secrets herself.

He got the snaps opened - first victory. He pulled her feet and legs out of the pajamas and rolled the fabric up. Below the pajamas, another form-fitting garment that hugged the bulging diaper close and unreachable greeted him.

"Oh, for cryin' out...kid, you've got more checkpoints than a damn airport." This time he found the second set of snaps fairly quickly. It was down to him and the diaper now.

Up close and without the many layers covering it, the smell was sharper. It was a physical presence in the room. Wendell felt his gorge rising and forced it back down, breathing slowly through his mouth as he examined the diaper with the care of a bomb technician.

"Come on, Wendell. You can decapitate a zombie, but you can't handle a little poo? Get over yourself." He found a strip of tape across one side of the diaper and gave an experimental tug. It came free, just like it was supposed to. There was an identical strip on the other side. He pulled it, too. The diaper fell open.

All the violence of the last few days, all the horror and pain and doubt he'd experienced, and all the dead bodies lying rotting in his wake could not have prepared him for that sight. If the smell had been physical before, now it hit him with a fist. Wendell reeled. Sheila cooed and kicked her feet happily. Freedom!

A cloth. A towel. A rag and some Clorox. He needed something to clean this kid up with. He batted around at the boxes and compartments on the table, seeking something, anything. He found a thick, warm blanket with a satin trim.

"Well obviously that's not it," he muttered. Still, he was on the verge of using it anyway when his hand brushed a white box on the table and it sprung open revealing soft, white, damp cloths in a white box, stacked one over the other like Kleenex. "Okay!"

An even dozen Soft Touch baby wipes lay wrapped up in the terrifying diaper. Wendell's hands trembled as he finished securing the new, clean diaper. He had expected it to be harder to do up the second diaper, but it proved to be the easiest part—he just reverse-engineered the process of removing the old one. Working backwards, he snapped shut all the snaps, wiped his hands off with another baby wipe, then—just to be safe—wiped them again. Then he picked up the baby and looked at her.

He had read somewhere that when newborn babies smile, it's really only gas. Smiling is a milestone for a baby, just as much as holding her own bottle and taking her first steps. Wendell looked into Sheila's eyes, and she looked back and smiled, a joyful, toothless smile.

"Buuuh!" she said.

"You know, you might be right," he replied. "Come on, Sheila. Let's get you out of here."

The doorknob jiggled and a single thump rattled through the apartment. Wendell held his breath. A low moan came from outside on the landing, then he heard the shuffling sound of feet moving off down the hallway. *Lesson One: Zombies have short attention spans.*

He'd made himself wait a full day in the apartment. Despite the dead man in the middle of the living room, despite the broken lock and the worry that the chair might not be heavy enough to repel a determined assault, Wendell was never one to rush into a situation without thinking it through first. He'd given Sheila another bottle and put her back to bed, where she'd quickly fallen asleep again. With no small amount of guilt, he himself had gone to sleep in the dead woman's bed. His night was fitful and full of nightmares in which Grace found him instead of the other way around. Each time he found her in the nursery, grinning a rictus grin as she lifted Sheila up to her jaws...

Each time he would snap awake and pad down the small hallway into the nursery. Inevitably, he would find the baby sleeping peacefully, one hand curled up near her mouth. Then he would check the chair at the door, drink a glass of water, and turn up the baby monitor in the bedroom a little more before laying down and waiting for another nightmare.

When the baby's cries for breakfast and another diaper change rattled him awake at the ungodly hour of five in the morning, he was a wreck. He felt like he hadn't rested at all. He found some instant coffee and a kettle in the kitchen. Since the living room had a corpse in it and the nursery carpet was stained with black goo, he took her into her parents' room and let her roll around on the floor while he huddled watchfully on the bed gulping coffee and trying to will himself awake.

In the daylight, he was able to get a better view of the street below. He could see the zombies as they wandered in their absentminded shuffle, and by counting the ones he could see and multiplying by ten he believed he could get a decent estimate for how many there were out of sight but waiting.

He was also able to learn more about Sheila and her patterns, and try to figure out how in the hell he was supposed to get her safely out of the building when she was as likely to start screaming for no reason as sleep peacefully. For leave, they must. Besides the dead body in the living room and the other in the corridor, there were shattered locks, splintered doors, the fact that the building itself was utterly unprotected and there was slim chance of finding anything edible or drinkable when the meager kitchen supplies ran out.

Sheila lived entirely on formula, though she eyed his modest breakfast of toast and jam with curiosity and, he thought, a slight envy. By the time the sun peeked over the tops of the buildings across the street, he was merely clumsy at diaper duty, rather than inept. When for no good reason at all she began to scream at the top of her lungs—she was fed, she was changed, he'd somehow managed to coax a burp out of her—he grabbed the first toy he saw, a bright pink bunny, and shook it in front of her face. The bunny made her scream harder, so he threw it and grabbed a purple octopus. All the while, he kept one eye anxiously on the door.

The octopus did the trick somehow. She fell silent, staring with wide eyes as little bells in its tentacles made a soft jingling sound. Her face wore an expression of rapture. When she fell asleep a few minutes later, he gently moved her and the octopus back to her crib, where she slept for almost exactly two hours. Wendell puttered around the tiny space like a caged lion.

Dusk was falling. He said a silent prayer and breathed a deep sigh of relief when the streetlights kicked on. The city's power was still holding. Back in 2003, a massive blackout knocked out power to the entire city and caused a chain reaction that led, within minutes, to blackouts across Ontario and the Northeastern United States. The cause of the incident was thought to be a bird flying into a transformer and a failure of the failsafes put in place to prevent that sort of thing. As a result, Toronto Hydro had installed backups on their backups and assured the public that such a thing could never happen again. As a result, even though there had been no one around to keep the system maintained, the power continued to flow, though Wendell knew that couldn't last. He only hoped that the lights stayed on long enough to get him and Sheila to safety. Night was still the safest time to travel; the dead would huddle around neon signs and streetlamps, staring with fascination at the lights and colors that played across their faces. For the most part, they would not even notice him walk by, unless he drew attention to himself. He had strolled right past a woman the night before, clutching his hammer with white knuckles, but the woman never turned from the neon diner sign. Her expression, now that he thought of it, reminded him of Sheila's face when he shook the purple octopus in front of her.

He had filled a diaper bag with everything he thought he might possibly need, including stacks of diapers and those infernal frustrating pajamas. He had located an old backpack and filled it to the brim with all the powdered formula he could find. Sheila dozed in the kitchen in a car seat with a carry handle. It was time to go.

Wendell looked around the apartment one more time for anything he might have forgotten, and his gaze fell on the stuffed octopus. He grabbed it and shoved it into the backpack, where the bells on its arms jingled threateningly.

There was a car half a block from the building, legally parked and undamaged in all the chaos. He had carefully broken into the apartment across the hall while Sheila slept, in order to get a look out the window at the back of the building, and had found the keys hanging from a hook right by the door. Returning to the other apartment, with fingers crossed, he'd leaned out the window and pressed the little lock button on the key fob. To his surprise and joy, the car up the street lit up and honked. He had no idea how far he could get before the snarl of derelict traffic stopped them, but it was surely better than trying to carry a baby through zombie-filled streets, neon signs or not.

The footsteps that had faded off down the hallway were still pounding in his head, more frightening in their absence than anything. Wendell went to the window and lowered the extension cord he'd prepared.

As the CD player glided slowly to the sidewalk on thirty feet of joined extension cords, Wendell noticed that the body on the sidewalk was still there, staring up at him with accusing eyes. *You'd better not let anything happen to her,* those eyes seemed to accuse, *or so help me I'll come back for you.* He looked away. The CD player touched the sidewalk with a soft thump; he felt the cord go slack. He knelt down by the socket in the wall and plugged it in.

The only disc he could find in the house was a CD of

children's music. Immediately, the street flooded with the sound of high-pitched children singing "The Ants Go Marching One By One". Almost instantly, figures began to move in the street, called away from their private meditations by the strange and cheery sound. He gave a count of thirty, then shrugged both shoulders into the backpack, slung the diaper bag's carry strap across his chest, and picked up Sheila's carrier in one hand and his hammer in the other. He hoped the sound had drawn away the wanderer in the hallway as well, but one way or the other, he had to leave now. Timing was crucial; he had no way of knowing how long it would take for one of them to pull the plug on the stereo, and then there would be a mob on the street, free from distraction and looking for something new.

He found nobody in the hallway or on the stairwell. His reconnaissance of the other apartment had shown him what he'd hoped he would find: the back of the building opened onto a wide alleyway that ran past the adjacent buildings and hopefully opened out back onto the street. With all of the zombies occupied in front of the building, he hoped to be able to creep through the alley unnoticed and emerge next to the car with all of the street's corpses clustered safely half a block behind him. He rounded the corner onto the ground floor and spun right, toward the back entrance.

A hand grabbed at his foot and he stumbled, barely holding onto Sheila's carrier. A low gurgling moan escaped from black toothless lips as he staggered forward kicking his leg out to try to free it. He looked down and saw, nestled in the crook between the elevator and the garbage chute, half hidden by a tasteless fake potted plant, the toothless old crone with both legs splayed out at odd angles behind her on the floor. His hand with the hammer was already descending, the hammer shattered the zombie woman's skull with a sickening thump and she dropped face first onto the carpet. Wendell's leg was suddenly free, and he raced for the back door as fast as he could go with Sheila in tow.

Outside, the air was cool and fragrant. A chill breeze blew through the alleyway, sending a tattered McDonald's wrapper skipping along past his feet. Other than the wrapper, the alley was empty. Dimly from somewhere to the left and around the corner, he could hear the faint tones of "The Wheels on the Bus".

As he hurried down the alley, Wendell found himself shivering. The night air was cool, but it was the cool of the approaching October whistling around the fences, that an unnaturally hot September was past and gone. Autumn was here in force. Wendell still wore only jeans and a light jacket. He would have to stock up on winter clothes soon, if he survived that long.

When he had gone what he guessed to be far enough he ducked down a side alley and in a moment was back on the street. About two blocks off to his right, the wipers on the bus were going swish swish swish, and the crowd gathered around the CD player could not have been more enrapt. To his left, the car was only a few paces away. He breathed a sigh of relief and started toward it, keys jingling in the hand that held the hammer.

He unlocked the car and opened the back door. Sheila's carrier was designed to strap into the rear seatbelt and he'd familiarized himself with the instructions during his long interminable wait in the apartment. He lifted her in and gently placed her on the seat. He was fumbling the seatbelt around the rear of the seat and beginning to realize just how different reading instructions could be from the real thing, when the sleeping baby suddenly awoke to the cold and the unfamiliar night. Her eyes blinked once, then snapped open wide with fear and confusion. She began to cry.

"No, no, no, no, nonono," gasped Wendell as he quickened his pace on the straps. He lost his hold on the seatbelt and it slithered back through all his effort and into its holster. He glanced behind him. One of the dead had turned away from the stereo and was gazing back up the street.

"Shhh, baby, shhh," Wendell whispered, "It's okay, we're almost there, and then I'll get you a bottle, just please, shhh." The baby only cried louder. Now, more of them were looking up. The music had lost its hold. The first one took a step in his direction.

Desperately he began to sing, his voice cracking.

"There is a young maiden who lives all alone," he sang, "She lives all alone on the shore-o." More heads were turning his way. "There is nothing she can find to comfort her mind, but to roam all alone on the shore, shore, shore." His voice, barely a whisper, cracked with fear, but it seemed to do the trick. Sheila's eyes found his, her cries didn't abate but they quieted. They were the only words he knew to the song, so he sang it again, softly, so that only she could hear.

"There is a young maiden." He looked back. Four or five of the zombies had turned and were moving in his direction. "She lives all alone." Sheila was whimpering now, a good sign, but the damage might already be done. "She lives all alone on the shore-o." The seatbelt clicked home in its lock. Sheila was quietly regarding him like he was a new kind of fish. He shouldered the rest of the bags onto the floor of the car and gently shut the door.

Crouching, he hustled around the back of the car and up to the driver's seat. He eased inside and had just closed the door when a hand slapped the windshield. He looked up and beheld a single glowing eye, inches from his own and separated by only a pane of glass. The other eye was, like the rest of that half of its face, gone, torn off right down to the skull. Tiny white teeth clicked at him. Black goo dribbled from its smiling, lipless mouth.

Wendell whispered, "Please," jammed the key into the ignition and turned. The engine started up with a roar, and now everybody left undead in the street was looking at him, headed his way. He jammed the car into drive and floored the gas. The car jolted, leaped, and sped off. The one-eyed man toppled off the hood and rolled beneath the wheels. Wendell never let off the gas. He was still singing as he drove away.

CHAPTER EIGHT

They walked in a single file. Tucker and Asshat came first, straining their leashes in opposite directions. Tucker, the big noble Lab, held his head up and sniffed the air. He made a good early warning for zombies; he would smell them far in advance and growl, fearlessly placing himself between the threat and his people. Asshat, the cringing, scrawny mutt, kept his nose low to the ground, and when he smelled a zombie, he would whimper and cower behind Dylan. Dylan held the leash, and Jesse walked beside him. Dylan's coat hung past his knees and the sleeves were cut off and tied back to fit his wrists. A goofy look, perhaps, but they didn't make firefighter's gear for twelve-year-olds, and this thick padding designed to protect skin from thousand-degree fires kept him relatively safe from bites.

Jesse's coat fit. His pants fit, his boots fit, his helmet fit, the four-foot steel bar he held in his hands fit. He looked every inch the veteran firefighter, and the others followed his lead accordingly. He only wished he felt as much in control as he looked.

Behind Jesse came Keith, red-faced, huffing and always

complaining. He'd had a fireman's coat as well, but he'd given it up after only a couple of hours for being too heavy. He carried the long steel pike he'd taken from the fire truck like a walking stick. Keith had resisted every move they had made so far, and threatened to leave once or twice a day. To Jesse's annoyance, he had yet to make good on his threat.

Last came black-clad Becca, bringing up the rear. Becca wore no fire gear, though she had gladly accepted the red axe from the back of the truck. Instead, she wore a motorcyclist's leathers: leather pants, jacket, long leather boots. Her face was hidden behind a black helmet. With her axe in front and a silver revolver slung low on her hip, she stalked behind Keith with obvious impatience. She would have left Keith behind in a heartbeat a dozen times if Jesse hadn't talked her out of it. He half expected her to leave all of them behind eventually. Of the four of them, Becca was the one he judged most likely to survive the coming dangers; of the four of them, she was the only one he feared.

Tucker growled and spread his large body out in front of Dylan's legs. Asshat whimpered and huddled behind his feet. Both dogs' hair stood straight up on their backs. Jesse tightened his grip on the bar and stepped in front. Tucker was staring at the mouth of an alley, all of his vicious teeth bared.

Jesse eased his way along the wall and peered around the corner. A single zombie leaned against a garbage can, staring at the glowing lights of the CN Tower blinking above the tops of the buildings. Jesse took a tentative step forward into the alley. The zombie didn't react at all. He was incensed in the play of light across the Tower. Slowly, with great care, Jesse came forward. Zombies at night were easier to kill, but caution never hurt anyone.

The thing's expression changed from vapid stupor to alert stupor in an instant. Jesse had crossed in front of the tower. It scrambled to its feet with surprising speed and came toward him, arms outstretched and mouth agape. The pickaxe end of the bar buried itself in its skull. The zombie dropped.

Jesse wormed the hunk of steel out of the wound and breathed a sigh of relief. Sometimes a blow to the head did them in, just like the movies said. Other times it seemed to have no effect on them whatsoever, and they came on regardless. It always chilled his blood to see one of the creatures, maimed by axe or crushed by thirty pounds of metal, stand and shake off the killing blow, only to attack and kill itself. After what happened to the Squeegee Kid, Jesse never took his eye off of even a dead zombie.

He motioned for the others to follow. When they joined him in the shelter of the alley, he said, "We need to start looking for a place to hole up."

The sky was beginning to change color. Dawn wouldn't be far off, and when it came they would find themselves much more popular.

Dylan nodded, obviously relieved. Since leaving their apartment three days ago, his brother's constant expression had been one of barely controlled terror. Jesse knew if it hadn't been for his reassuring presence and—utterly false—confidence, Dylan would have snapped on the evening of the storm. Jesse looked at Becca, expecting a fight, but she just stood there without a word, faceless behind the helmet visor.

"Stop now? Are you kidding me?" To Jesse's surprise it was Keith who spoke up, Keith who had predicted they would all be dead before the night was through. They had found him huddled behind a newsstand counter in Queen Street Station two days before, and not an hour went by that he didn't wish they had taken a different route. "We're almost there. What the hell are you thinking?"

"Listen," said Jesse. "The sun's going to come up soon. It's taken us all night to get this far, and there's no telling how long it'll take to get through the last dash. Also, I don't know if you've noticed, but it's getting a lot more crowded around here." They were right smack in the middle of the downtown core, the most populous area of the most populous city in the country.

Becca flipped up her visor and regarded Keith with cool contempt. "What's your hurry anyway, Keith? The boat doesn't show up until midnight. You want to get there at six in the morning and sit around in the open for eighteen hours?" Without waiting for a response, she slid the visor back down. A faceless mirror reflected Keith's pudgy face back at him. For Becca, the discussion was over. Keith looked around to say something, thought better of it, and stepped back further into the alley. Jesse couldn't be sure, but he was fairly certain he heard Keith mutter, "Fucking kids," under his breath.

The clouds were tinged with ominous bloody red; the sky was definitely lighter and everything on the street was colored the same crisp, pale blue of an autumn dawn when Jesse saw the big red S looming overhead.

"A hotel?" hissed Becca. "That's a lot of rooms to clear, Jess."

"It'll have food," he argued. "Beds, running water. We only have to clear out the ground floor and one room, then we'll have a locking door behind us. I don't know about you, Becks." She absolutely hated when he called her that. "But I could use a shower."

She trained a practiced eye on the hotel's front entrance.

"The doors are still intact," she said. "They won't hold up to a heavy beating, but they can still be locked. If the lobby is clear, we could make it to the main office and go from there. I don't know if it's the best choice, though."

Jesse pointed across the street. A man sat staring at the neon OPEN sign of a cafe. He was beginning to fidget, to glance around. The sign wasn't the brightest thing around anymore; the spell was wearing off.

"I think it's this or nothing," he said. "We'll be fighting our way through if we wait too long."

"Okay," she said. "Let's do it."

Jesse opened the door and stepped through, holding his bar at the ready. Becca followed, holding Asshat's leash in one hand. He'd left Dylan and Keith in the protection of the larger dog. Asshat wouldn't be much in a fight, but as a canary in a mine shaft his cowardice was an effective early warning.

Nothing loomed up out of the shadows in the lobby. A Ficus plant and a luggage trolley huddled together by the elevators, on the other side a pair of couches brooded in the darkness. It was frighteningly normal, and yet Jesse couldn't shake the feeling that something was wrong. He peered into the darkness of the lobby with his heart hammering in his chest for a long moment before his mind came to grips with the fact that there was darkness in the lobby.

When you got used to the fact that every electric light left on when the infection struck was going to stay on indefinitely, the idea of walking into a public building in darkness was an alien concept. It threw Jesse right off, and even Becca seemed disconcerted, standing indecisively off to one side before shaking her head and pushing on into the murk. Jesse followed. They split up and searched the lobby, finding nothing but a strange collection of office supplies scattered near the far wall by some tan couches.

Jesse motioned the others inside. They huddled by the check-in desk while he and Becca searched the rest of the first floor.

After a ten-minute search, Jesse came back and announced that the floor was clear. Dylan smiled with relief, but deep inside he couldn't shake the feeling that something was wrong, and some mangled creature might leap out of a shadowed alcove, biting and tearing.

Two things caught Jesse's attention during his brief patrol of the first floor. Both were doors.

One door was closed. The other was not.

The door that was shut stood off to the left of the check-in desk, down the hall that led to the rooms. It had a coded electronic lock on it—five digits to push, hundreds of possible combinations. On the floor in front of it, lay the twisted and smashed remains of what he assumed was the inner door handle. He gave the door a wide berth. Even though he had no way to ever get it open, something about it made him uneasy.

The door that was ajar led to Room 117. He stared at the gap between door and jamb for a long time. He ought to have gone back for Becca, or at least for Asshat. Instead, he slid the door open and went in.

It was a standard hotel room: two beds side by side, TV bolted to a laminated wood cabinet, Gideon Bible in the drawer. One bed was rumpled, as if someone had slept there recently, but there was no other sign of life. Not even a toothbrush in the bathroom.

They could stay here. Without danger of trying random

doors to see if they were attacked, without having to figure out the electronic key card machine. Only two beds meant someone would have to sleep on the floor, but they had become used to sleeping in shifts anyways.

They could shower.

Even in the growing chill of early autumn, Jesse's thick clothing made his body a sauna. He'd been sleeping in the heavy gear for days, never feeling safe enough to take it off, and he probably stank like week-old fish. He couldn't imagine how Becca was managing in her head-to-toe air-tight leathers.

The four people and two dogs filed into the room. Becca, who had drawn the lucky short straw and got to shower first, strode wordlessly into the bathroom and slammed the door. Dylan dropped onto one of the beds and was instantly asleep. Keith sat down on the other bed and began waiting for his turn to shower, playing with the TV remote.

"Hey, look, all the movie channels are unlocked!" he said.

"Keep it PG-13, Keith," said Jesse. "Mixed company, right?" Keith muttered something about where Jesse could stuff his mixed company and kept paging through movie titles. Jesse laid the dogs down by the door and positioned a chair where he could watch it. He lit a cigarette, something he'd explored as a hobby before but was now pursuing as a serious endeavor, because who gave a fuck about cancer now? He smoked, sipped water, and tried to stay awake.

The dogs lay curled up together—the big yellow one curved protectively around the wire-haired mutt terrier. Asshat whined and pawed the air, running from something in a dream. Jesse watched him and thought about the Squeegee Kid.

The Squeegee Kid was hardly a kid, looking on the far side

of twenty-five, and by the time Jesse met him outside a comic book store on Queen Street he'd traded his squeegee for a tire iron he called his brain stick. He wore his thinning hair cut long, knee-length lace-up boots and a black trench coat, and ran around with a mangy dog. He looked like he'd originally set out to become a super hero and fallen on hard times when he discovered that it didn't pay well.

They never learned his name, and he never called them by any of theirs. Dylan and Jesse, he just called "Fuckers" and Becca he addressed as "Fine Ass Jailbait Bitch". He was a lazy, offensive, homeless white guy trying to act black. For some reason, Jesse liked him a lot.

They had been moving slowly through the downtown area, always traveling south toward the lake. Such a short distance, maybe a four hour walk on a sunny fall day, but it had taken them days. Ages of anguished waiting, hidden behind dumpsters or underneath burnt-out cars, for one of the creatures to move along. Endless rerouting and doubling back to avoid large congregations of the dead. And scouting ahead, leaving the others in what they hoped was safety while either he Becca or he and the Squeegee Kid—they couldn't stand one another and never went anywhere together— moved ahead to find the best route. It was slow, frustrating going, so when the Squeegee Kid suggested taking the PATH, it fell into the growing list of things that seem like a good idea at the time.

The PATH was a network of tunnels, basements of skyscrapers, and long underground corridors that connected most of the downtown subway stations with each other and with most of the major buildings. The halls were most often lined with enterprising little shops, making it something of a vast underground mall. The Squeegee Kid's idea was that the

PATH would be less crowded with zombies and it would be easier to see them coming. They could go all the way to Union Station underground and make up all their lost time. It made sense to Jesse. The idea of getting to the wharf in hours instead of days was tantalizing, and too good to be true. Along the way they wound up losing the Squeegee Kid and getting saddled with Keith.

They'd been under the city for only an hour when everything went wrong. The PATH was less infested with corpses than the streets but was also brilliantly lit with fluorescent light, and with no night to hide in, the four of them stood out like beacons. Then, when they rounded a corner on a long corridor leading out from the subway and found themselves facing a mob of the dead, there was nowhere to hide, and nowhere to run.

Forced to fight their way back to the subway station through a second group that had turned up suddenly behind them, they took shelter in a tiny coffee kiosk. Jesse, Becca, and Dylan were able to ram the bars down on the security cage, but when they turned around they saw the Squeegee Kid locked in combat with a brown-shirted Tim Horton's employee. The Kid broke free long enough to deliver a solid blow to the forehead with his brain stick that caved in the front of the woman's skull and sent her staggering into a shelf of rock-hard old donuts.

"Yeah!" he screamed. "That's *right*, you fucking fuckface! Suck on this!" He turned back to the others with a big shit-eating grin. "Now that's how you—"

Behind him, she stood up. Despite the gross trauma to her skull and the black ichor seeping out of it, she launched herself at the Kid and buried her teeth deep into his tattooed neck.

Jesse flailed about with his baseball bat while the Squeegee Kid screamed and tried to push her away with weak hands. Jesse hit her over and over, until finally with a blow that broke the bat in half, her neck snapped and she released the Kid to fall lifeless to the tile floor. After that there was nothing to be done but to sit on the floor while the Squeegee Kid's life gushed out all over Jesse's jeans, to wait for his eyes to turn white, and then to brain him with his own brain stick.

They went back out the way they came in. Along the way they stopped at a newsstand for water and found Keith huddled behind the counter.

In Jesse's eyes, it was a very poor trade.

The Kid's mangy dog didn't really have a name, but the Kid called him Asshat often enough, as in, "Hey, look at that asshat over there. Come here, asshat!" that he responded as well to it as to any other name. They could have called him Fuckface and the dog would have responded just as well, but that just seemed mean. At any rate, he'd taken well to Dylan's dog and, for his own part, Tucker seemed to be as protective of the little dog as he was of his small master, so that was all right.

Jesse sat in the dim light of the hotel room, smoking and watching the dogs dream, thinking of things no seventeen-year-old should have to think about. *At least we're safe for the moment*, he thought.

He was wrong.

He didn't know what lay behind the door by the check-in desk. He didn't know about the hotel's other guests, or about its sole surviving employee. He didn't know about Ontario Hydro and its failsafes.

If he had known, he would have packed up and left that moment, and never mind about the hot shower.

CHAPTER NINE

A keening cry pierced the darkness, and Wendell Jenkins shot up out of bed. He was across the room and fumbling a bottle into the microwave before his brain actually awoke.

The suite was luxurious and large, with room both for the massive king-sized bed and the ratty old playpen he'd found in a storage closet. Wendell crossed to the playpen and gently lifted Sheila out, holding her to his shoulder as he carried her across to the little table. She stopped her crying and gazed at him wide-eyed, as if discovering a strange creature for the first time. On an impulse, he gave her a quick kiss on the cheek. "Mm-wah," he said.

Though he knew you were supposed to talk to babies, he always seemed at a loss for anything to say. The tiny little bundle of wails and poop was baffling to him, and he felt more awkward speaking to her than to any adult he had ever met. Unwilling or unable to descend to the "goo-goo boo ju-boojy-boo" of accepted baby talk, he felt even more awkward talking to her the way he would an adult. For the most part, he engaged in a one-way conversation full of questions she

could not possibly answer, "Are you hun͟
diaper need changing?" "Did that burp feel g͟

Wendell retrieved the bottle from the ͟
looked at the time on the glowing green displa͟
As much as he hated to admit it, he was up for ͟   ͟w.
He flicked the switch on the coffee pot and carried Sheila and
her bottle back to his chair. As she drank, he sang. Any song
he could think of, she didn't seem to care. As long as it had a
tune, she was content to listen. Wendell always felt more
comfortable singing to her than talking.

"I know a girl," he sang. "Who always...huh. Guess I
don't know that one." He chuckled to himself, but she
seemed not to notice. Her hands played up and down the
sides of the bottle and her throat continued to work up and
down, devouring the nipple. Her eyes closed in contentment.

When the bottle was empty, Sheila's eyes seemed to grow
heavy and her chest started to rise and fall more gently. When
he was sure she was asleep, he gently lifted her over to the
playpen. Setting her down was the hardest part, and time and
again he'd fumbled the pass enough that her eyes shot open
and the crying began. Ever so gently, he lowered her down to
the blankets, paused a moment to adjust the balance, and let
his hand slide out from beneath her head. She lay on her
back, eyes closed, arms up by her head, chest rising and
falling softly. He watched her a moment before backing away
and tiptoeing back to bed.

No sooner had he lifted the covers to his chin than he
heard her begin to wail. *Oh well*, he thought. *It was worth a try.*

He let her roll around on the floor and play with her
octopus while he filled a mug with coffee and set about
waking up.

Lesson One: Babies are predictable only in their unpredictability.

It was the morning of their third day at the Downtown Sheraton. They occupied the very spacious penthouse suite on the very top floor, for Wendell had decided that if he had to hide out from marauding zombies for the rest of his life, he could at least do it in style. He'd quickly discovered that no matter the size and suggested opulence of a penthouse suite, it was still a hotel room, complete with hard beds, bad coffee, and furniture bolted to the walls.

The black sedan had managed to bring them into the downtown core of the city before becoming ensnared in the last and greatest traffic jam of Toronto's illustrious history of traffic jams. Thousands, if not millions, of cars all locked up bumper to bumper in the last days of the city's death throes, trying to get south, trying to get north, trying to get anywhere but where death waited. Now they sat dark, abandoned, a massive maze where the dead were the rats and he and Sheila the cheese. How grateful he had been, then, to see the huge red S looming above it all, so near and so safe. Locking doors and plentiful supplies—provided it wasn't yet occupied.

Inside, he'd discovered a building suspiciously devoid of zombies. His explorations revealed a well-stocked freezer and bar, lots of occupied rooms already conveniently marked with barge black Zs across their doors—*stay out of those*—and one dead hotel employee lying face down in a plush leather chair in a spacious office, a bottle of whiskey and a bottle of bleach next to his head on the large desk.

He'd learned how to use the electronic key card machine in the office to make a master room key and a couple of spares, stocked the penthouse fridge with as much food as he could carry, and wheeled the manager out the back door and left him to the ghouls. Since he was still collecting methods of death, he took careful note of the bleach-and-whiskey cocktail on the desk. Three fingers of each, and repeat as necessary. Effective but unpleasant, and without the elegance and simplicity of the window method employed by Sheila's mother. He decided it wasn't for him.

Though he found himself unexpectedly with a reason to live in the form of a tiny little person, he still had it in his mind that he would eventually go back to his original plan: find Grace and put her out of her misery, and then die himself. How he was supposed to accomplish that with Sheila in the picture he was unsure, but surely he was in no fit state to raise her, was he? Granted, he was doing all right with the day-to-day, when keeping a baby happy and keeping one alive were essentially the same thing. Eventually though, she would need to learn to walk and talk and ask questions, and Wendell—all alone and always on the run—could hardly see himself succeeding at that. There had to be other survivors, somebody more fit. Or sooner or later the army would make their big push, reclaim the city, and he could hand her off to more capable hands.

So he told himself, even then not believing it.

For now, she was happy and miraculously healthy. That was the main thing. And now, sipping his bitter coffee and watching her shake the purple octopus and gurgle at its musical jingling, he found himself strangely content. Thoughts of suicide seemed far off in the growing light of a new dawn, academic rather than real.

When he'd finished his coffee and changed her diaper—something at which he was already becoming something of a pro—he began preparing for his daily rounds. The food in the fridge was almost gone and would need to be replenished. Maybe if he was feeling ambitious, he'd fry himself some eggs and have a real breakfast. Subsisting on cold cuts and bread was fine, but with a huge empty kitchen just waiting downstairs, a hot meal would make him feel civilized again.

Wendell put Sheila back in her playpen while he showered and dressed again in the same dirty clothes. Eventually, he would have to locate the laundry facilities. Then he got Sheila's carrier out of the closet.

On his first day, he had thought he could just leave her sleeping while he did his chores. The door was locked and she always slept for exactly two hours, so if he hurried back he would be more than fine. He'd tossed out the old manager, filled his arms with sandwich paraphernalia, and checked that the halls were still blissfully empty before he went back to the top floor.

When he'd gotten there, though, he'd found to his horror that the little light blinked red and the door refused to open.

He'd tried again, with the same result. He'd tried putting the card in backwards, upside down, tried rubbing it on his shirt before sticking it in. Stupidly, he'd tried pounding on the door, which only produced an anxious cry from the now wide-awake baby trapped in the room.

It had been a desperate, frantic fifteen minutes as he ran back down fourteen flights of stairs to the front desk to re-code the card. When he returned to find Sheila still alive and fallen back asleep, he nearly wept with relief. Now she accompanied him wherever he went.

Wendell set the carrier down on the floor beside the playpen and reached inside the pen. When he lifted Sheila to his shoulder again, she turned her head to his, planted a wide-open mouth on his stubbled cheek, and made a sound.

Twenty minutes later, when the rising son burst through the penthouse window, it found Wendell Jenkins sitting on his king-sized bed, staring down at the infant cradled in his arms with wide-eyed wonder.

He would have sworn before a judge and jury that the sound she had made when she kissed his cheek had been "Mwah."

They had themselves a little party in the restaurant kitchen. Wendell wasn't much of a cook, but he could manage eggs and bacon when he had to. With Sheila's carrier propped up on the counter, he cooked while she watched.

He was in a better mood than he had been in ages. He sang as he cooked the bacon, and when he pulled out the eggs he astonished them both by juggling three of them for about eleven seconds. Sheila's mouth was a wide O of amazement as the eggs seemed to float in midair, and she laughed out loud, in pure, innocent joy, when he fumbled one and it landed with a wet splatter across the floor.

"That was pretty good, wasn't it?" he said. "You should see what I can do with glass. I once knocked over a whole shelf of wine glasses Grace's grandmother gave her. She didn't think it was that funny, but I bet for you it'd be comedy gold."

Wanting to hear the trilling sound of her laughter again, Wendell capered around like an idiot while the eggs fried. He danced, he sang, he made silly faces at her, and even launched into a bout of the hated baby gibberish. But while he was able to coax a smile or two from her, and even a little giggle, it seemed nothing he could think of had anywhere near the humor potential of a single splattered egg.

"Oh well," he mused as he ate his breakfast. "I'll find out what you find funny. I've got nothing but time." He tidied up his dishes and piled them in the sink. He looked around for a cloth or something to clean up the egg on the floor, then thought, *Why bother?* There was no one around to impress. He left the mess where it was.

Wendell filled a plastic shopping bag with fruit, meat, and bread. He looked for one brief, longing moment at the bottles poised so invitingly along the bar, before the memory of the hotel manager's final cocktail turned him away with a shudder. Instead, he topped the bag off with more packets of coffee grounds before picking up the carrier and heading back upstairs.

Fourteen flights of stairs is wonderful exercise. Wendell absolutely would not risk the elevator—who knew how much longer the electricity would stay on?—so by the time he reached the penthouse, he was exhausted. The baby, too, was starting to yawn, and after guzzling another bottle and lying back in a fresh diaper with her purple octopus jingling beside her, she slept. Wendell stretched out across the bed, relaxed, and completely failed to doze off.

It was a frustrating fact, known to most new parents, that when the grown-ups wanted to sleep, the baby wanted to play, but by the time the baby nodded off, the grown-up found himself wide awake and staring at the ceiling. There was nothing to read but the Gideon Bible, and with corpses wandering around outside eating good God-fearing Christians, he didn't expect to find anything of inspiration in its pages. Instead, he thought of Grace. He wondered where she was right at that moment. He had no doubt she was dead, but what was happening to her mind, or, for lack of a better word, her soul? Was she alive inside the zombie somewhere trapped in an unending horror as her body stalked and devoured the living? Or was she at peace, either in blissful nothingness or else surfing the cosmos in a new body of wings and light? Could he ever find her again? Amid the conflicting torments of these thoughts, his eyes finally grew heavy and he slept.

And dreamed.

He was running. Ragged limbs in bloody clothes reached out for him from everywhere.

He raced through a gauntlet of the dead, desperately dodging them at every turn, their eyes always showing right in front of his face, their teeth always too close. He ran down King Street, a magical King Street where every landmark he had passed on his four-day trek was crammed into a single block: The sporting goods store, the convenience store, the concrete husk of an abandoned building. Here, a zombie with no face leered out of a car door at him with a gaping mouth full of gristle. He fled from Sheila's mother, her eyes empty and full of reproach.

Sheila! Where was Sheila?

He darted on and they fell behind him, though he knew that every ghoul he passed was joining up behind his back and carrying on the pursuit. He should have been able to outrun them at a clip, but he was too slow. Too slow.

He came to a wall. A dead end. He couldn't go either left or right. Somewhere, Sheila was crying. He wept, knowing he could never reach her. From behind, a weight on his back, and the first tearing pain as sharp teeth tore into his neck.

Wendell shot out of bed, drenched in sweat. Beside him in the playpen, Sheila was awake, and ready for lunch.

CHAPTER TEN

Becca shot awake with a thin prickling of fear in her heart and the feeling that something was terribly wrong.

She sat up on the floor between the two beds and reached for her axe and pistol. The clock on the nightstand read 12:15. The room was dark, but around the edges of the drawn curtains she could see a thin pencil line of brilliant light. Outside it was another glorious fall day.

Becca's clothes were clammy with sweat, but she couldn't tell if that was from the head to toe leathers or the dream. Every time she shut her eyes, she was back in the dark, back in the pulsing bass and laser light. Every time she shut her eyes, all she could see was the barrel of the gun as she it slid between her teeth.

Everyone was still asleep when Becca stood up. On her left, Keith sprawled in a starfish shape across one whole bed. Dylan was on her right, curled up like a baby and whimpering, visiting an unknowable horror of his own. She looked to the door. Tucker and Asshat both watched her from their pile of fur and tangled limbs. Jesse slept slumped back in the chair.

Becca picked her way with light feet toward the door. As soon as she passed Jesse, his head snapped up and he looked at her. Worried. Wounded.

"Where are you going?" He didn't mask the fear in his voice. After all these days together, he still expected her to abandon them at the first opportunity. *What do I have to do to prove myself to you?* she wanted to shout, but held her tongue. The old Becca would have cringed, kowtowed, and apologized for anything it took, anything to gain acceptance. The old Becca had spent three days sobbing with a gun in her mouth, and emerged as the new Becca.

"Going to get something to eat," she said instead as she buckled the selfsame gun to her waist, "Want anything?" Jesse's eyes narrowed. There was, however, nothing he could say. Becca was going to do what she wanted, regardless. "Take Tucker with you," he said. She nodded, patted her thigh once, and when the dog was at her side, she left without another word.

The dangerous silence of the hallway did nothing to make her feel better. She didn't like this hotel. It was too big and guarded too many secrets, and they'd only done a cursory search of one floor before declaring it safe. To Becca, it wasn't safe. It was more dangerous than the street, all the more because of the illusion of safety.

Night could not come fast enough.

Tucker growled at a door set into the wall on its own. She dragged him away. The door was locked and she didn't have the combination, but the prickle of fear became an itch, and she saw teeth in every shadow. She walked on to the restaurant kitchen, Tucker padding along at her side.

Moments after she passed by, the door to the main stairwell swung slowly open.

She dumped some soup into a pot and turned on the gas. The hotel might claim to have a five-star chef, but from the cans stacked in the pantry, the soup of the day was usually Campbell's Chunky. Whatever, it smelled good. Her stomach rumbled as she stirred.

Tucker whined in the corner, and she looked over to see that his back legs were shaking.

"Piss wherever you want," she told him. "I'm not taking you outside." He looked at her and whined. He wouldn't go on the floor, he was too well-trained. Becca left the soup bubbling and went into the bar. A TV above the bar was somehow still picking up HBO on the satellite. The sound was off, but Peter Dinklage was giving an impassioned speech to some medieval men. In the unnatural silence, the room seemed to hold its breath. Becca found a newspaper in a trashcan. *Civil Unrest turns to Riots* the headline read. She opened it to the political page and dropped it to the kitchen floor, where Tucker immediately, and with great relief, pissed all over the Prime Minister's face.

"Good boy," she said and knelt down to ruffle the thick fur of his neck. "You know your politics, don't you boy?" She looked across the room at her pot of soup and froze. Fear soured in her throat.

On the floor next to the range was a broken egg. It was still wet, the yolk still bright yellow. It was fresh.

They were not alone in the hotel.

Becca hefted her axe in both hands. The prickle of fear was screaming now, and she knew her first intuition was right.

They needed to leave.

Now.

Wendell stared at the food in the mini-fridge for a long

time. Finally, he decided he was sick of sandwiches after all.

"Hey, Sheila!" he called out in the direction of the playpen, and steel-blue eyes smiled at him. "What do you say to another kitchen party, kiddo? Since we had so much fun the last time."

"Guh!" said Sheila emphatically. He set about bundling her into her carrier, chatting all the way. Suddenly, the conversational floodgates had opened and he was much more comfortable talking to her now that he knew she liked him. They left the suite and began the fourteen-story trek down to the kitchen. Wendell was thinking about the cans of soup he'd seen in the pantry.

Later, it would occur to him that had he not bought into the illusion of safety, if he had only stayed put and choked down a sandwich, things might have turned out differently. He would realize that the most momentous moments often boil down to insignificant choices. Choices you can never take back.

Wendell Jenkins chose the stairwell, and his fate was sealed.

The last of the hotel's employees stood in the hallway, letting the silence breathe around her.

She stood an inch above five-foot fall with short dark hair and almond-shaped eyes. Alone, forgotten, abandoned to her conscience, she haunted the building like a ghost, rattling her chains and dusting the surfaces with lemon Pledge.

The dreams had begun shortly after David drank his last scotch. She had lived in such terror of him, of his singular ability to destroy her life with a wave of his hand and a scratch of his pen. He could fire her so casually—and it would be casual, too, like the casual way he had shut the door on Rob. She had watched him do it, watched him turn and meet her eyes with no trace of guilt or sadness. Even then, she had done nothing, only backed away with her fear of him so alive in her heart.

She busied herself, she got lost in cleaning, in making up rooms no guest would occupy. As long as her hands were busy, she was mindless. She would not sleep. When she did, for only minutes at a time, allow her arms to drop and sleep to seize her, she would see Rob, alone and bloody, pleading to her from behind the door. "Please," he'd say. "Please, it's so dark."

She would jolt to her feet and find uses for her hands once more. Anything was better than seeing the reproach in his eyes.

Today she had finally fallen. In the basement, while mopping the hallway that led between the hotel gym and its pool, she had collapsed where she stood, and awakened hours later with a bruise on her face and water all over the floor and soaked into her clothes. The sleep had left her even more exhausted than before, but she awoke with a purpose. She knew what she had to do to clear her conscience. Soon she would be able to sleep again.

She rapped softly on the luggage room door. After a moment, she heard a scrape, and then a single thump back. Rob. He was alive.

Her fingers found the numbered buttons, the code every staff member was told and ordered to memorize. She would let him out. She would say she was sorry. Then, everything would be all right.

Yvonne punched the last number. The knob turned free in her hand. She beheld walls of shelving, painted with blood.

Fifty-six white eyes gazed at her with malice.

At the same time, the lights went out in the city of Toronto for the final time.

That the power would eventually fail completely, had been an inevitable fact from the moment the crisis began. Even with the city's millions of dollars in upgrades, capacitors, and automatic shunting systems, the grid could not have kept humming forever with nobody minding the store. The miracle was that the lights had stayed on this long.

In fact, the power had been steadily failing all around Toronto for days, and a good many neighborhoods were already dark. On the day that Wendell Jenkins established himself in the Sheraton's penthouse, a capacitor overloaded and exploded two buildings down from the one he'd managed and cared for these eleven years. The resulting fire burned through the night, obliterating more than half the street and leaving the rest in darkness. It reduced to melted slag the faded pink carpet he had so diligently fought with and cremated the body of a woman who had loved her son too much to live.

The fire also forced five men out of their sanctuary in a camping and hunting supply store; and those five men were now left with nothing to do but walk away, well-armed, well supplied, and dangerous.

Wendell was midway between the fourth and third floors when the lights abruptly shut off, leaving the stairwell in impenetrable, inky blackness. It was so dark, it seemed bright. Colors exploded behind his eyes as they tried to adjust to the sudden absence of any kind of light at all. Wendell froze in place on the stairs, one hand gripping the reassuringly cool metal banister, the other held tight to Sheila's carrier. Shapes danced in front of him, wavered, and vanished.

He cursed himself for not being prepared. He'd brought no flashlight down with him, not even a cigarette lighter. He'd been too hungry and too happy, too safe and deluded to think that things would not carry on just as they had. In fact, he'd begun for a brief, shining moment to forget that he was surrounded on all sides by death and danger. Now he would have to brave the dark, alone.

Not alone. Almost immediately, Sheila began to scream in terror. The sudden and oppressive darkness was too much for her to comprehend.

"Shhh," Wendell hushed. "It's alright, it's alright," to no avail. She might not even have heard him. He took the few steps down to the third-floor landing, set her down, and fumbled with the clasps to her five-point harness. "Shhh, Sheila, shhh, it's okay, I'm here, it's okay," he repeated over and over as he lifted her out of her chair and held her to his chest. Her screams were a physical pain in his ears, her tiny fists beat at his shoulder, her tiny heartbeat hammered in her chest.

"It's okay. It'll be okay, we just have to get downstairs. There are windows there, it won't be so dark. You'll be—"

He froze in fear. Above and below him, he heard the click and creak of doors opening.

All throughout the building, behind every door marked with a Z, the TVs had suddenly shut off. Every single door was opening out into the halls now, their occupants free from distraction and drawn to a new sound.

The cries of an infant.

Wendell stood in indecision on the landing. His left hand held Sheila close to his chest, his right grasped the reassuring weight of the hammer hanging from his belt. He needed to get Sheila out of the stairwell.

The penthouse was the only place he could be sure they would be safe, but it was eleven flights back up the pitch dark stairs. The lobby was only three flights down and would offer light at least, but little in the way of shelter. He didn't know where to go. Sheila continued her shrieking in his ear.

One flight up he heard over her scream the unmistakable thump of a foot on the landing above, and then a low, chilling moan. His decision was made for him. Wendell spun on the landing and yanked open the door that opened onto the third floor.

It was better than in the stairwell, for at least there was one window at the end of the hall. It was curtained, and only a thin dusky light escaped it, but at least he could see the shapes that filled the corridor.

They had left the frying pan but jumped feet first into the fire. Wendell raised his hammer and ran the gauntlet of hands and teeth.

Let me find an open door. Let me find an open door. It was no use. As each corpse stepped out into the hallway, the heavy doors swung shut behind them with a series of resounding thuds.

One night on his honeymoon, Wendell had gone out to get ice and been horrified to hear the unmistakable click of his door swinging shut. He'd stood in the hallway in just his boxers, holding an ice bucket and feeling fairly stupid. It had taken a few terrifying minutes before he'd been able to wake up Grace. She had laughed her musical laugh and let him back in.

No one was laughing now, though, as Wendell waded his way through the hall, dodging and lashing out with his hammer when one of the dead came too close. All the while the baby screamed.

Before him stood an unmarked door. He saw a thin ray of hope and grasped at it: a storage room. He had found Sheila's playpen in an identical room, and the door had been unlocked. Wendell breathed a prayer, grasped the knob, and pulled.

The merciful door swung open. Wendell pushed inside, slamming the door behind him.

The door wouldn't close. He looked down and saw a green-colored hand, streaked with black, wedged between the door and the jam. With one hand on the baby, the other on the knob, he kicked awkwardly at the hand, but it grasped and clutched and felt no pain. He cried out in fear and pushed the door open again, and brought it back home with all his strength. He heard the snapping of bones, but still the hand clawed and grasped at him. He did it again, and the hand went limp and boneless. When he let it free it slid out of the gap and he was able to slam the door.

They were in darkness once again.

CHAPTER ELEVEN

Jesse woke to a sound he couldn't place. It was dark in the room. A thin square of daylight was visible around the curtains. The door to the corridor was ajar.

Jesse remembered. He'd left the door ajar so Becca could get back in. None of them had key cards. He yawned and stood up, glancing at the digital clock. He wore his heavy firefighter pants and a green T-shirt. His jacket hung across the back of the chair.

Still groggy, it took Jesse a moment to realize the clock wasn't lit up red. He turned back to the door. The sound that had woken him was coming from the dog, who was staring at the dimness beyond the open door with a steady, endless whine. Jesse looked down and saw that the dog had urinated on the carpet. A prickle of worry crept into his brain. The door opened.

"Becca?" he said. "Is that you?"

The door thumped in his hand again. There was no lock. Wendell held the knob in a white-knuckled grip and sobbed. He stood in pitch dark, trapped behind a door with no lock, with a screaming baby in his free hand. Outside, a crowd was growing, drawn to the cries of the baby, and would keep coming as long as she screamed. They would never lose interest or grow bored. Eventually, the door would be wrenched from his hands. And to think, only a few minutes ago, his only concern in the world had been soup.

Awkwardly, with his right hand still clutching the doorknob, he crouched down and lowered the squalling baby to the floor. Over his right shoulder, he still carried her diaper bag and he rooted around the items inside looking for something he could use to calm her. He tried the bottle of formula he had prepared earlier, but she screamed around the nipple and seemed not to notice it was there. The same thing happened with the pacifier, except that after she spit it out, he dropped it into the darkness. He had plenty of diapers, but no hands to change her. It didn't matter. It wasn't hunger, or gas, or her diaper that was causing her distress, but terror. She was feeling his terror and adding it to her own. How long had she been screaming now? He didn't know if it had been five minutes or an hour and a half since the lights went out.

Her cries were taking on an exhausted peal now, and he held on to a desperate hope that she would simply tire out and scream herself to sleep, but it wasn't likely. He had learned in the course of only a few days that babies have an inexhaustible energy for wailing. The more she cried, the more she would need to cry, and her cries would kill them both.

The door lurched open. He'd let himself relax his grip without realizing. He yanked it shut again and held on as hard as he could. His hand ached with the effort and he knew his fingers would be white around the knob.

If I lose my grip, we both die, he thought. He tried

desperately to think. He shoved his free hand into his pockets, looking for anything useful. His hand closed around something soft and cool. Wendell's blood went cold and he wondered just what kind of coward he was.

The door juddered.

The baby shrieked.

Wendell stared into the inky dark.

In his hand, he held a plastic bag.

Becca was crossing the bar when the lights went out. The ground floor was well-lit with daylight from numerous windows, but the sudden failure of the overhead lights and the oppressive silence that followed in the absence of the never-noticed hum of electricity only added to her sense of unease. Then she heard a far-off moan—the low, mournful sound of trapped air escaping from dead lungs. Tucker whined.

Becca ran. The dog loped along beside her down a long corridor hung with sconces that would never light again. When she reached the lobby she gasped and ducked behind a Ficus plant. The lobby was swarming with corpses.

"Shit," she muttered. There were at least twenty zombies between her and the others. She could only hope they'd had the sense to lock the door.

Tucker growled. A posh, well-dressed woman, right at home in the Sheraton's plush decor—if not for the blood on her blouse and the deep gash that spread from one side of her throat to the other like a bloody diamond necklace—had turned her blank eyes toward Becca's cover. She realized with horror that while she was more or less out of sight, the big yellow dog stood out in the open of the lobby. She stood up and bolted for the nearest door she could see. Tucker followed.

They were in pitch darkness. Before the light left completely she saw they were standing at the bottom of a stairwell.

"Come, Tucker." Becca reached into her jacket pocket and pulled out an iPhone. She kept it charged every chance she got, not because she expected a call, but because the screen made for a handy flashlight that wasn't so bright as to be noticeable. Its pale gleam cast a ghostly glow on the silent steps that marched steadily upwards. Together, the girl and the dog climbed the stairs.

She would go up one flight, she decided, cut through the second floor and find the other staircase. It opened right next to the room where Dylan, Keith, and Jesse were hopefully still safe. If she could get to them, they could regroup and fight their way out of the building. Just as she was nearing the second floor landing, however, the door swung open. Becca crouched down and hit the button that killed the phone's screen. A moment later, a pair of soft, glowing white eyes appeared above her, seeming to dance in the dark. They slid over the top of Becca's head and moved on without interest. She heard footsteps begin to mount the stairs above her. The zombie was going up. It was focused on something else and had not even seemed to notice her or the dog.

The zombie had been called. Somewhere upstairs, something had found something interesting, something to be excited about, and every creature in the building was answering the summons.

She heard it, too. Faint and far off, but echoing in the deep silence. The desperate wail of a small child.

"Fuck," whispered Becca. "Where the hell did the *kid*

come from?"

"I'm sorry," said Wendell. He wasn't sure who he was speaking to: Sheila, her mother, or to Grace. God knew he was about to fail them all.

His eyes were adjusting to the darkness just enough that he could make out the complete absence of anything useful in the tiny closet. Towels and bed sheets, a maid's cart. What could he do with that? Wave a towel at the zombies like a bullfighter? Roll the cart down the hallway and hope they would chase it? He had run out of options and he knew it. He could just make out the dim shape of the tiny body on the floor. His responsibility, his charge.

Now his victim.

You're a coward who hides while people die.

Her cries stopped for one merciful second and the only sound was the huff-huff-huff of her breathing, and the thumps and moans from outside the door. But then, the oppressive silence in the suffocating darkness came rushing in on her, and she began to shriek with renewed vigor. So much for hope.

He was down to exactly no choices. He had a baby, a hammer, and a plastic bag. That was what his world had shrunk to.

It would have been easier to stop thinking of her as a person, to turn off emotion and go cold. But of course, he couldn't. She was a person, a little girl who preferred a stuffed octopus to a teddy bear. She was a soft kiss on his grizzled cheek and a peal of laughter at a dropped egg. She was alive.

"I'm sorry," he said again. "It'll be easier for you this way. It will be quick, at least, and painless. Better than what's waiting out there." He was glad the room was dark, for he wouldn't have been able to see through the blur of tears.

He would wait, he decided, until he could not hold his grip any longer. It wouldn't be long now, the pressure on the other side of the door was growing stronger.

Softly, even though she couldn't hear it over her own cries, he began to sing.

"There is a young maiden, she lives all alone..." But his voice was choked and the words were lost in a croak.

The wailing of the baby was coming from the third floor. Becca nearly tripped over a pair of fallen bodies on the landing. Their necks were broken—it looked as if they had followed the call in the darkness and pitched right over the railing above. She opened the door and entered the hallway.

A crowd of zombies was gathered around a door in the middle of the hall. She guessed about ten or eleven of them— more than she could handle alone, but their backs were all to her and they hadn't yet registered her presence. She choked up on her axe.

The first few were no problem. She simply walked up to the last one in line and chopped hard into the back of its neck. When it dropped to the carpet, she moved ahead to the next one. She took out five of them this way, but the sixth turned to the sound of the wet *thwok* as her axe lodged in the fifth zombie's skull. It was the worst possible timing. She tried to raise the axe, but it was locked in the meat of the zombie's skull. As she struggled to pull it out, the other one came for her.

A yellow blur and a throaty growl, and Tucker was between her and the zombie. The zombie came forward, and Tucker sank his teeth into its leg. With a moan, it pitched forward onto its face. A chunk of black-lined flesh tore out from its thigh under Tucker's teeth. With a mighty heave,

Becca finally yanked the axe head free and buried it again in the fallen creature's skull.

It was a short-lived respite, as two of the ones attacking the door turned toward the dog's growl. Tucker looked poised to attack, but she called him back with a stern whisper of *"Here!"* The dog would, she knew, fight to the death for her, but outnumbered against creatures that felt no pain or fear, death would come very quickly.

There were four zombies left, two on the door, scrabbling at the steel-reinforced wood, and two advancing on her. She backed off a few steps, Tucker in heel position at her side, and let them come to her.

She jabbed the first in the face with the butt of her axe and the woman fell back, stumbling. Tucker charged at the second and Becca moved so that the zombie was between her and the dog. When it tried to twist to get at both of them at once, Becca shoved her axe into its chest and it toppled to the floor. He was easy to take out, lying prone on the stained carpet. She spun around in time to catch the other woman as she found her footing and came back around.

The blue carpet had a growing stain of black ichor spreading across it now. Becca stepped around the bodies to get to the door. Two zombies still grappled with the knob, impeding one another so neither could actually open it. These were the two who were seeing the most red, whose bloodlust for the screaming baby and whoever else was in there was so strong that they noticed nothing else, not even a bright red axe that came whistling through the air right at their rotting heads.

And it was over. In the sudden silence Becca grasped the doorknob and pulled with all her strength.

The man who crouched on the floor was a man ready to

meet his death. He blinked into the dim light in total confusion for a moment, and Becca suddenly realized how odd she must look, dressed all in leather and wearing a motorcycle helmet that hid her face completely. She was probably the strangest thing he'd ever seen, especially when he'd been expecting a swarm of the ravenous dead. No words passed between them. She glanced past him to find the small body on the floor behind him, and in that instant, they both realized that the cries had stopped. The man's eyes widened in horror.

"NO!" he screamed and yanked the plastic bag off of the baby's face. She was still, her eyes closed, her mouth slack. "No! Please, God, no. It wasn't that long, please."

He picked her up and cradled her to his shoulder, sobbing, "Come on, Sheila, wake up baby. Please wake up."

CHAPTER TWELVE

It hadn't been that long. It couldn't have been long enough. The world was upside down. What had seemed a final mercy had become, in the space of a few seconds, an awful and completely unnecessary murder.

He rocked her. He bounced her. He covered her face with his tears. She did not move.

Wendell leaned down and blew into the baby's nose. All at once her body jerked. She snorted, then coughed, and let out an ear-splitting wail.

He clutched her to his chest and wept with relief. It was the same cry, the same brain-shattering noise that moments ago had damned them both to death.

It was the sweetest sound he'd ever heard.

"Are you hurt?" asked the woman in black. She was a murky silhouette in the doorway, faceless and gripping a dripping axe. Behind her lurked the shadow of a dog.

"No," said Wendell, his face still streaked with the tears of mingled relief and terror, "Thanks to you, we're both fine. I don't know where you came from..."

"I came from downstairs. If you're not hurt, get up. We

have to get moving."

Without another word, she turned and walked away down the hallway. Feeling awkward and disoriented, Wendell followed. She walked with a wary confidence Wendell did not share, although the dozen bodies strewn around the hallway indicated that confidence was earned. He followed behind her, doing his best to keep the baby calm. It was easier now, in the light and the absence of immediate danger. He fed her a bottle as they walked, and before they reached the black hole of the opposite stairwell, exhaustion had taken her and the bottle's nipple fell out of her mouth. She slept peacefully, her chest rising and falling against the crook of his arm.

The woman threw open the stairwell door and vanished into the darkness. Wendell cradled Sheila and stood with the yellow dog, who watched him with wide brown eyes and no trace of malice. After a few moments, the woman returned. A cell phone was in her hand; its screen lit the dim corridor with a pale glow.

"It's clear," she said. "Here, Tucker." The dog padded to her side. Wendell followed, but stopped short when she started down the stairs.

"Um," he cleared his throat. His voice sounded reedy and plaintive in the echoing stairwell. "If you want, I've been staying in a suite in the penthouse. It's safe, and big enough for two, and..." he trailed off when she turned the visor of her helmet onto him, and he saw his own silhouette reflected coldly in the mirror that was her face. She stared at him for an awkward minute.

"Ew," she said. Wendell felt his cheeks flush and was deeply glad he was nearly invisible.

"I'm sorry. That came out wrong. I didn't mean... I mean, it's a safe place to stay, that's all."

"No it's not," said the woman. "It's ten floors up a pitch black staircase in a building crawling with corpses. You go if you want and good luck. I've got people downstairs." She turned and continued down the staircase. "I only hope I didn't kill them all when I saved you instead." Wendell looked back through the door at the bodies that littered the hallway. He shivered, then turned and followed her rapidly receding light down the stairs.

The staircase spit them out on the back end of the hotel's main floor corridor. Dozens of bodies were scattered up and down the hall. Black viscous goo stained the carpet as far as the eye could see in either direction, all centered around one door, splattered with gore.

Moving with a deadly purpose, the woman squelched her way through the carnage and pounded on the splattered door with a gloved hand.

"Jesse!" she shouted. "Open up, it's me!"

After a moment, the door cracked open and Wendell wondered what kind of faceless crowd he'd hooked up with. The man's face was entirely covered by a white balaclava, under a firefighter's domed helmet and over a firefighter's thick yellow coat. Only his eyes were visible, but they spoke volumes, as they softened in relief at the woman's return, then widened in surprise when they fell on Wendell and Sheila.

"Well," said the fireman. "Looks like we're not the only ones with a story to tell." He stepped inside and beckoned for the three of them to enter.

"First things first," said Jesse, lighting a cigarette. "We need to clear the corpses out of this building."

He sat in a chair by the door, his helmet resting on his lap.

Wendell fussed with the baby over in a corner, welcomed in but mostly ignored by the odd little group. He was utterly shocked when the tall, broad-shouldered firefighter had unclipped his helmet and yanked off his balaclava. The teenage boy's face poking out from the heavy, bulky coat looked startlingly young. Then the black-clad woman pulled off her own helmet to reveal a face even younger than Jesse's, framed by messy dark hair.

"You're just kids!" he heard himself say. The girl, introduced to him as Becca, fixed him with a look of such cold contempt that Wendell found himself missing her helmet.

"So?" she said, "Hey, show of hands—who killed a dozen zombies today, and who locked themselves in a fucking closet?"

That put an end to any friendly chitchat they might have been considering, and opened up the floor for arguing, which both Jesse and Becca seemed to enjoy more than wearing masks and killing zombies.

"Are you crazy?" said Becca to Jesse. "We need to get out of here as fast as we can!"

"It's going to be ten times worse out there than in here," argued Jesse. "Besides, with the power out, we need a new game plan. There won't be anything to distract the corpses from us anymore. It's going to be just as bad at night now as it is in the day." He took a long, luxuriant drag on his cigarette, then blew the smoke out tenderly. "Maybe worse."

"Doesn't anybody want to know what I think?" said Keith, a balding, red-faced man and the only other adult in the room.

"No!" said Becca and Jesse at once. When the fighting started, Keith had locked himself in the bathroom. As far as the teenagers were concerned, Keith was on the same level of respect as Wendell.

"Okay, okay," said the man, holding his hands up. "I just think he's got a point, that's all."

"Thanks for that," said Jesse. "But I don't need your help here. Why don't you go hang out in the bathroom while we figure this out?"

Keith's face puckered. He opened his mouth to retort, but closed it again and returned to staring sullenly out the window.

For Wendell, it was like being at somebody else's family dinner—awkward, uncomfortable, and confusing, made worse by the fact that he'd never been so happy to see people again, yet never wanted so much to be alone. The baby slept peacefully in the crook of his arm. He couldn't bear to look at her. All he could see when he watched the slow rise and fall of her chest was the shopping bag that had very nearly stopped it. He was utterly wretched.

"Besides, we have a baby to worry about now," he heard, and snapped back to reality. He hadn't been paying attention to the teens' bickering, but now he saw they were both looking at him.

"What about it?" snorted Becca? "He's not with us. He might not even be going to the boat."

"He's with us now, Becks," said Jesse, "For better or worse, just like Keith. We're not just going to leave them here." To Wendell he said, "What do you think? Are you going to try for the boat with us?"

"What boat?" asked Wendell, totally confused.

"See?" said Becca, "He doesn't even know what we're talking about."

"Haven't you been listening to the radio?" asked Jesse.

"It's been repeating on all the emergency channels. The ferry docks at Queen's Wharf every night at midnight, to bring any survivors to the island. That's where we're going."

"Why would you want to go to the island?" demanded Wendell. "That's where this whole thing started. It must be crawling with zombies."

Jesse smiled. "Not any more. Apparently, the corpses are all gone. They've got food, water, weapons, space for hundreds of people to live comfortably. The military won't let anyone leave the city, the whole place is surrounded and no one will come in, but they're airdropping supplies to the island. It's like a little town out there.

"There were four hundred people living there before the outbreak. Most of them are gone now, and their houses are empty and waiting to be filled." He looked over at Dylan, who sat stroking the two dogs. "We're hoping our mom might be there."

"Yeah," said Becca. "And we might not get another chance soon. What if the ferry doesn't come any more? The power outage might scare them off."

"In that case, they might not come tonight either. They need to change their plans to work with the power failure, same as us. We could be stranded on the wharf if we leave now. Meanwhile, we have a safe place here to hole up for a couple of days, and all we have to do is clear it out."

"You're being stupid, Jesse. Stupid and afraid. We have to go."

Jesse's eyes narrowed, but he held his temper.

"You can leave if you want to, Becca. You always could. But I'm not going anywhere." He moved away and sat down in his chair by the door, and lit a cigarette.

Discussion over.

"I have an idea," said Dylan. He had sat silent through the whole argument, stroking Tucker's head and watching the floor. Now he spoke up, a thoughtful look on his young face. All eyes turned to him. Dylan blushed when Becca looked at him, and Wendell guessed he was nursing a preteen crush on the older girl.

"Well," he said, dropping his eyes to the floor. "I have an idea how we can get all the zombies out of the hotel."

"Go ahead Dill, what is it?" said Jesse.

"Well, like, it would take forever to kill them all floor by floor, right? Not to mention the mess they make. But what if we could just get them all to leave?"

"What are you gonna do," said Becca. "Play them all a song and lead them into the lake?"

"Kind of," he said. "I could prop open one of the back doors and then yell up the stairs until they hear me. I only need to get the first floors' attention. After that, the rest will pick up the signal and follow the others down. Then I run out into the parking lot and you lock the door behind me. I lose them in the traffic jam and come back in the front door. I'm pretty fast, you know."

"It's... a really good idea," said Becca. Dylan beamed. "It won't get all of them out, but it would take care of most of them, and then—"

"No," said Jesse sharply. "It *is* a good plan, Dill, but it's too dangerous. You stay here. I'll do it."

"Like hell!" said Dylan. "It was my idea! Anyway, I'm way faster than you. You smoke too much. You'd get taken down for sure."

"I'll do it," said Wendell before they could start fighting again. "I'm not very fast, but I'm usually pretty good at getting around these things." Becca raised her eyebrows at that. "When I'm on my own," he added.

Before anybody could argue, Wendell crossed the room and sat on the bed next to Dylan. "Could you hold Sheila for me?" he asked.

"M-me?" said Dylan, wide-eyed.

"She's sleeping. She'll be easy to take care of. I'll be back before she wakes up." He smiled. "But she likes to be held."

Dylan stared in mingled wonder and terror at the sleeping baby.

"Okay," he said. Wendell instructed him how to hold his arms to let the baby rest in them, and propped a pillow beneath the boy's elbow.

He stood up. "Thank you. I know she's in good hands." To Jesse he said, "Block the door behind me so nothing gets into the hallway. I won't be long."

Jesse considered Wendell for a long moment. Wendell was shocked by how pale the young man was. Finally, Jesse seemed to reach a decision about him and, wincing as he bent down, lifted a heavy steel bar from beside the chair and handed it to him.

"You might need this," he said.

Wendell took the bar in his hand. It was heavy, thirty pounds of solid forged steel, with a pickaxe on one end and a pry bar on the other, both stained black from violent use. Wendell knew what it was immediately.

"This is a Halligan bar," he said, surprised.

"Are you a firefighter?" asked Jesse. None of them had ever seen the strange tool before Jesse pulled it out of the abandoned fire truck.

Wendell smiled. "I almost was, once. They showed us this in training. Outside of a hose, this is a firefighter's favorite tool." He moved away from the others and took a few practice swings with it, liking the feel of it, the weight of its swing. "It's also the best zombie-killing weapon I've ever seen. Thank you."

A moment passed between them. Wendell felt a strange shiver run up his spine. Something very powerful and irreversible had just happened, and it frightened him. Somehow he felt Jesse wasn't just lending him the weapon.

"Come on," said Jesse, "We'd better get going."

Wendell hefted the Halligan and put his hand on the door latch.

"Wendell." He turned. Becca was glaring at him, her hand on the butt of her pistol. "If you don't come back, I'll track you down and shoot you."

He nodded. "Thank you." Then they left.

Wendell stood in the dark, at the bottom of the back staircase he had so recently followed Becca down.

Jesse had wished him luck, shaken his hand, and said, "I'm glad you're here. Becca won't admit it, she thinks of herself as a one-woman army, but we're going to need you."

"Thanks," he'd replied. "It kind of looks like I need you guys, too."

"Listen, if it comes down to a fight, be careful. Sometimes when you hit them in the head, they don't go down the first time. It can surprise you."

Wendell smiled back. "You have to get them in the back. Base of the skull." Jesse looked puzzled. "I'll explain when I get back."

"It's a deal. Try to come back. Alive." Then he'd shut the door, leaving Wendell in darkness.

In truth, Wendell was glad to do anything that would shake off the stench of his cowardice. Luring the zombies out of the building wouldn't make up for nearly killing Sheila—nothing ever would—but it was a start. And if he somehow didn't come back, well, the kids had her diaper bag, and extra bottles in his suite upstairs, and of course the fabled boat to an island free of terror. She was in better hands than his. Some small part of him even considered leading the zombies out the door and then just running, leading them a merry chase until they caught him, far away from here.

Off to his right, invisible in the darkness, was the heavy fire door. "Leave it shut until you've got their attention," Jesse had said. "You don't want to attract anything from outside back in."

Wendell shook off dark thoughts and focused on the task at hand.

With the pry bar end of the Halligan tool he gave the metal banister a ringing whack. The gong sound of metal on metal reverberated up and down the stairwell.

"Hello? he called into the darkness, rattling the Halligan against the rails, "Come and get it, gang! Dinner is served, you sons of bitches!"

He stopped banging. Silence came rushing back in to fill the cavernous space. Somewhere above, he heard the creak of a door opening. Wendell put his hand on the fire door's handle and waited.

A wet, meaty thump sounded three feet away from him, and he jumped back with a cry. He fell backwards against the door and it swung open, spilling warm September daylight into the stairwell.

A body lay prone on the concrete floor. In the dark, the zombie hadn't bothered to look for the stairs, but toppled right over the railing to get to him.

Another body came plummeting down from up high and

splattered next to the first. Wendell felt himself grin.

"Come on, you bastards!" he yelled, and stepped back out of the way.

Inside, it began to rain people.

There was one last body.

Rather than try to climb the mound of corpses that now lay broken on the bottom step and trying to force the door that Jesse had so carefully blocked off, Wendell jogged around to the front entrance after all. Inside, he found Jesse crouched over something in the hallway near the lobby.

"Is she with you?" he asked Wendell.

"I've never seen her before. I would have guessed she was one of yours."

"No," Jesse reached out with a gloved hand and rubbed a smear of black goo, revealing a rectangular gold-colored badge on her shirt. Yvonne, it said. "She worked here."

The woman was unconscious, which was lucky. She was still alive, which was not, at least for her. What was left of her ruined body was covered in jagged wounds. Thick black grime commingled with her still bright red blood.

"That poor woman," Jesse said, and reached down to touch her. At that moment Wendell saw something wriggling, wormlike, in the black blood.

"Don't touch her!" he cried. Jesse jerked his hand back as if stung. The wormlike thing reared up and seemed to search the air for a moment, then it dropped back down and disappeared inside the viscous goo.

"Jesus Christ," Jesse said.

"We need to put her out of her misery," said Wendell. "If she wakes up, she'll be in agony. If she doesn't...she still will."

"Becca's got that precious gun," said Jesse angrily. "But she won't spare the bullets. I don't know what she's saving them for, but it isn't to put people of of their misery."

Wendell hunkered down on the carpet. "So we wait," he said. "I've done this before."

Jesse nodded. "Me, too. It wasn't something I wanted to repeat."

They waited. It wasn't long.

CHAPTER THIRTEEN

They took Becca's now-reheated soup—*Thank God for gas ranges*, thought Wendell—and a case of Canadian from the bar, and retired to Wendell's spacious suite for a celebratory lunch. There wasn't much room at his small table, but there were plenty of chairs and couches to go around.

Becca didn't drink. She barely sat, prowling the room, looking through the peephole, checking the locks again and again, looking out the window at the street below. Even at rest she was on the move, her eyes never staying still. She was like a caged cat. Wendell wondered what the last two weeks had done to her, and what she'd been like before.

Dylan didn't drink. Although he'd accepted with a mix of surprise and curious pride when his big brother handed him the brown bottle, after a couple of sips he set it aside. It tasted bitter to him and a little sour, and he honestly wondered what adults saw in the stuff.

Wendell didn't drink. "A woman got me drunk and then tricked me into killing her so she wouldn't become a zombie," he said. "I would've done it anyway, if she'd asked, but it's the kind of thing that sobers you up quick and sours the taste of beer."

Jesse didn't drink. He sat an open beer bottle next to him on the table and hoped no one noticed that he never touched it again.

Keith drank enough for all of them.

It was an afternoon for stories. Jesse and Dylan took turns recounting their adventures before meeting up with Becca and the others. Peppered with details that were either grossly exaggerated or shamelessly stolen from one or another action movie—"Dylan, you did not jump off a building." "Yes I did! Just before it blew up!"—their story contained within the grain of truth of a daring and deadly escape from a high school overrun with teenage corpses. Keith told a much less embellished story of stopping for a paper on the way to the subway and finding himself hiding for his life behind the till. Jesse looked expectantly at Becca, but she pursed her lips and said nothing. Wendell gathered that the black-clad girl with the messy dark hair and barely controlled temper was something of a mystery to the entire group.

Then it was his turn. Eight eyes were on him intently—four of them green and earnest, two of them red and bleary, and two brown and narrowed with contempt. He swallowed, wished he had a drink after all, and began.

He told them about Ellie, and his long walk from a tenement near King Street East. He told them how Sheila's mother very nearly toppled out the window onto his head, and finding Sheila.

He didn't tell them about Grace.

"Backwards out the window," muttered Jesse, almost to himself. "That's...very smart."

He told about the old lady's attack, and they chuckled darkly when he got to the part about kicking her teeth across the nursery.

"Then, I bundled Sheila into a car, and drove as far as I could. It brought me here. You know the rest."

"Why did you say you had to hit them in the back of the neck?" asked Jesse. "All the movies say to get them in the head."

"Not the back of the neck, the base of the skull." Wendell rubbed the soft spot where his hairline ended. "The movies aren't completely wrong, but it's not the brain you're after, it's the brain stem."

"What's the difference?" said Dylan.

"You don't need a brain to live," explained Wendell, trying to recall his high school biology. "Some animals don't even have a brain, but in most animals, their entire brain is basically the bottom part of our brains. The lizard part. The part that handles all of the basic functions we don't think about, like keeping the heart beating. The impulses that come from the brain stem are the basic ones."

"Like moving and eating," said Jesse. "Even if we don't need to think, we still have a need to do those things."

"And fucking," said Keith. "And shitting. Those are animal impulses, too. So why don't zombies fuck?"

"Who says they wouldn't if they could?" said Wendell, realizing he was talking out his ass for the sake of it. "I think if a corpse was capable of emitting sex hormones, another corpse might try to have sex with it. I mean, a cat goes into heat, another cat smells the pheromones, and they go for it. But if a male cat doesn't smell the pheromones of a female cat in heat, sex doesn't even enter its brain."

"And who knows whether zombies shit?" said Dylan. "Have you ever followed one around?"

"They smell bad enough," said Becca. "Maybe they're

crapping all the time."

Keith laughed out loud, a hearty, merry sound that seemed out of place coming from his mouth. In the adjoining bedroom, Sheila stirred at the sound.

"This is great," said Keith. "We're sitting around drinking beer and debating whether zombies shit. All we need is a bong and a tape player playing Zeppelin, and this could be my old dorm room!"

Everybody laughed at that. After a quiet moment, in which Dylan picked at the fraying label of his beer bottle, he finally raised his head and asked, "What do you think they are?"

"I don't know," said Wendell. Jesse caught his eye.

"Remember the worm?" he asked.

Wendell shuddered. How could he possibly forget? It had joined the long list of things he would see in his nightmares.

"What worm?" said Dylan.

"There was something squirming on the body we found today," said Jesse. "Like a worm or a maggot. It was gross."

"It came out of a puddle of that black slime that drips from their mouths," added Wendell. "I'd guess she had a lot more of them already working their way up her bloodstream."

"Do you know," said Becca suddenly, "why pregnant women can't scoop the cat litter?"

"What?" said Jesse. "Where did that come from?"

"When you get pregnant, you can't go anywhere near old cat litter," she explained. "Because there's this parasite that breeds in cats, and you can get infected with it. Adults aren't affected, but it'll fuck up a baby."

"Okay," said Jesse. "So?"

"So what happens is, the cat craps out the parasite's larva, and the crap gets eaten by rats. The parasite grows up inside the rat's brain. But here's the creepy part." She crossed the room, picked up a beer, and took a long swig, her first of the day. "The parasites only live in rats, but they only *breed* in cats' stomachs. So they take control of the rat's brain and make it want to get eaten by the cat."

"Creepy," said Keith.

"How do you know all that?" said Jesse. Becca took out her phone and waved it at him.

"I had an awful lot of time on my hands when this all started," she said. "The networks were still up, so I googled zombies. I found a lot of creepy stuff. Did you know there's a tiny fly that lays its eggs on bees' heads? Then the larvae burrow down into the bees brain and take it over, too. Did you know bees have been dying off all over North America? They're starting to think this fly might have something to do with it. And who wants to guess what this little fly is called?"

Wendell raised his hand like a kid in school. "The Zombie Fly."

"Exactly," she said. "Of course, the Zombie Fly and the rat parasite don't make their hosts eat one another, but it just goes to show there's a lot of weird, awful stuff out there."

"Well, whatever it is," said Wendell. "It's not natural." The others looked at him quizzically, and he went on. "Think about it. These things have killed most of the population of a major city in only a couple of weeks. They spread too fast. Four to six hours after a bite, and the victim is reanimated." Jesse looked up at him sharply. "Reanimated, hungry and capable of infecting others."

"I mean, thousands of people, maybe even millions, dead in a couple of weeks? If we're the rats *and* the cats for these things, in a very short time they'll use up their food source and die off."

"No," said Wendell darkly. "Somebody *made* this. And then, whether by accident or on purpose, they let it out into a city of six million people."

Jesse jumped to his feet suddenly. He swayed and had to put a hand on the table to steady himself.

"It doesn't matter," he snapped, "We have to work with what we know, and get to the boat as soon as possible. Hit them in the back of the head." He began to move shakily toward the door. "Wish I knew that earlier."

"Where are you going?" asked Becca.

"I'm going…for a smoke," said Jesse, and left. The door slammed behind him, leaving silence in its wake.

"He's acting really weird," said Becca.

"He's drunk," chuckled Keith. "Kid can't hold his beer."

"No," said Wendell. He was thinking of how pale Jesse had looked. How he winced with pain when he bent down. He was thinking of Ellie, dolling herself up so she didn't die alone. "He's trying to hide it, but I think something's wrong." He looked at Dylan. The poor kid was staring at him with wide eyes. "Dylan, I'm sorry. I think your brother's been bitten."

"No," said Dylan, "No, it's not possible."

"Shit," Becca looked at the clock on her phone. "It's four-thirty. The power died at just after twelve."

"We don't have much time," said Wendell.

They found him on the roof. Wendell, Becca, and Dylan burst through the access door to find Jesse sitting on the ledge. His firefighting gear lay in a pile beside him with the yellow helmet on top and the Halligan bar leaning against the ledge. Without his bulky clothes, wearing only jeans and a green T-shirt he looked very young indeed.

"Shit," he said through his teeth as he struggled to light a cigarette in the autumn wind. "Dylan, I didn't want you to see this." The center of his shirt was torn open and drenched with blood from a wound that wouldn't close. To Wendell he looked just as Sheila's mother must have looked, sitting alone on a ledge, smoking away his last moments.

"Oh, Jesse," cried Dylan. "Why didn't you tell me?"

"What good would it have done, Dill? There's nothing we can do about it. I'm sorry, I was careless."

Jesse looked out over the span of the city laid out before them. The lowering sun bathed the dead buildings in a spray of rose gold, and a warm breeze ruffled Jesse's hair. In the distance beyond the dark skyscrapers lay the dappled face of the lake.

"It's nice out," he said. "I was always afraid I would die cold. You gave me a good idea, Wendell. I was going to pull you aside and ask you to smash my head in for me, but this is better. This way I can just…float away."

"You stupid fucking moron," said Becca. "I should have been there."

"Maybe," said Jesse. "Maybe if you had you would have told me to keep my coat on, even if we were safe. You would have made me lock the door. You were always smarter than me. But if you had, where would *he* be? Or the baby? At least you got two for the price of one this time." He swayed for a dizzying minute, then steadied himself. His eyes locked on Wendell's.

"Those are for you," he said, gesturing at the thick clothes. "You're a little taller than me, but they should fit. The boots, I don't know. You've got pretty big feet. The coat will keep you safe, though. Don't take it off. Ever."

"Th-thank you," was all Wendell could think of to say.

"I don't have much time left," said Jessie. "Dylan, try not to be sad. You're…you're the man around here now. You've gotta be strong." He hugged Dylan tight, and Dylan's shoulders shook as he sobbed against his brother's chest. "I'm so proud of you, Dill. You, too, Becks," he said as he gently pushed Dylan away.

"Fuck you, Jesse," Becca came to stand behind Dylan, wrapping her arms around him. "I hate when you call me Becks."

"I know," said Jesse, smiling. He leaned back. Then he was gone.

PART THREE
THE BOAT

CHAPTER FOURTEEN

There was a momentary silence following Jesse's fall. The sun dipped lower on the horizon, staining the clouds neon pink and orange, while off to the east, where the deep purple of night was closing in, the skyscraper walls were becoming flat silhouettes and the city was about to see stars for the first time in years. Dylan stood frozen in place, staring at the spot where his brother had sat just moments before. A dozen emotions fought for control of his face. Becca dropped to her knees beside him and took him wordlessly in her arms. He buried his head in her shoulder and sobbed.

Wendell stood off to the side, unnoticed and horribly out of place. Relaxing in his suite earlier, sharing drinks and jokes, he had begun to feel almost at home with these strangers. He had begun to feel a kinship with them, at least a sense of being in the same terrible place together. Now he felt like a stranger intruding on a very private grief. The best thing was for him to leave, quietly, but he could think of nothing he could say or do to extricate himself.

In answer to his prayer, the roof door swung open and Keith walked out.

"Wendell," he said. "The baby's moving all over the place and talking to herself in her sleep. I think she's going to wake up soon."

Keith looked around then, and took in the sight of Dylan weeping on Becca's shoulder, and Jesse's clothing lying in a pile by the ledge. "Oh," he said. "Oh God. Dylan, I'm so sorry. I can't imagine how you must feel—"

Dylan broke free of Becca and charged across the gravel-covered roof. "Bastard!" he screamed, and Keith fell back against the boy's fury. "You coward! You hid in the bathroom, and now Jesse's dead!" He fell on the older man, beating at Keith's raised arms with savage fists.

To his credit, Keith did his best to stay level and calm. "Dylan," he said. "Calm down, son. I didn't kill your brother."

"You could have helped him! You could have helped us both! Instead, you hid like a baby while we fought for our lives. You're a...a Goddamn WORM!"

"Hey!" Keith snapped. "Did I lock you out? Did I leave you to die? No. I called to you. I wanted you both to get in there with me. We could have locked the door and kept quiet, and they would have forgotten we were there and moved on. I tried to save you. But you had to go running off like a cocky fucking *kid*." He was beet red, sweating and shaking with days of pent-up fury. "You kids think this is all a big video game, that if you stay alive longer it means you get better hit points and cooler weapons, but you don't. You just get more tired, more stupid, and more likely to make a mistake.

"Yeah, I hid. There were dozens of them out there, it was the smart thing to do. But no one ever listened to what I thought, did they? Jesse always did what he wanted to do. It's his own fault he was bitten, and if you had gotten killed, it would have been his fault, too." Keith stood shaking, glaring down at Dylan, who glared right back. The thing of it was Wendell couldn't easily say that Keith was wrong.

Becca strode over and pulled Dylan away by the shoulders. Dylan resisted, then seemed just to melt with exhaustion, all his energy spent in anger. She led him over to a blocky ventilation box and had him sit down. Then she turned to Keith with eyes hard and pitiless.

"You stay far away from us. It's a big hotel. You can find someplace else to sleep. Tomorrow we'll try for the boat, but I don't want to see you or hear from you until then. Got it?"

Keith met Becca's stare for a moment, then shook his head. "You know what?" he sighed. "That sounds just fucking fine by me." He turned away and left the roof with his shoulders set.

Wendell, meanwhile, had edged away from the confrontation, toward the ledge of the roof. His foot brushed something soft and he looked down to see that he'd nearly walked into the pile of gear Jesse had left behind. He knelt down to examine it, the enormity of the young man's final gift overwhelming him. The heavy clothes would weigh a ton, and be sweltering hot even in the cooling weather as September waned, but the thick fabric, piled on in multiple layers specially designed to protect sensitive skin from scorching heat, would be almost impossible to bite through. Jesse had been right. This might save his life.

Wendell heard an ominous click and looked up. He found himself staring at the black eye of a .45 revolver's barrel.

"Put it down," Becca said. Wendell dropped the coat, raised his hands, and backed away.

"He told me to take it," he said lamely. Becca wasn't moved.

"He did. I didn't."

It occurred to Wendell for one heart-stopping moment that he may have been rescued by a lunatic. Becca's eyes were cold and her jaw was set in a grim hard line. He had only known her a few hours, but he had seen her fight with murderous fury, and between Jesse and Keith her nerves had to be worn to a fray. He had no doubt that she was capable of shooting him dead over a coat.

"What makes you think you deserve to wear that?" she demanded. "Do you have any idea what that coat means?"

"I know it has sentimental attachment for you both," he said, trying to keep his voice steady and reasonable. "I didn't mean to—"

"It's not what it means to me," she said, holding the gun steady. "It's what it says to everyone else. Every single person you meet wearing that won't see a sad forty-year old man. They'll see a fireman. A goddamn hero. You put that on, and everybody will assume you're in charge. They'll defer to you. They'll think you're our leader."

"And you think that will take away from you somehow?" he said, trying to understand the direction she was going in. What was she talking about?

"I don't give a fuck! I followed Jesse because he knew what he was doing most of the time. If someone else comes along who wants the job and I trust them, it's theirs. But if you're wearing that coat, it's you everybody will be looking to, so it better be you who's in charge. You don't get to wear it until I'm convinced you deserve it."

"Okay," said Wendell. "How do I do that?"

She lowered the gun, put it back in its holster, and fixed him with her deadly gaze.

"Why were you going to kill the baby?" she demanded,

and Wendell's heart sank. Hadn't she been there? Hadn't she seen what he'd seen? Wasn't that enough? But no. She was going to bring it to the front, make his private hell a public one. He heard Dylan gasp, and realized that part of the story had been left out of their retelling. Dylan stared at him in horror.

"Becca, we were all alone," he said. "I didn't know anyone else was in the building, let alone that you would hear us and come to the rescue. As far as I knew, we were both about to die, and it was going to be horrible. What would you have done?"

She considered. "If you had no other options, letting her die quietly and cleanly would have been the kindest thing you could do." Wendell relaxed. "But," she continued. "If the kid stopped crying you would have been safe. If the kid had died, you would have been able to wait until they left and go on your merry way, just like Keith said. I'm sure that thought crossed your mind."

There it was. The words he had been dreading to ever think to himself, the cold truth rushing in on his denial. Had that thought crossed his mind in those desperate minutes in the dark? Of course it had. But had it affected his reasoning? He couldn't be sure.

His hesitation was answer enough. Becca nodded.

"There's no shame in that by itself. I would have thought it, too. But here's the thing, Wendell. I don't know you. I can't assume you're a good guy just because you're alive, and that's so rare in the people you meet these days. Bad people are bound to survive, too. It all comes down to the why. One way, you're a human being in a bad place doing what he thought was right. The other way, you're a coward who would murder a baby to save his own ass.

"So what was it, Wendell? Kindness or cowardice? Were you killing her to save her, or to save yourself?"

He sighed. "I don't know." Becca's eyes widened; it was obviously not the answer she was expecting.

"Well, you're honest, at least," she said. "But until you can answer that question, the coat stays right where it is."

Sheila was indeed up, and outraged at having woken up alone. She had rolled to the edge of the playpen and her face was pressed right into the mesh as she screamed at him. If her shrieks could contain words, they would all be words no mother would want her child to know. Her blue eyes glared.

"I'm sorry, I'm sorry," Wendell muttered, dumping two scoops of Similac into a bottle filled with vending machine water and shaking it up. While screwing the nipple on one-handed, he reached in and gathered Sheila up with the other.

"Urrreuh! Urrreuh!" she screamed in his face.

"It's coming. Just hold on a sec." He shifted her in his arms and plunked the nipple between her outraged lips. Immediately, she stopped. Her throat worked up and down as she gulped greedily, and her eyes gazed up at his, softened. All was forgiven.

While she drank, the suite descended into twilight. Wendell watched her drink as the shadows grew, and pondered Becca's question. *His* question, if he was being fair; she had said nothing to him that he hadn't thought himself.

Those minutes in darkness had been minutes of chaos. He could remember nothing clearly besides his hand slick with sweat on the door handle, the thumps of the dead beyond, and Sheila's petrified, inconsolable wail. Of the thoughts that had run through his head, disjointed and random like a radio set to scan, he could remember almost nothing. He knew he didn't want to die. For all that he had thought of suicide in the past week, for all that he had planned his own death and even gone about collecting different ways to do it, in that moment he had never felt life flowing through him so precious and needful. He had realized he did not want to die, and that damned him.

But wanting to live and willing to murder were not necessarily the same things. Could he truly have sunk so low in the space of only minutes? Low enough to hold his own life above the life of a child he had only that morning begun to love? He watched her eyes follow the shadows around the room. She seemed to have forgotten the storage room completely, although he suspected they would both return there in their dreams.

He did love her, a stranger's child thrust on him by chance, perhaps the closest to a child of his own that he would ever have in this darkened world. He wanted to believe that he would die for her, that he would do anything to protect her, but the coward always wants to believe he is brave until the moment of courage comes, just as the adulterer wants to believe he is faithful, until the offer of soft flesh away from home proves his true nature. Wendell's memories were of terror, and in terror he might well have proved the weaker.

Given time, he knew he would find a way to reconcile his version of events to shape a story he wanted to believe. Becca was wrong. The important truth wasn't the why, but the almost, and when one day he looked back on the day he nearly killed a child, he would recall that he had done it to save her from a much more awful fate. He would almost believe it, too. In the end, it wouldn't matter. But deep inside, in a place he could never acknowledge was even in him, would remain the question: *Did I?*

Sheila swallowed the last drops. The nipple made the squeezing sound of sucking air. Wendell plucked the empty bottle from her lips and draped her over his shoulder. He patted her gently on the back as he paced the room, and saw with a start that the twilight had deepened to almost-full dark. He could no longer easily read the words on the side of the Similac can. Soon it would be dark as pitch in the room, and in all the chaos of the day he hadn't managed to find time to look for a flashlight, or even some candles.

"Damn," he said. *Now what?*

As if the universe had read his mind, there came a knock at his door. He opened it to find Dylan outside, holding a pair of over-sized flashlights. His eyes were puffy and red, but his tears were dry.

"Becca went shopping," he said and handed one of the lights to Wendell. Then he turned and hefted a garbage bag and brought it through into the room. Inside were bottles of Aquafina water, a package of diapers, and a Mars bar.

"Thank you," said Wendell. "That was very thoughtful."

"Well, it was Becca, not me," he said. "She was worried about the baby."

"In any case, I appreciate it," said Wendell. "I…um…I don't know if it means anything, but I'm sorry about your brother. He was a good man."

Dylan sniffed. "He was the best." He shuffled his feet. "Well, goodnight." And he left Wendell in darkness once again.

Wendell shut the door quietly. Sheila dozed against his shoulder, one chubby arm wrapped around his neck as though he were the one who needed comforting. He set her back in bed and sat down at the small table, staring into his soul by the light of a Coleman flashlight. His arm brushed a bottle beside him, and without thinking, he raised it to his lips and drank.

The beer was warm and flat. It took him a moment to realize it was Jesse's untouched beer from that afternoon.

"Oh hell," he groaned and buried his head in his arms on the table top. He wept for Jesse, a brave kid cut down by a single moment of carelessness. He wept for Dylan, all alone in the world. He wept for Grace, for Sheila, for the world.

Mostly he wept for himself.

Dylan found Becca in the lobby, frowning at the doors. Outside, true night was falling on a city unknown to darkness.

"I hate all this glass," said Becca. She had unearthed a bicycle lock that she'd used to secure the double doors, but the wall of glass that surrounded the doors made it an empty gesture.

"What's it like out there?" asked Dylan.

"Creepy," she replied. "The good news is, the way their eyes glow, you can see them before they see you. The bad news is, that's all you can see. Just pairs of tiny white eyes, everywhere." She shuddered. "Let's get out of here." They went together back to the room they had slept the morning in. Dylan didn't like sleeping in the room where his brother had been bitten, but the only other option was to force another locked door or sleep in the hall.

"We'll be out of here tomorrow," Becca said, but that didn't make it any better. Dylan threw a couple of steaks from the rapidly thawing freezer at the two dogs, who lay in their usual place by the door. Turning, he saw the chair that Jesse had sat in. It still faced the door, as if his brother might walk in at any moment and take up his sentry position. Dylan kicked it as hard as he could. The chair toppled over, leaning at an awkward angle against an in-the-wall ironing board, He turned to find Becca watching him. "Better?" she said.

"No." he answered. He still wanted to kick something else. "Why would he do that?" he blurted suddenly, to his own surprise.

Becca sat down on the bed. "Jesse made a mistake, Dylan. It could happen to any one of us. It wasn't his fault."

"No, not Jesse," said Dylan, "*Wendell*. He seemed like a good guy. Why would he hurt the baby?"

Becca sighed and put a leather-clad arm around his shoulder.

"Let me ask you a different question," she said. "Let's say we leave here today and run into a pack of corpses. A big one, and we're surrounded. We hide in...I don't know, a car, but they're all over. Around the car, on top of the car, the only reason they're not inside yet is they haven't figured out glass breaks. There's no help coming, and we can't fight them off." Dylan gulped. Becca un-holstered her pistol and weighed it in her hand. "Now, I've got enough bullets in this to do for all of us, and corpses don't really care whether you've alive or not when they start to eat you. What would you rather have? A quick way out, or a slow one?" She holstered the weapon again, and smiled grimly. "Personally, I'd take the bullet."

Dylan nodded. "So he really thought he was doing the right thing," he said. Becca nodded. "In that case, why did you give him such a hard time?"

"Because there's more than one kind of person," said Becca. "And we can't just assume that everyone we meet is going to be the right kind of person. I don't want to wind up in a situation where he looks at us and says, 'Sorry, guys, it's you or me.'

"See, Jesse and I trusted each other. You and I, we trust each other. I even trust Keith, because I know he'll always run away, so I can count on him to be reliable and run away every time."

Dylan scowled. "Keith's an asshole."

"Keith was right, for a change. You should have hidden. What the hell were you thinking, fighting thirty corpses just with the two of you?"

"There were only five at first. The rest showed up when we were finishing them off."

"Okay, look. The next time you look up and see twenty-five zombies coming at you, you run away and hide in a bathroom, got it?" He nodded. "You and I need to stick together now, Dill. You've gotta be smart. No mistakes."

"Okay," he said. "No mistakes. But what do we do about Wendell?"

"I don't know about Wendell yet." She sighed. "He could either be a big help to us or he might get us killed. We need to watch ourselves, and wait and see. Now let's go to sleep. Tomorrow's a big day. The biggest."

Dylan lay down in the dark room and pulled the blankets over his shoulders. The room seemed cold and threatening, and he felt very alone. He didn't think he would ever fall asleep.

He felt arms encircle him and hold him tight.

"Becca? what are you—"

"Shh," she whispered. "Just lie down and go to sleep."

In spite of his grief and his fear, Dylan felt himself smile just a little. The smile died on his face almost immediately, though. A memory of his brother, and something he had said once about Becca.

"Becca?" he whispered. "You're not going anywhere, are you?"

He could hear her frustration in the dark. "Do I look like I'm going anywhere?"

"No," he said. "It's just, Jesse said—"

She sighed. "Jesse wasn't right about everything, Dylan. Go to sleep."

He snuggled into the warmth of her, feeling safe for the first time in weeks.

"Hey Dylan."

"Yeah?"

"If you try to cop a feel, I'll throw you out the window."

CHAPTER FIFTEEN

Wendell was startled by a knock on the door. The room was pitch black except for the small circle of light cast by his flashlight. He had no idea the time, but it was certainly nearer to midnight than morning.

The light spilled over a half-dozen empty bottles, casting long-necked shadows across the carpet and against the curtained window. Wendell Jenkins' time on the wagon had come to a screeching halt.

The knocking continued, quiet, polite, but insistent. He stood up, wobbling a little, and thinking the place *was* just like a university dorm, with people dropping by to chat at all hours of the night.

Out of habit, he looked through the peephole in the door. Of course, he saw nothing but a wide circle of black. Stupid. He reached for the hammer he still kept in his belt. There was no telling who might come calling, especially if his supposed allies were sleeping away another danger.

He opened the door a crack and pulled his hammer. Zombies were never so polite as to knock, but the others' arrival had driven home the fact that there were sure to be more survivors in the city, some certain to be not as nice.

A circle of light hit his face and fell back down. In the glow, he beheld a pudgy face with a two-week growth of beard, small, searching eyes, and a lopsided grin.

"Do you know how many doors I had to knock on before I found your room? This place is a maze in the dark."

Wendell lowered his guard and let the door swing open. "Evening, Keith," he said. "What can I do for you?"

Keith raised his other hand, brandishing a bottle as if it were a weapon.

"I'm getting shitfaced," he said. "I'm halfway there already. Figured since you're the only person here legally old enough to drink with me, I'd see if you'd changed your mind about the sauce."

Given the general opinion of Keith around the hotel, it was just as likely he had decided to visit Wendell because he was the only person who wasn't already set on hating him.

"Come on in," he said, and stood aside to let Keith's circle of light enter the room, followed by the bottle of Jack Daniel's.

"I see you got started without me," said Keith, looking around at the pile of beer bottles that had grown since their aborted afternoon party. "No shame in it, man. The way I see it, if you can't get up to your worst at the end of the world, when can you? Besides, who's left alive to judge?" He winced as his mind caught up to his mouth and he realized what he'd said. "I'm sorry, Wendell. For all I know, you had a wife and kids before this. I'm not thinking too clearly, you know?"

Wendell nodded. "I've got some coffee mugs around here somewhere," he said. He crossed the room to where the double doors separated this room from the room where Sheila still slept and gently closed them. Drunks get loud, and

Keith was already whispering at rock concert volume. He fished out a couple of mugs from the pile on the desk and handed one to Keith.

"Did you?" he asked as Keith poured generous shots of whiskey for each of them.

"Did I what?"

"Have a family? Before this?"

"Not really. An ex-wife in Rosedale. If she's a zombie it only means the alimony can stop. No kids. I never had the knack for them. Never wanted any of my own."

"I couldn't tell," said Wendell.

Keith chuckled. "Yeah, you can see by the deep paternal bond I've built up with these kids what kind of a father I would have been. It cuts both ways, though, you know? They hated me from the first glance." He lifted his mug to his lips and downed the whiskey in one shot. His eyes found Wendell's, and Wendell knew he was about to ask the question that had been driving him to drink all night.

"Did I kill that boy today?"

Wendell sipped gently at his mug. The whiskey went down smooth and bitter and warmed him from the stomach on out. "I don't think so. You were all asleep when the attack started, weren't you?"

"Yeah. First thing I heard when I woke up was, 'fucking zombies guys, get up!' That shoots you out of bed better than a kick in the crotch."

"And when you woke up, was Jesse wearing that big coat of his?"

"Yeah."

Wendell thought for a minute. "Then he was bitten while you and Dylan were still sleeping. He fell asleep with his coat off and the door open because he thought you were alone in the building. After he was bitten, he put the coat on so no one would see the bite. He hid it all day."

"So there was nothing I could have done?" Behind the fog of drunkenness, Keith's eyes were beginning to shine with a kind of desperate hope.

"No," said Wendell. "Under the circumstances, you're not responsible."

"Oh, thank God." The relief that washed over Keith's face was so spontaneous and genuine that Wendell was forced to re-evaluate his entire opinion of the man. It seemed that sometimes first impressions don't always paint the best picture.

"I mean, we never liked each other, but I never wanted him to die! Did you know he saved my life?"

"Yeah, I heard the story today, remember?"

"He saved my life more times than I can count. Becca wanted to cut me loose as soon as we got out of the subway, but he made her back down. That leather-jacket bitch would have left me alone on the street to get eaten alive." He reached for the bottle with unsteady hands and filled the mug almost to the top. After a few glugs, he was calmer, if far more wobbly.

"I mean, what ever happened to respecting your elders?" he said, and Wendell was surprised at how quickly the old Keith could come back. Sometimes first impressions do paint an accurate picture.

Keith was staring at Wendell expectantly, and Wendell realized he had meant the question seriously.

"I think," he began, parsing his words carefully. "We're not in a world anymore where respect is automatic. It doesn't matter anymore how much money you make or what floor of what building your condo is on. For these kids, survival is the most important thing, and how much respect you earn depends on how good you are at staying alive."

"Bullshit," said Keith. "I'm great at staying alive and so are you. We think and we run and we hide. That's what makes us the best. We're prudent. We should be right on top of things if that was the case, not playing Us versus Them with a couple of teenagers. It's fighting and killing zombies that matters, and at that, buddy, we suck."

You're a coward who hides while people die.

"I'm not that bad," Wendell started to protest.

"Oh no? How many zombies have you killed? I've killed two that came too close to my hiding place. It wasn't easy, either. Jesse knocked out twenty corpses *today*. Could you do that?"

"I'm sure if I had to…"

"You did have to, Wendell, and you didn't. You ran and hid, and so did I. And it was the right thing to do, but they don't see that, and they never will.

"I don't like kids much, but I remember being one. I remember how it felt. They're not in the middle of the worst disaster in history, they're on a fucking adventure. But it wouldn't matter anyway. They're kids. Every day is an adventure to them. I used to have that. I used to get excited by *thunderstorms*. I'd stand facing the clouds just as the wind picked up and I'd feel so alive, like something huge was just about to happen. I wanted to say something like 'so it begins' every time the rain started. I remember life being an adventure *every day*. Now I work in a bank. I take the same train at the same time and I buy the same damn bagel and coffee and read the same newspaper, and I try not to think how much of it doesn't come close to exciting me.

"That's why they hate me. Because I'm old and fat and not

on the adventure anymore. And that's why I hate them. Because they still are."

"Look, these kids saved our lives," said Wendell. "If it wasn't for them, you'd still be huddled under a cash register in some subway station, and Sheila and I would be worse than dead. You could be a little grateful."

"Oh, I'm grateful, all right. I'll sing their praises to the heavens and anyone I meet. But I don't have to like them, and they sure aren't making it easy for me to try. You neither. Becca hates you, and she'll make sure Dylan does, too. We're second class citizens now, my friend, and you might as well get used to it."

He poured more Jack into his mug and offered what was left of the bottle to Wendell. Wendell waved it away. His head was already foggy, and he could feel the beginnings of nausea coming on. At the same time, he felt the beginnings of an idea, one that might even begin to make amends for what he had done and nearly done today.

"What if we weren't?" he said.

"Huh?" Keith was swaying rhythmically back and forth in slow circles. He was obviously very drunk and close to passing out. Wendell was certain Keith would be sleeping on his couch tonight.

"What if there was a way to even things out? I mean, by all rights we should be the ones protecting them, not the other way around. You should have their respect because you kept *them* safe. And there might just be a way you and I can do that."

"How?" said Keith.

Wendell grinned. "Do you feel like an adventure?"

CHAPTER SIXTEEN

Outside the penthouse window, sheets of driving rain pounded the glass, but still the thin morning sunlight spilling through the clouds and the open curtains stabbed into Wendell's head. He was reeling from the effects of last night's drinking. All he wanted to do was climb back into bed and never move again. Unfortunately, babies don't care what you did the night before, or how bad your hangover is.

Sheila squirmed and fussed on the bedspread in front of him. Her diaper sagged with the weight of her latest efforts, but she stubbornly fought against his efforts to change it. A syncopated pounding beat against his temples.

"Can I help?" said Dylan. Wendell had asked both he and Becca to join him in his suite for breakfast.

"Sure," he said. "You'll need to know how to do this later tonight." He showed Dylan how to pull off the little yellow tabs and open up the diaper.

"Oh, gross," said Dylan. "That's the size of her!"

Wendell chuckled. "Now comes the fun part. You've got to clean it all off." He handed Dylan a wet wipe. "Wipe from the front to the back. You've gotta get all the little nooks and crannies in there. Go ahead, grab another one if you need. Use all the wipes you want. We've got lots."

"So you really want to go through with this?" said Becca from behind him. She was scowling out the window, keeping a silent vigil on the street far below. A light rain had begun to fall, and a mist was rising.

"It makes more sense to me than marching blindly into the night," said Wendell. "If we all go for the boat, we'll be easy prey. I can't fight off zombies and carry the baby at the same time."

"Yeah, we've both seen that," said Becca.

Wendell ignored that. "Look, the more of us that go out, the better the chances are that one of us will be killed. But if Keith and I can make it to the boat alone and convince them to bring us back an armed escort, we can show up with the cavalry and be away safe before dawn."

"I get that part," said Becca. "And I like the whole 'show up with the cavalry' idea, I'm just not sold on the part where I have to trust all our lives to you and Keith."

"Would you rather take the chance of Dylan being bitten along the way?"

"I'd rather go myself."

"You and Keith?"

"I'm not going anywhere with him. Or you, for that matter."

"Then you go off alone, get killed in the middle of Lakeshore Boulevard, and no one ever knows what happened to you? If two people go, one has a chance of getting through, even if the other one doesn't make it."

"Of getting through and catching the ferry! Who's to say you wouldn't just jump aboard and leave us here?"

"Come on, Becca," said Wendell. "You have to trust

someone sometime. If anything, do you really think I'd leave Sheila here, after everything I've been through with her?"

"From what I saw yesterday, yeah!" she snapped. It hurt, but Wendell looked her dead in the eye without flinching.

In a calm and level voice said simply, "You're wrong, Becca." Then he turned back to Dylan and the newly diapered baby.

"Okay," said Wendell to Dylan. "This next part's the tricky part. There's all these little snaps, see, and they all have to be lined up right..."

Becca fumed behind him, but he ignored her and concentrated on Sheila and the boy.

"Can I hold her?" asked Dylan when they were done.

"Of course," said Wendell. Dylan took the girl in his arms and rocked her gently. Suddenly the weight of the world disappeared from his face and he smiled. Sheila smiled and cooed at him.

"She makes me feel better," he said. All of a sudden, he was crying softly. "I miss Jesse."

Wendell sighed. "Dylan, what you're going through right now...I can't even begin to find the words to help you through it. All I can tell you is I know how you feel."

"How? You didn't lose your brother last night."

"No," said Wendell. "My wife. Last week." Dylan stared at him, horrified. From the window, Becca turned to regard him, and he could see he'd surprised her, too. "I still talk to her sometimes," he continued. "No, I'm not crazy. I know it's not really her. It's just me imagining what she would say and telling myself things I want to hear, but it helps sometimes."

"How... how did she die?" asked Dylan.

"I don't know. I wasn't there. I had it in mind that I would go find her, if, you know, if she was walking around still, and..." He couldn't finish the thought.

"Put her to rest?" ventured Dylan.

"Exactly. I think she would prefer that. I know I would, if it came to that. I know it's a stupid idea, trying to find one zombie in a city full of them, but it was something to do. It kept me going.

"The point is," he went on, shaking off the sudden wave of melancholy that threatened to settle on him. "That you're not alone, Dylan. Everybody who's left alive has lost somebody to this plague, or whatever you want to call it. I lost a wife, Sheila lost a mother, you lost your brother—"

"And my mom," Dylan said. "We're not gonna find her on the island. She was working at the hospital."

Wendell winced. "I'm sorry, son."

"It's okay. I kind of knew for a while now. It was just something Jesse said to keep us both going. It doesn't even really hurt anymore. I mean, maybe it will later, if I make it out. But right now I just keep thinking about Jesse." He began to cry softly again.

With a very serious expression on her tiny face, Sheila stuck out a searching hand toward the boy. Her fist closed around his nose and she yanked with surprising strength, and giggled. The sound broke the morose tension in the room, and Wendell was relieved to see Dylan laughing. He lifted her and kissed her cheek.

"I always wanted a little sister," he said.

Wendell laid a hand on his shoulder. "I'd say you've got one now."

The rain came to a stop around noon, and gave way to glorious sunshine. Knowing that each sunny day might be the last, not only for the season but forever, Wendell carried Sheila up to the roof. He made her a little play area out of pillows and blankets and with a tablecloth for a sunshade. She sang to herself and sucked on her feet while Wendell practiced with the Halligan.

Becca had forbidden him Jesse's gift on pain of bullet, but she hadn't specifically said that he couldn't use it while on the roof. Besides, thought Wendell, if he ever did have the chance to use it, his arms would need exercise if he was going to be able to use the heavy bar to any effect. So with no one around to say no, he lifted the Halligan and tested its weight with a solid swing.

Before his late life career as a low-paid building superintendent and handyman, Wendell had enjoyed a storied and diverse working life. He'd worked in construction, been a delivery man for a paper company, and even spent a lonely and frustrating stint in Alberta working in the oilfields before a trip to Toronto and a chance meeting with a friend's friend named Gracie made him move home and settle down for good. Working numerous heavy jobs had given him strong arms and a broad back, but with even one swing of the Halligan he could tell that he would have a hard time if he had to fight too many for too long. It was *heavy*. It gave a satisfying swing if he used it like a full-handled axe, and the multiple different heads on it meant that both ends could be used as a weapon at once, smashing with the pickaxe end and jabbing with the pry bar end. But that was action movie stuff, the kind of fancy moves that would only come with a lot of practice, if at all. In the meantime, his arms tired quickly and he could already feel the burning in his biceps and forearms. It was an excellent weapon—the best he could ever hope to find—but he was a fool if he believed he would live long enough to master it.

"You promise you'll come back?"

He spun around and dropped the Halligan. She was standing behind him, next to Sheila's makeshift cabana. He hadn't even heard her come up. The expression on her face was one he hadn't seen before. It wasn't snarling or contemptuous. For the first time since he'd met her, she looked her age, a sixteen year old girl who was scared shitless.

In answer, Wendell reached into his back pocket and pulled out his wallet. He handed it to Becca.

"Open it," he said.

Inside, besides a twenty-dollar bill that was now as good as worthless and a driver's license he hadn't used in two years, was a tattered and much-handled photograph. It showed a woman of about thirty-five, with creamy chocolate skin and long, flowing hair blowing in the wind. She was laughing at something off to the left, and her face was lit up with joy.

"I'll be back for Grace," said Wendell. "You can trust that."

She nodded. He believed she almost smiled. She took the picture out of the wallet, tucked it carefully in the top pocket of her jacket and handed the wallet back.

"You can take the whatchacallit bar," she said. "You'll stand a lot better chance with that than with your little hammer."

"Thank you," he said. "You know, I'll have an even better chance if I wear the coat and helmet, too."

"Do you have an answer to my question?"

"No," he sighed. "A lot of things went through my mind at once in there. But does it really matter, Becca? If it was the only choice I had, does it matter what I was thinking when I made it?"

"It matters," she said.

"Okay," said Wendell. "Okay."

They stared at each other. Wendell could tell that she had something she wanted to say, but couldn't find the words. He had a thousand thoughts running through his own mind, but he didn't think anything he might say would ever make anything better.

"Well," he said lamely. "Sun's going down."

"Yeah," she said. "Better get going if you're going."

He started to walk away, off the roof. At that moment, the roof door swung open and Wendell jumped, bringing Jesse's Halligan up to strike. But it was only Dylan.

"I just wanted to say good luck," said Dylan. "And don't worry, we'll take care of Sheila."

"Thank you, Dylan," said Wendell. "And don't worry. I *will* be back."

"I know," he said.

Wendell turned to look at Becca, who stood stock-still. Her eyes glared, but her mouth quivered, and Wendell could tell she was torn by some dark thoughts he couldn't even imagine. He wondered if he would ever get to find out Becca's story, or if he would even want to know.

"Grace was pregnant," he blurted suddenly. It surprised him; he hadn't meant for those words to come out. "She was pregnant with our first child. She left that morning for an ultrasound. I didn't want to find out what we were having, but I knew she was going to."

The children said nothing. Dylan had tears in his eyes and Becca was staring at the gravel on the floor of the roof. "I wanted so badly to be a father," he went on. "I thought I'd be so good at it. But look at me. Three days with a baby and I come seconds away from killing her. Maybe it's better the baby won't ever be born."

Dylan came up beside him. To Wendell's shock, he wrapped his gangly arms around Wendell and squeezed him in a bear hug. "I think you would have been a great dad," he said.

Becca looked up from the gravel. "You should get going." She sniffed. "It's a good plan, Wendell. It's really the best option. Just make sure you don't fuck it up."

He had to smile. Coming from Becca, it was the nicest thing anyone could say.

Then it was time. Wendell slid his hammer into its familiar spot in his belt, slung Sheila's now-empty backpack over his shoulder, and turned to the door. He looked back at them, once, three children whose hope fate had placed in his hands. For the first time since coming up with this plan, Wendell felt afraid. If he made a mistake this time, they would be the ones to suffer. Wendell smiled for their benefit, grabbed the Halligan by its shaft, and walked out the door into the dark.

He'd left them his flashlight; he would need both hands free. By feel and memory he made his way to the stairs, fourteen stories of inky darkness unbroken by light or windows, and that would be the easiest part. His boots made heavy echoes in the shaft, an ominous drumbeat leading him on toward death.

CHAPTER SEVENTEEN

His relief when he came to the relative brightness of the lobby was palpable. He was surprised to see Keith already there, looking as bad as Wendell did and holding his seven-foot steel pike like it might be a fish. He had half-expected Keith to back out at the last minute.

"I was starting to think you'd chickened out," said Keith, and Wendell had to laugh. He found the dour, irritable man was growing on him by the minute. The fact that he'd kept his word and showed up said a lot for him.

"Are you ready for this?" asked Wendell.

"Hell no," said Keith. "This is the dumbest thing I've ever done. But if we're going, we might as well go, ready or not."

"That about sums for me, too," said Wendell. "Let's get going if we're going."

They crept out the fire exit on the kitchen side. The door opened onto a wide alley leading up to the loading dock.

"This would be a bad place to get caught," whispered Wendell. High walls flanked the alley on both sides, and an abandoned delivery truck blocked the entire rear escape.

It was a dead-end.

"Hold the door open," Wendell said to Keith. "I'm going to make sure the coast is clear."

"How do you like that," muttered Keith. "We might get eaten right outside the door."

Wendell moved cautiously up the alley, stopping periodically to listen for approaching footsteps. The sun had dipped below the skyline, and long shadows stretched from skyscraper to skyscraper, but there was still enough golden autumn light to see by.

He peered around the corner. Not five feet away stood a zombie, staring right at him. Wendell jerked back with a gasp, and braced for the inevitable charge. When after a few moments nothing came around the corner, he crept back and peeked again.

He was a middle-aged man, with greenish skin and a sunken face. In the deepening shadows of gloaming twilight, every bone in his face was set off in sharp relief. He looked like an animate skeleton. It took Wendell a stunned moment to realize that though the creature was facing directly into his hiding place, it hadn't noticed him. Its eyes were cast high above his head.

Gradually, he noticed there were other figures on the street, all standing alone, all gazing intensely in the same direction. Something about the unity of it, the unspoken coordination, sent a shiver up Wendell's spine. Slowly, keeping one eye on the skull-faced man for as long as possible, he turned to see what they were all looking at.

Before him stood a skyscraper, a towering wall of mirrored glass looming high over head. Its mirrored surface caught the setting sun as it lowered beneath the distant horizon in an explosion of orange fire. He looked back at the figures on the street below and chuckled to himself. What had seemed to him to be a telepathic convergence was nothing more than the zombie's natural inclination to look at pretty lights. He searched around the garbage at his feet until he found an empty pop can, and hurled it across the street. It landed with a deafening clatter, but nobody moved. He waved for Keith to join him.

"They're occupied for now," Wendell said when Keith was beside him. "But they won't be for long. Let's go, right across to the other alley, fast as we can."

They leapfrogged their way from alley to alley at a running crouch while the sun set fire to walls of glass, and in this way passed by a mob of nearly a hundred corpses, until they made it to the door of the convenience store Becca had located the night before. Just as they were ducking inside and easing the door shut behind them the sun disappeared for good, and the fires went out.

"We won't have it that easy again," whispered Wendell. "Now we'll need to start getting inventive." He took the empty backpack and crossed to the cigarette counter, where he began dumping cartons of cigarettes and cases of Zippo fluid into the bag.

"Smoke much?" said Keith.

"Nope. Never got into the habit. You?"

"I've been quit for six years," said Keith, though he was eying the wall of cigarette packs longingly.

Wendell finished his shopping spree with three boxes of matchbooks and a pair of water bottles, zipped the bag shut, and threw it back over his shoulder.

"Need anything else?" Keith shook his head. "Then let's go be heroes."

Even now, Grace was helping him.

Full dark had fallen. The utter absence of light was much worse on the ground than it had been from the Sheraton's penthouse. The buildings were obsidian slabs only visible where they sliced across the purple starless sky. Amid them, here and there the lantern-lights of glowing eyes seemed to float above the ground.

Wendell and Keith were huddled behind a trash can on Front Street. Up ahead, blocking their path, a large clot of zombies meandered about. Wendell wasn't sure how well their searchlight eyes could see in the dark, but they hadn't yet taken notice of the two men crouched by the curb. Wendell was busy pouring the contents of a full bottle of lighter fluid into the trash.

"Here," he said, handing Keith a cigarette. "Light this for me. The last one made me yack."

The way Grace was helping him this time was through her love of a certain type of television show—the kind where genius forensics detectives with electron microscopes for eyes used their skills to solve crimes the regular police would be baffled by. Grace ate up these crime scene shows in all their various forms, and there always seemed to be more of them. In one particular episode, the laser-eyed investigators were trying to figure out how a killer could possibly have blown up a hospital oxygen tent and murdered its sole comatose patient while being in a completely different part of the hospital when the explosion had occurred. The answer had surprised Wendell, and stuck with him all these years, a little tidbit of useless knowledge he was now putting to good use.

A match flared, and the cigarette sprang into life. Keith coughed and handed the cigarette to Wendell, who carefully wrapped a book of matches around the filter and set it down on top of the butane-soaked garbage.

"Go!" he whispered. Keith grabbled his cumbersome pike and followed Wendell across the street. They hid behind an upside-down Prius and watched.

It usually took about five minutes. The cigarette slowly burned down to the filter, igniting the matchbook. The sudden heat of twenty-five matches flaring up at once was enough to explode, say, the pure oxygen contained in an oxygen tent, or in this case ignite a garbage can full of lighter fluid. Soon the trashcan was a roaring bonfire, and in the unnatural darkness it lit the entire street. The fire did its job; within minutes every zombie in the area was gathered around it like hobos in a railyard. Keith and Wendell moved freely past the group.

In this manner, with tiny acts of petty arson, they had made it nearly half-way to the docks without once having to fight the dead.

Almost.

As Keith rounded the bend into the alley they had picked for their next cover, a dark figure sprang out at him. He tried to bring his long staff around to defend himself, but the seven-foot pike was too long and cumbersome. It was designed by firefighters to break second-story windows in safety, not for close-quarters combat. Too heavy to get a good swing and too long for him to pull back for a stabbing thrust, all Keith could do was hold the creature at bay as its teeth gnashed inches from his face. As they grappled in the mouth of the alley, Wendell came up behind and brought his Halligan to bear, driving the pickaxe end hard into the dead man's neck. With a loud wet crack, the zombie went limp and dropped to the pavement.

Keith was shaking. The entire incident had lasted maybe thirty seconds, but he was breathing as if he'd run a mile, and his face dripped with sweat. Wendell put a hand on his shoulder.

"Are you still with me?" he said.

"Shit," said Keith. He dropped his pike with a loud clatter and rubbed at his face with both hands. "That was too close."

"It's a good thing there was only one of them," said Wendell. "We need to find you a better weapon. That stick of yours is useless."

Front Street, like most of downtown, was littered with abandoned vehicles and scattered with debris. If it had been a major artery it would have been bumper to bumper traffic, like Yonge Street up ahead.

Wendell moved slowly among the darkened hulks of cars and trucks, barely able to make out the very nearest vehicles. Behind him, Keith watched as he vanished from sight, suddenly realized he was standing alone in a dark alley, and hurried down the street in the direction Wendell had gone.

He found him standing beside an overturned tow truck. The tool box on the side of the truck was knocked open, and the street was littered with its contents. With a grin and a flourish, Wendell presented Keith with a five-foot long tire iron.

"Seek and ye shall find," said Wendell. "That's a breaker bar. It's got a good reach and a nice swing. Swing it like a baseball bat, and go for the neck."

Keith gave the breaker bar a couple of practice swings, liking the feel of it already. "Why the neck?" he said. "I thought you said the back of the head was the sweet spot."

"It is," said Wendell. "But it's a very small area to be trying to hit under pressure. If you can't get behind one, break its neck, and it'll still go down. It won't matter if they're still biting if they're paralyzed. Just step over it carefully and walk away."

Feeling much more confident with a weapon he felt he could actually defend himself with, Keith followed Wendell as they crept out into the Yonge Street intersection. Here the clog of vehicles was the worst either of them had yet seen. Yonge Street was the longest street in the world, and ran in a more or less straight line north out of the city and through dozens of smaller towns before it turned into Highway 22 and disappeared in Ontario's northern wilderness. Anybody who had seen the backlog on the Gardiner Expressway would have turned and made their way to Yonge Street in the hopes of finding a way out of the rapidly dying city. Wendell didn't even want to think about how many people had met their grisly end trapped in this hideous gridlock, helpless to do anything but watch the waves of corpses roll over them and hope the glass and the locks would hold. The number of empty, shattered windshields he could see just before him said that they hadn't held for long.

"This isn't going to work," he whispered. "They're jammed up from one end to the other, all the way across the sidewalks."

"Why can't we just skirt along the edges?" said Keith. "There's bound to be ways in between the cars. Room enough for two people, anyway."

"Not a chance," said Wendell. "I've been through one of these before, and it wasn't nearly this bad. If we hit a dead end, we'll be sitting ducks, and there's going to be people in cars who've reanimated still trapped in their seatbelts. It'll be like walking through a minefield."

"Well, what do you suggest, then? We've only got two hours. Who knows how long they'll wait around if there's nobody there."

"If we don't make it tonight, we find someplace to hole up and try again tomorrow night. The kids'll worry, I bet, but we'll still make it." Wendell thought a moment. "That's Union Station up ahead. There's a sky bridge that goes right from the concourse to the CN Tower and the Skydome."

"Rogers Centre," corrected Keith.

Wendell snorted at the new name. "It'll always be the Skydome to me," he said. "Look, I know you barely just got out of a subway station, and it's going to be very dangerous, but I think it's our best bet."

"Lead on, boss," said Keith. "At least inside we'll have lots of places to hide if something goes wrong."

CHAPTER EIGHTEEN

The grand concourse of Union Station could not be seen, but it could be felt. Immediately upon entering the huge doors, Wendell felt it in the air, a vast sensation of space. He knew from memory that it was an enormous room, several stories high and wide as a football field, with corridors branching off in all directions from this central spot. Somewhere ahead lay stairs that led up to the southern end of the PATH system, and the sky bridge to Toronto's two most famous buildings. Where were they in all this darkness? He wondered if he had made a mistake.

"If you see anything glowing," he said to Keith. "Hit it as hard as you can."

They moved off straight ahead, toward where he remembered the stairs to be. He thought they were at the end, beyond endless arrays of ticket booths and sales kiosks. Thousands of people moved through this concourse every day, but Wendell hadn't been here in years, and only when friends happened to have extra Blue Jays tickets.

He slammed up against something at waist height, driving the wind from his gut. He'd smacked right into the main

189

ticket counter.

"Where are you going?" asked Keith.

"I'm trying to find the stairs," he wheezed.

"There's no stairs on the concourse," snorted Keith. "When's the last time you were here?"

"Not for a while," he admitted.

"Then fucking ask! The stairs to the sky bridge are off to the right, past the computer kiosks."

"Okay," said Wendell. "Lead on, boss. Looks like you're the point guy now."

Keith led him to the side of the great room until he felt the hard plastic frames of a large bank of kiosks. By feel, they crept along until Keith felt brick under his hands. They had come to the enormous arch at the back of the building that led toward the baggage claim, the food court, and the stairs going up. Keith peered around the bend, then turned to Wendell.

"There's eyes out there," he whispered. "I saw maybe three, but there's probably more."

"Okay," Wendell said. "We stand back to back and go slow. I don't know if they can see us or not, so don't attack unless you have to. Stay at my back. If we get separated, we'll never find each other."

Back to back they edged out into the corridor. Wendell's blood went cold when he saw the ghostly eyes floating in the ether. They were far away, only pinpricks of light at this distance, though neither of them could find any frame of reference for how far away exactly they were. Wendell's eyes played tricks on him in the dark; he saw trails where the eyes passed his vision, and imagined hundreds more where none were. At his back, he felt Keith's muscles tense and heard the whoosh of air as he swung his breaker bar at nothing, and realized he was seeing things, too. The real eyes, the ones that stayed put and didn't dance around his vision like will-o-the-wisps, moved in their stately pace or stood perfectly still, staring at nothing, all in complete, unnerving silence. Wendell shivered, trying to watch all of them at once, knowing that each pair of eyes was connected to unseen teeth and certain death.

They were nearing one now; two floating orbs of ghostly light grew larger on his left. The moment of truth was coming—could it see them? For all he knew he was a bright red glow of pulsing life in its vision. Then again, it might be as black in here to the zombie as it was to him, and they might just glide by, unnoticed. Wendell watched the eyes come closer, closer still. Still the creature made no sound, not a moan or a hiss. Now it was a few paces away.

Now it was right in front of him. Wendell stared into the center of its eyes and realized he could see the outline of a ghostly cornea, limned with purple veins. Then the eyes slid by on his right, the zombie still staring into the ether, seeing who knew what.

Then there was deafening clatter and an audible curse as Keith stumbled against something in the dark. Wendell watched with horror as the eyes he had so easily passed a moment before suddenly snapped his way. From the unseen mouth of the zombie, a low, mournful moan floated through the dark to be joined by others. Wendell looked around him and saw eyes everywhere, not three or four, but dozens, all snapped to attention and staring his way.

"Shit," he said and swung the Halligan into the middle of the floating eyes. The light went out. He backed up, pushing Keith forward and away from the unseen obstacle. More lights were headed their way. He felt Keith tense up and swing, heard the echoing *thwock* as the blow hit home. Something thumped to the ground.

"Keith," Wendell whispered. "Go slow and stay at my back, but *move now.*"

They inched their way through the murk. The zombies were still advancing, but they were heading toward the spot where the sound had originated, and Wendell hoped they could slide by the bulk of them undetected.

"We have the advantage," he whispered. "We can see them by their eyes, but they can't see us."

"That's great, professor," whispered Keith. "Then wouldn't it be a good idea to shut the fuck up?"

They edged their way left through the middle of the corridor. Up ahead was a large grouping of zombies, their eyes all clustered together and coming forward fast. Wendell grabbed the back of Keith's belt and pulled him backward away from the group. He stopped where he was and watched as the floating lights continued on down the corridor. He saw no more eyes up ahead.

"I think we're in the clear," he whispered. "How far to the stairs?"

"I don't know," said Keith. "I don't know where we are. We might have passed them."

"We'll just have to keep going. There's no point retracing our steps until we're at the end of the corridor. What side are they on?"

"The far left," said Keith. "My way. They take up half the hallway, if we haven't passed them already we'll fall right onto them."

Wendell backed up until Keith signaled they were at the other wall. Then they started forward again, back to back.

This time it was Wendell who tripped. Something soft and

yielding met his foot and threw him to the floor. The Halligan banged off the tiled floor as he landed. He rolled and got to his feet, when he saw something glowing right near the floor. The zombie he had tripped over was crawling toward him. He felt no presence behind him. He had lost Keith.

Wendell slammed the end of the Halligan down on the crawler's head. The lights in its eyes went out, but he became aware of more eyes, dozens more, all on the floor, crawling his way.

He backed away from the oncoming crawlers. One at a time, he could easily have taken them out, but so close together, the chances that one would get past his Halligan and sink its teeth into his leg were too great. From the other end of the corridor, he heard a chorus of moans. The crawlers had called in the others. Wendell backed up against a wall. Nowhere left to go.

"Keith?" he whispered. "Keith, where are you?"

"I'm here," came a voice ahead of, and above him. "I found the stairs."

"Get down here! I'm surrounded."

"Hold on," said Keith.

He couldn't hold on. Wendell dropped his backpack and felt around inside until he found a bottle of lighter fluid. He ripped the cap clean off and started dumping butane on the tiles in front of him. When the bottle was empty, he struck a match and dropped it.

Orange flames instantly lit up the corridor. He could see the zombies crawling toward him, lit up in stark relief. A dozen paces away, an enormous staircase rose up two stories, but a teeming, writhing pile of crawling zombies with broken legs splayed out at impossible angles was clambering over each other to cross the floor to him.

The lighter fluid would burn out soon. Wendell pulled another bottle out and dropped it into the middle of the flames, then ran the other way into the Yogen Fruz he could now see was directly beside him. He ducked behind the counter just as the second bottle caught fire and exploded, showering wet flame and orange light across the corridor.

That's good, thought Wendell, at least the zombies would head toward the fire and not his hiding place. The bad news, of course, was that once the fire burned out and left him in darkness again, every zombie in the building would be between him and the staircase. *Lesson One*, he thought. *Worry about the immediate problem first.*

From his vantage point, he could see the first of the crawlers approach the burning pile on the floor. Its clothes immediately caught fire, but the creature did not react. In fact, it bathed in the fire; having forgotten what it had originally been chasing, it saw the fire as its goal, and having reached it, reveled in it. He saw other zombies walk right into the flames as well. The guttering fires did little damage to them—lighter fluid burns hot and fast, but disappears quickly. It gave Wendell an idea.

He had three bottles of Zippo fluid left. He pulled one from the bag and felt around by hand until he found the drink cooler under the counter. He reached in and grabbed a bottle, popped the cap and dumped out the liquid on the floor. It smelled like juice.

Come on, dishrag, every counter has a dishrag. He fumbled around in the dark. He found it by smell, a long-abandoned, moldering cloth that hopefully was dry enough to do the trick. He poured the lighter fluid into the juice bottle, then shoved the rag down the mouth of the bottle. With his miniature Molotov cocktail ready, Wendell zipped up his bag, stood up, and lit a match.

The rag caught fire instantly, but so did the fluid he'd spilled on his hand. Pain erupted along his arm, and he nearly dropped the bottle. He saw ahead of him the faces of the nearest zombies turn toward the light. With all his strength, he hurled the bottle down the hall, away from the stairs.

It exploded in a shower of flames and burning plastic. Utterly invisible again, he watched the walking zombies turn away from him toward the new source of light. The mob ambled away, and the slower crawlers followed.

When he thought enough of them were behind him Wendell dashed out of the yogurt shop, running at top speed through the darkness to where he knew the stairs to be. Just as he reached them, he heard a rumbling crash up above him, and dived out of the way just before something large and very noisy rolled off the stairs past him.

Wendell took the stairs two by two. He was panting when he reached the top, but found that there was enough light from enormous windows to just make out the silhouette of Keith standing before him.

"What the hell was that?" he demanded.

"A garbage can," said Keith. "I thought it might clear a path for you."

Wendell was glad Keith couldn't see him roll his eyes. What it had done was nearly brain him, not to mention attracting all the zombies he had just successfully lured away.

"Come on," he said instead. "Let's just get out of here."

CHAPTER NINETEEN

Queen's Wharf stood silent as a tomb, and that made Wendell nervous.

All along, the further south they went the more concentrated the zombies had become. By the time they reached the Gardiner, that massive overpass that dominated traffic along the Lakeshore, it had become impossible to get by with distraction and misdirection alone. They had had to fight their way through several small groups to get past the gridlock on Lakeshore Boulevard.

Now, though, as they rounded the bend of the last building, another hotel, and stood staring at the empty wharf, there was not a figure in sight.

"What time is it?" said Keith. Wendell was growing more and more impressed by Keith as the night went on. Despite his poor physique and tendency to take longer to catch his breath than Wendell would have liked, and despite his own admission that he was a coward, Keith had proven himself a staunch ally time and time again. He had saved Wendell's life twice as they fought their way beneath the Gardiner, in the artificial cave that occurred when one road ran directly beneath another for endless distances.

Wendell checked his watch. "Quarter to twelve. We made it. Just barely."

"So where is everyone?"

To that, Wendell had no answer. All he knew was that he felt exposed and vulnerable, and he began to wonder whether the boat was just a fantasy Jesse and Becca had dreamed up.

"We'll just have to find somewhere to hide and wait," he said. They moved toward the enormous wrought-iron gates that closed off the quay from the street. Suddenly Keith grabbed his arm.

"Look," he said, pointing to the east. Between the buildings and far away, a giant orange glow lit the sky.

"Something's on fire," Wendell mused. "That explains why there's no zombies here, anyway. They all followed the light."

Wendell put a hand on the gate and pushed. It moved about a hand's span and then stopped short. He looked down and swore. The gate was sealed by a heavy chain that wound around several times and was secured a massive padlock.

"Why the hell would they lock us out?" roared Keith. Wendell looked at the padlock. It was a Yale lock, but the biggest he'd ever seen, and to his surprise and relief, the key was in the tumbler.

"Zombies can't open locks," he said. "We'll be safe inside, even if they don't come tonight." He turned the key and began unwinding the heavy chain as quietly as he could. They crossed through to the other side, and Wendell shut the gate and relocked it.

There were no benches or anything else to break the monotony of the quay, just plenty of cobbled space for ticket holders to queue up for the ferry. Wendell and Keith sat on the pier itself, dangling their legs over the water.

"Nothing to do now but wait," said Keith. "Give me a cigarette." Wendell handed him a full pack. He still had a dozen unopened packs in his backpack.

"Shit, man," Keith said, striking a match. "I was quit for six years, then one night with you and I'm back at it again. Why did you have me light all those cigarettes for you? Why didn't you just make some of those exploding pop bottles like you did in the station?"

"Honestly, I didn't think of it," said Wendell, rubbing the sore skin of his burned hand. "I wish I had. If I'd had time to make a better cocktail, I might not have burned myself."

Keith smoked and Wendell watched the black water wash against the pier. For a while, they said nothing. Wendell checked his watch. Five after twelve. Where was the ferry?

"Let me ask you something," he said as Keith fished a second smoke out of the pack. "I know it's a little late for second guesses, but what if this boat isn't all it's cracked up to be?"

"What do you mean?" said Keith around his cigarette. He lit a match and dropped it in the water. "Shit."

"Well..." said Wendell, "Look, we're way too far into this for anything I say to sound stupid, but at the risk of sounding stupid, have you ever seen a zombie movie?"

"I saw one or two. It was never my thing. What does it matter? We're living one now."

"That's my point," said Wendell. "Half the time, in a zombie movie the heroes will fight their way all the way through the undead looking for some safe place. When they find it, it turns out to be a trick, and the place is being run by bad guys who turn out to be way worse than the zombies."

"Humans are the real monsters, right? So you're afraid that

this island is going to be some kind of trap? What would be the point of it, Wendell? I mean, why go out of your way to rescue people, risking your own life every time, just to use them for some evil plot?"

"I don't know," said Wendell. "I just think we should be on our guard, that's all."

"Okay, what about this?" Keith took a long drag and sent a flicker of burning ash across the water. "Look, I farted my way through university. I was there to meet girls and make my parents happy. So I took a lot of easy courses. You know, the kind where you sit in a lecture hall and watch movies for three hours and get a grade based on showing up? In one of them we watched a couple of zombie flicks, and the professor was all about how zombie movies are all really hidden-message movies beating their audiences over the head with some important truth or whatever. In that case, wouldn't the message always be about how we are our own worst enemy?"

"I suppose," said Wendell.

"Wendell, they're movies. They're made to tell a story. These people are real people, and real people either don't give a shit about each other, or they genuinely want to help out. Nobody in real life concocts elaborate schemes to lure unsuspecting victims into their bizarre trap."

"Yeah, well, nobody in real life dies and then wakes up and starts eating his friends, but here we are." He sighed. "I guess you're right. *Lesson One: Don't look a gift horse in the mouth.*"

They sat in silence a while longer. Finally, Keith said, "What about the other half of the time?"

"What?"

"You said half the time the heroes get to a safe place only

to find it's run by bad guys. What happens the other half of the time?"

"The heroes find themselves a safe place to hunker down and wait it out," said Wendell. "And the bad guys show up there."

"Huh." said Keith. He took a final puff and sent the shortened filter arcing across the water. "I got a more pressing question for you. What if the boat doesn't show up?"

But Wendell was already standing up. Out on the water, far in the distance and floating above the darkness just like zombie eyes, were bright white floodlights, coming closer.

The white-painted and white-lit ferry *Thomas Rennie* drifted into the quay and came to a bumping stop against the line of tires hung from the pier. Instantly a flurry of activity swarmed around the boat. A white-clad crewman threw a line around a pole and pulled the ferry fast. Two other crewmen lowered the ramp, which was the entire back wall of the ferry, to the dock. Before the ramp touched the cobbles, a dozen figures in body armor were moving over it, silently following a well-practiced routine as they spread out to the corners of the enclosure.

Wendell and Keith were the only civilians standing on the pier. They stood together in the middle of the activity, feeling quite a bit like an afterthought instead of the whole point of the operation, as the soldiers—or whatever they were—fanned out and, communicating with hand signals, created a wall of armed men around the enclosure.

Finally, a figure stepped alone off the ferry and approached them. Tall and unarmed except for a sidearm pistol, the figure was clad in police riot gear and a helmet.

Around its waist, in place of a belt, wound a thick chain. As the figure neared them, Wendell could see that it was a woman. She removed her helmet to reveal a serious face with light-colored hair tied up in a severe bun.

"Well?" she said. "What are you waiting for?"

Wendell pursed his lips. He had been concentrating on getting here to the wharf, but in all this time, he had never actually figured out what to say when he got there. The woman looked exasperated.

"Look, man, we don't have all day here. Are you coming or not?"

"Well, that's the thing…" said Wendell. It was a poor start. The woman rightly believed that he and Keith were wasting her time. Before she could berate him for it though, Wendell blurted out what he had come to say in a jumbled rush, and to hell with how he worded it. "I need your help," he said. "I've got three more people holed up in a hotel near Church and Richmond. We were hoping you could send someone to get them."

"You're joking. You're a joker, right? You realize we're risking our lives just being on this side of the lake to pick you up, but sure, we'd be happy to go wandering around on streets crawling with zeds to pick up your friends!"

"*We* made it," said Wendell.

"Yeah, so why didn't they?" She turned back to the boat. "If they're not here, they aren't coming. Get on the boat or don't."

"They're children!" Wendell blurted. The woman stopped short with one foot on the ramp. Her shoulders slumped, and she sighed.

She turned back and fixed Wendell with a dark-eyed stare.

"You'd better come talk to the captain," she said.

Captain Talleck turned out to be a short, ebullient man with a red beard and a thick Newfoundland accent. He led them up to the bridge, which was a four-foot square wheelhouse on the top deck of the ferry, and offered them a beer.

"You come a long ways, b'ys, take a rest an' have a cold one," he said, handing a can to each of them. He was wearing jeans and a North Face jacket, but Wendell imagined he'd look right at home in a yellow Nor'easter on a turn-of-the-century whaling ship. He liked him immediately, but it was obvious that, despite his generous attitude and fast speech, this man was the absolute master of his boat. The woman who had brought them up stood at ease in his presence, but she didn't sit, and she jumped to answer his every question, even though, as Wendell had learned, she was not a cop or a soldier, but a civilian like himself.

"We'll be staying here for an hour to see if anyone else shows up," said Talleck. "So I can take a bit o' time to tell you something about us, and why we can't help you.

"We've rescued nearly a hundred people in the last week and brought 'em to the island," he said. "There's a bustlin' little community over there, but they aren't all made of strong stuff. They won't come back to the city for nothin'. I got everybody brave enough to volunteer for rescue duty on this boat, but even most o' them aren't willing to go past the gates o' the wharf."

"But these are children," urged Wendell. "Two kids and a baby!" Talleck smiled sadly and shook his head.

"If they can get here, I'll take 'em to safety, b'y. But I might lose every one o' my people savin' your three kids, and the kids might still die. A lotta kids have."

"You can't just sit here—"

"I can do whatever I want." There was steel in Talleck's voice as he cut Wendell off. "Look, I know you're upset, an' it's a credit to you that you're willin' to fight for these kids. But we've survived this mess, an saved as many as we could, by not bein' stupid and takin' risks. If I had an army, I'd go out and carry every little baby out of every building in the city, but I don't have an army. I got twelve people, and the army won't even come in here."

"You've talked to them?" cut in Keith.

"Yeah, they're on the radio all the time. If you stand at Hanlon's Point an' look out south you can see the lights o' the Navy ships out on the lake. They got the city surrounded on all sides, by water an' by land, and they aren't letting anybody in or out. The country's declared martial law under the War Measures Act, an' we're in what they call a state of extended quarantine. But they talk to us every day, and they've dropped supplies to the island for us."

"And is it true that there aren't any zombies on the island?"

"It's true. The zeds all wandered into the lake, all of 'em in a group, 'bout eight days ago."

"I find that very hard to believe," said Wendell, fuming.

"Trust me, b'y, I was there. We put in to Ward's Island for what was supposed to be our last trip, evacuating whoever was left after the police an' the National Guard were overrun. Soon as we dropped the ramp, we were swarmed. I was just a crewman. My job was to check that all the life jackets were in their cubbies, every trip, every day, even though no one ever used' em. It was the dumbest job I ever had, an even before the zeds came along, I was plannin' on quittin'. When they rushed the boat, I pushed out a pile o' life jackets an' hid in an overhead compartment for about four hours. When I come down, the ferry was empty. Everyone was dead, an' wandered off. I found the captain right here, bangin' into everything and groaning. Hit him over the head with an oar, an' I don't miss him much. He was a right bastard, and never could stop telling the same goddamn Newfie jokes whenever I was around.

"Anyways, I backed out o' the wharf an' started back for shore alone when I started hearin' worse things on the radio back on the mainland. Last thing I heard before the static cut in was my dispatcher at the terminal dyin' right there on the open air.

"I was stuck. Couldn't go home, couldn't go back to the island. I dropped anchor a hundred feet from the island terminal an' shut off all my lights. For five days I sat there, not sure what to do. I saw a couple boats make for open water, but the Navy was already there. I hears 'em call out on the radio that anyone tryin' to run the blockade would be sunk. I'm sure a few tried it anyway.

"That's not the first time I've heard that," said Keith. "The night Jesse and Becca picked me up we all sat huddled in a bathroom and watched the news on Becca's iPhone. They had machine gun nests at Yonge and Steeles and were firing on anyone who tried to cross the boundary."

"Yup," said Talleck. "It's a state of emergency the likes o' which no one's ever seen before. Government's main goal is to stop the spread an' keep it contained to just this city. Official word is, anyone still inside city limits is considered to be already dead and infected. Terrible, but you gotta see the bigger picture.

"Anyway, there I am, moored within spitting distance o' the island shore when I starts to see all these zeds show up right around sunset. They're linin' the shore as far as I can see. Hundreds of 'em, all starin' at me, it seems. I'm thinking, fuck, now what, an' wonderin' if they can swim, when all of a sudden, every man, woman, and child of 'em just walks right into the water like goin' for a stroll. They don't stop when the water gets up to their heads, either. Go right on underneath. Couple of 'em floated up, but they can't swim so they just drifted there, face-down. Rest of 'em just kept on walkin'."

"Why would they do that?" said Wendell. "It doesn't make sense."

"Sure it does. You ever seen the city from the island at night? I'm sure you have, it's on every postcard. The whole thing's lit up. Great big floodlights under the CN Tower, the Skydome, half the buildings on the shore. All kinds of bright cotton candy colors. It's gorgeous."

"So they were just following the pretty lights and walked right under the lake?"

Talleck shrugged and sipped at his beer. "It's what they do."

He threw the empty can into the trash and stood up. He shook Keith's hand, and Wendell's. The look in his eyes was regretful but determined.

"We'll be pullin' out soon. You two are the only ones to show up, so we'll be goin' back empty. I suppose we'll see less an' less stragglers now the lights are out. I'm sorry I can't help you, son. I wish I could, I do."

"I don't understand," Wendell said. "You've got weapons, armor, guns, for Christ's sake. We made it here by ourselves with nothing. You could burn through half this city and bring everyone left right to you, but you'll just leave empty instead?"

Talleck frowned. Turning to the woman who had stood

silent this whole time, he said, "Dana, hand me your gun please." Dana didn't hesitate, un-holstered the weapon and passed it to him butt-first. It was a police-issue automatic, and Talleck flicked the button that dropped the clip out the bottom. He handed the ammo clip to Wendell. Inside was a single bullet.

"The cops on the island didn't go out without a fight," said Talleck. "They used everything they had and died anyway. When we took back the island we scrounged up everything we could find, but it wasn't much. Each of us has enough ammunition to do for ourselves if things get bad, and that's it. I have enough people with me to hold the wharf for long enough for a few people to get through to the boat if they're on the run when they show up. Exactly enough. I don't have enough of either people or supplies to go into downtown and bring back your kids safely, and if we went and didn't come back, the night ferry would be done, and nobody else would be comin' out either. I'm sorry."

Wendell seethed with frustration. To get all this way, with safety just a boat ride away, and be turned back...

"Sir."

Talleck and Wendell both turned to look at Dana, who was standing with an odd look on her face, as if she didn't like what she was about to say but couldn't stop herself from saying it.

"Sir, what about the beacon?"

"What beacon?" asked Wendell.

"The fire on the Gardiner Expressway," explained Talleck. "It's our new system for keeping the zeds away since the power went out."

"One volunteer goes across early in a motorboat," said Dana. "And pours gasoline all over a couple of the cars jammed up in that traffic. The fire spreads fast—you'd be surprised just how much on a car will burn, and when it hits the gas tank, whoo!"

"Yeah, we saw it on the way in," said Wendell. "What's your point?"

Dana ignored him, speaking only to Talleck. "Sir, I'm on beacon duty tomorrow night. I'll already be inside the city. I could meet them halfway."

"Dana, I can't tell you to do that," said Talleck. "It's too dangerous."

"You can't tell me not to, either. Isn't that right? We go as far as we're willing, and no farther. Well, I'm willing to go halfway." She turned to Wendell. "At King and Bay Street there's a Scotiabank branch right on the corner. One of our people used to work there, he showed us how to manually open and close the vault. We've never used it, but it's there as an emergency bunker in case one of us winds up stuck north of the Gardiner. If you can get the kids there, I'll meet you after I set the fire, and get you back here."

"Well, what do you say?" said Talleck. "It's not an army, but Campbell's the best we've got. If anyone can get you here, she can."

Wendell wanted to wrap Dana Campbell in a bear hug and spin her around. Instead, he held out a hand, and they shook. "Thank you," he said.

"Just don't get me killed," Dana replied, and left the bridge to begin securing the ferry for her return trip.

Wendell bounded off the ferry's ramp onto the cobblestones.

"We've got a long way to go," he said to Keith. "It'll be morning when we get back." There was no answer, and

Wendell suddenly realized Keith was neither beside him nor right behind him. He turned to find the man standing on the ramp with a hangdog look on his face Wendell didn't like.

"Come on, Keith, we have to go. The kids are waiting for us."

Keith shuffled his feet and looked at his shoes, but made no move to come forward.

"It's just," he started. "Look, we came to get help and we did. But it's one thing to come all the way here and go back with a SWAT team like we thought we would. But to go halfway across the city again, twice, alone? It's more than I can handle."

"You're not coming." Wendell was dumbfounded, but in the back of his mind, he realized he shouldn't have been surprised. Keith was careful. He was nothing if not prudent, and he would always look out for himself first.

"It's nothing personal. I don't get along with the kids, but I don't want anything bad to happen to them." He shrugged. "I'm just not willing to die for them, that's all."

Wendell sighed. "Fine," he said. "I understand. It's like Talleck said. 'Some people just aren't made of strong stuff.'"

Keith gave him a rueful smile. "You know, when we were in that hallway at Union, if I could've found a closet to climb into and scream 'til I was blue I would have. We did good, you and me. We made a good team. I just don't think I've got another one of those in me."

"It's not a problem," said Wendell, but of course, it was. He took off his backpack and threw it to Keith. The lighter fluid and matches were all gone, but there were still several packs of cigarettes inside. "Who knows if they've got smokes on the island."

Keith caught the bag and gave him a grateful look. "Be

careful, Wendell. I know you won't be pleased to see me when you get to the island. But believe me, I'll be glad to see you."

Wendell nodded. He left Keith standing on the deck of the ferry as the crewmen raised the ramp and prepared to cast off, and walked out of the gates into the night alone.

PART FOUR
BULLETS FOR MY FRIENDS

CHAPTER TWENTY

"Shouldn't they be back by now?" demanded Dylan.

Becca looked at her watch. "If the ferry showed up on time it's only been a few hours. It might take them all night to get to us."

Dylan paced the floor of Wendell's suite in an endless circle. He was keyed up, too scared and excited to relax. Sheila had fallen asleep hours ago, and by rights, Dylan should be getting his rest, too, but he just couldn't turn off his brain or stop the ulcer-like tension in his gut.

Becca sat on the floor, playing Solitaire by flashlight. She had tried to get Dylan to sit down and play Crazy Eights or something, but to no avail.

She felt surprisingly calm. For the first time since she burned her way out of the Kat's Ass nightclub, her fate was in someone else's hands. And while the thought rankled that Wendell and Keith were not the most reliable two people she could think of, for a change it felt nice to let someone else do the work. They were safe, they were secure on the fourteenth floor, and if the men didn't follow through or didn't make it, she would find some other way to get Dylan and Sheila to safety. Serenity was an odd feeling, but she thought she could get used to it.

"Where are they?" cried Dylan for the fortieth time.

"Dylan!" Becca shouted. "Here!" She grabbed a bottle of vodka and rolled it across the floor to him. She had grabbed it from the bar thinking it might calm her down, but found that not only did she not need the calming down, she didn't want it either. The Becca who had loved sneaking straight vodka from her parents' pantry was gone, apparently.

"What do I do with this?" said Dylan.

"Pour it into a cup with some juice," she ordered. "Drink it. It'll help you relax."

"Will it, really?" he asked.

"You're twelve. It'll knock you unconscious in about ten minutes. Just drink it slow. You don't want to get sick." She stood up and gathered her flashlight and her axe. "Drink one and then try to sleep. I'll check on you in a bit."

"Where are you going?" he asked.

"I'm going for a run," she said.

Becca didn't fear the dark. She walked confidently down fifteen flights of stairs to the Sheraton's basement. The hotel boasted a small fitness center, just a few treadmills and some weights, next to the pool. The power was off on all the treadmills, of course, but you could still run on them. Before she went into the gym, however, she poked her head into the pool to make sure Michael Phelps was where she'd left him.

The pool was a cavernous empty space, pitch black like the rest of the hotel. A single flashlight was perched on the lip of the pool at the center of the deep end. It shone into the murky water. Beneath the water, the circle of white light illuminated a pair of reaching arms and wide-open white eyes.

They had discovered Michael Phelps on their belated second tour of the building, the one that, if they had taken it first, might have saved Jesse. He was the only zombie left in the hotel as far as Becca could tell, a thin young man in black swim shorts standing on the bottom of the pool. He couldn't figure out how to work the ladders, but just to be on the safe side Becca had placed a flashlight at the end, to keep him focused on the deepest part of the pool and safely well beneath the water.

Becca closed the door on him with a sad little feeling. He was really a pathetic creature, lost and confused. She almost felt sorry enough to give one of her precious bullets to him, but she had none to spare for the dead.

She walked into the gym and set her axe down against the wall. Climbing up onto one of the treadmills, she set her flashlight in the space usually reserved for a water bottle and began to jog. The belt moved under her feet, moved by her strength rather than electricity, and the slow scraping of canvas over steel rollers was the only sound aside from her breathing. Her pants stuck to her legs as she began to sweat—running in leather was hot, hard work, but just standing in leather was uncomfortable enough on its own, and she'd grown used to it. Besides, she rather guessed she smelled awful enough no matter what.

Becca increased her speed, and reached up to shut off the light. In the dark, she ran as hard and as fast as she could, and in her mind she was always running through the Kat's Ass nightclub.

Sixteen-year old Becca Bowman, pre-zombies, cared about only three things: boys, dancing with boys, and pissing off her parents. So it was that on a school night, armed with only a halter top, a pair of low-rise jeans, and a decent fake ID, she had lined up with her friend Ashley at the door of the newest club on Spadina. It was a garish place, the kind that opened to great fanfare on a Friday and was usually gone by the following Tuesday. The neon sign out front depicted a cat-like woman in heels and fishnet stockings, and it blinked back and forth as she appeared to wiggle her cat's tail at the street. But it was the newest place, and Ashley especially had to be onto all the newest trends.

Ashley didn't like Becca much. She was a sidekick, a hanger-on whose job it was to gushingly agree with everything Ashley said, no matter how inane. That was all right with Becca, for while Ashley never shut up, Becca was a quiet girl who kept most of her thoughts to herself. To be completely fair, Becca didn't like Ashley very much either.

As soon as the bouncer let them in—with a wink and a "You sure you're nineteen?"—Becca managed to lose her friend in the crowd. She would bump into her later, maybe, when they were both a little drunker and easier to tolerate, give her an enormous hug like they'd been apart for decades, and say, "Oh my God, this place is so *crazy!*" For the moment, she made her way to the bar.

Becca wasn't tall, blonde, and ditzy like her friend, but she still had no problem finding people to buy drinks for her. It wasn't long before she was enjoying a healthy buzz and feeling the bass pounding from her feet to her chest.

The dance floor was getting frantic, and Becca was starting to think about making her way over and joining in. It must have been a new dance, she thought, some kind of a wave. The far end of the dance floor was rowdy, jumping and thrusting and shoving, with the effect moving outward in a ripple. Becca was wondering if it looked more fun or violent when somebody pushed free of the throng and ran, stumbling and shoving, out the door.

Now others were running, shoving, falling, and Becca's alcohol-fogged brain was starting to register that this *wasn't* a dance. She saw terror in the eyes of one girl, and realized that the day-glo purple stuff on her face was blood shining in the blacklight.

The entire club was in chaos now. People were running for the doors, but more were coming in—people in torn and filthy clothing and wearing glowing contact lenses. She saw a girl that she thought was Ashley—she had Ashley's long blonde hair and pink skirt—run off the dance floor and straight into a pair of the new arrivals. They grabbed her arms and pulled her to them and the girl screamed. Becca was horrified to be witnessing what she thought was an assault right in the middle of a downtown nightclub. But when one of the glowing-eyed men lifted his head to show the blood that soaked his mouth, and the blonde girl slumped in their arms, she realized it was even worse. One of the men crouched down and started picking at her body while the other took off lunging after a young man in a fedora. It was equal-opportunity slaughter.

Still more came pouring through the door, attracted by the pulsing neon sign and drawn in by the pounding bass and laser light. Becca was sober in an instant. Whatever was happening, she was on the wrong side of the building. She needed to get out of there. She still stood at the bar, where some people still hadn't noticed that anything was going on. One man leered drunkenly at her with hazy, but human eyes.

"Hey baby, whatsa matter? Wanna drink?" he slurred. She pushed past him. There were white-eyed figures coming her way. She shoved past a pair of scantily clad serving girls dressed just like the girl on the sign, complete with tail.

"Bitch!"

"Watch it!"

She didn't stop. Behind the bar was a door, an Employees Only sign above it. She burst through it. On her right was the rear service door. She saw white-eyed figures pushing through it, grappling with the screaming staff. Becca turned left and ran. The corridor ended at a narrow staircase. Without a second thought she ran up it and threw open the only door at the top.

She found herself inside a dingy office, just a chair, a desk, and a mini-fridge. Above the empty desk was a giant window back into the club, so the club owner could look out over his creation and be sure that everything was going well. Through the window, Becca could see that things were *not* going well. The carnage on the dance floor was horrendous. Bodies lay everywhere, and still more white-eyed creatures came in. She suddenly realized that if she tried to run out the front, she would be killed. She wanted to scream.

Between the screams and the music that still pounded out of the club's speakers she never would have heard it, but something made her turn her head just in time to see a man's foot in an expensive shoe on the top step just outside the door. She didn't look to see if the man was alive or dead, she lunged at the door and slammed it shut. There was a thump on the door as she threw the bolt in the lock, and the door shook, but held.

Becca pulled out her phone and dialed 9-1-1. She almost screamed with relief when the line picked up, but what she heard wasn't the standard, "What's the nature of the emergency?" that TV had led her to expect. In fact, she heard nothing. A click, and then nothing.

"Hello?" she said. Her voice in her ear was the voice of a frightened child. "Hello, is anybody there?"

"*Uuuuuuuuuuuuhhhhhhhhhh…*" she heard, and in the background, a slurping sound. She screamed and hung up.

The pounding on the door went away eventually, but the party continued all night. If the police arrived, she never saw them. Possibly, they didn't make it through the front door. Probably by this point, there were more places like the Kat's Ass in the city than there were cops to respond to them all. She watched through the window as the creatures rounded up the last of the living and began to feed in huge groups. She saw a stream of people rush through the doors to the bathroom, and was glad she hadn't been stupid enough to try to hide in there. She saw a screaming man cornered next to the bar, then a dozen or more of the things were on top of him. She couldn't see what they did, but when they finally moved off to look for something else to do, there was nothing of the man but bones, a wet smear, and a bloodstained Affliction shirt.

Eventually, there was nobody but Becca and the endless party. The strobe lights never turned off, the lasers never stopped jumping, the music—pre-mixed on a computer playlist—continued on an endless loop. The zombies, mesmerized by the constant shifting lights, were always on the move, bumping into one another, grinding on one another, sometimes rocking in place as both tried to get past the other to get to some other place. The dance floor spilled out onto the bar floor. Everywhere, the dead danced.

Becca sobbed on the floor for what felt like hours. No one heard her. No one was coming. She searched through the desk drawer and found it empty except for a bottle of Wiser's and the silver gun. She put the gun back and drank the rye, trying to black out, but she was sick instead.

She paced the floor. She nursed her sick stomach with water from the mini-fridge. She played Angry Birds on her phone until the battery died and left her in darkness. She wanted to call her parents, but she resisted the urge. They couldn't help her anyway, and she couldn't bear the thought of what she might hear at their house instead.

She began marking time with Britney Spears. Since the music was on a loop, "Scream and Shout" blasted across the club once every three hours or so. The song was accurate, at least. Every time it came on, she wanted to scream with the awfulness of it all.

After one "Scream and Shout", the pounding on the door stopped, the zombie having grown distracted by something new. After two "Scream and Shouts", her phone died. It was after five "Scream and Shouts", that she put the gun in her mouth for the first time.

She sat that way, on the floor of a scummy office in a dingy nightclub with the barrel of a gun scraping the roof of her mouth while tears streamed down her cheeks and Scream and Shout pounded in her ears, for what felt like hours but was only minutes. She still remembered the taste of the gun, the taste of pennies and oil. In the end, she couldn't pull the trigger. It turned out she was more afraid of what would come next than she was of the zombies below.

She took the gun out of her mouth and drank the rest of the rye, sobbing the whole time. This time she finally did pass out, into merciful oblivion. She didn't know how many "Scream and Shouts" she slept through, but when she woke up on the floor with her head pounding and her mouth full of ash, Britney was singing again.

She tasted the barrel of that pistol a total of four times in those three days. The first time that she failed to pull the trigger, it was fear that stopped her, but as the hours ticked by, the fear began to blossom into anger. Anger at herself, for not taking what she felt to be the only possible action, anger at her family for letting her wind up here, and anger at the people who ran this city, for not being able to protect her. Eventually, the anger turned cold. She ceased to be a scared teenage girl. She became nothing but her anger, and a cool determination grew where the rest of her used to be.

She realized she had been right the first time. She was doing herself no good lying here sobbing on the floor. She needed to take action. She took the gun out of her mouth for the last time and stood up.

The sound of the deadbolt sliding back sounded enormously loud to her, despite the music. For a second she hesitated, sure that the noise had attracted a dozen flesh-eating zombies to the top of the stairs. She opened the door anyway.

The staircase and corridor were empty. Becca went cautiously down, eyes darting back and forth. The music was louder out here, and she realized the office must have had some kind of cheap soundproofing. If it had been this loud in there, she likely *would* have gone mad.

Something came out of the shadows below the stairwell, and the shock caused Becca to fire wildly into the void. The flash was blinding, but the gun didn't even make a sound over the probably illegal noise level in the club. The zombie seemed to grin at her as its jaws widened and its eyes glittered. But Becca's fear was gone, the last of it burned away by the force of the gunshot as she realized that she was not helpless. Calmly, she stood with the gun held in front of her.

She didn't need to aim; the zombie obligingly walked right into the barrel and she fired into its mouth.

There was no one behind the bar when she crawled in on her hands and knees. The bar was darker than the dance floor, and most of the dancers were drawn to the pulsing lights. Becca crawled around the bar and began pulling bottles off the shelves.

The bar was well stocked with cheap booze, but Becca knew enough high school science to know she needed the good stuff, hundred proof or better. There had to be a cache of expensive liquor somewhere. What did VIPs drink when they showed up? Then she saw the cupboard above the beer cooler.

Bingo.

She took a pile of bar rags and began shoving them into bottles as fast as she could. She had five Molotov cocktails made up in as many minutes, when suddenly she realized her mistake.

The bottles lined the floor like an alcoholic's ideal suicide, but she had no lighter. Becca didn't smoke and had never felt the urge, but now she'd have given anything for a Bic lighter.

A movement to her right made her whirl. A black shoe stepped around the bar, followed by a leg that ended far too high up under a pink miniskirt. Becca watched in horror as Ashley, her very best frenemy in the whole wide world, tottered up behind the bar where she hid.

Ashley was a mess. She was wobbly; her corpse had forgotten the trick to walking in high heels. Her mouth dripped black vomit down her chin, and her hair was tangled up and greasy with the stuff. There was nothing unusual about any of that; Ashley usually looked like this at around four in the morning. What could not be ignored were the multiple jagged wounds that peppered her flesh, or the glittering diamonds of her luminous eyes.

What had driven her, of all people, to wander back to the bar, Becca never knew. A last vestige of recognition and a desire for her friend to join her now? A last vestige of a teenage alcoholic's urge to belly up to the bar and have a shooter? Or just terrible, terrible luck? Whatever the case, she saw Becca and came for her. Becca, huddled at the far end of the bar, reached for the pistol, but stopped. Bullets were going to be hard to come by if she got out. Better to use it as a last resort than as a first choice. Instead, her hand closed around a bottle of Glenlivet.

Ashley's footsteps sped up as she sensed she was nearing food. Her ankles teetered dangerously but she didn't fall. Becca grabbed another bottle and rolled it down the bar. It caught Ashley's toe in midstride and the obstacle was finally too much for her balance. She toppled face first to the floor, never even putting out her hands to catch herself.

She looked up at Becca, eyes glowing over a broken nose. She was only inches from Becca now, but they were on the same level. Becca raised her bottle and brought it down hard on the back of her friend's head. The impact drove Ashley's face back into the wood, but she came up again. One pink-nailed hand closed around Becca's ankle.

Down came the bottle again, and again. Becca beat her best friend's skull to jelly, in the bar where the party never ended. On the last blow the bottle shattered, sending hundred-dollar whiskey spraying everywhere, but the zombie finally dropped to the ground. Becca looked at the husk of a thing that days ago had been her friend, and knew that she was finally at peace.

"Bitch." she said.

A sudden inspiration made her turn the body over. Ashley smoked like a chimney, but never bought her own cigarettes. She was content to allow lustful guys to keep her smoking all night long. She did, however, keep a pink Zippo lighter under her bra, a possession she was very proud of. Becca fished around like a horny fifteen-year-old until she found the lighter, stood up, and lit all five rags at once.

There was a crowd headed her way. They were almost on her when she threw the first bottle. A hundred and fifty glowing eyes watched the flaming bottle arc across the room to shatter and explode against the far wall. Becca ducked back down, but couldn't resist the urge to peek back up.

The flames were burning the wood floor of the club, and all of the zombies that had been advancing on her hiding place were now wandering back down toward the fire.

Becca picked up her four bottles with their burning wicks and crossed over to the rear exit. She set one aside for her way out, but the other three she hurled into the jam-packed room. The computer sound mix shattered into the fire, and Britney Spears was replaced by the whine of overloading feedback. The bar burst into flames. Becca hefted her last bottle and locked eyes with a young zombie right in the middle of the dance floor.

"Stop." She hurled it with all her might.

"Fucking." The bottle soared over the heads of the burning zombies.

"Dancing!" The bottle shattered.

Becca went out the back door into a cool and fragrant September evening. She was undisturbed; anybody on the street was at the front of the building, watching the flames. She broke into a curio shop across the street from the club and watched long into the night, as the Kat's Ass burned to the ground.

Drenched with sweat and panting hard, Becca stepped off the treadmill. In the deep darkness of the basement gym, lights flashed and danced in front of her eyes from the exertion. If anything, though, Becca was glad for the darkness. The citywide power failure meant places like the Kat's Ass would finally be silent.

She plucked her light from its coaster and flicked it on her watch. It was nearly four a.m. Even if Wendell was coming back tonight, it would be smart to get a couple of hours of sleep, and after an hour of hard running, she was finally tired enough that she thought she might. Becca followed the pale white circle of her flashlight beam up the stairs.

Halfway up the second flight she heard a sound that chilled her blood and made her freeze. It was coming from the door to the lobby, and it was the sound of shattering glass.

CHAPTER TWENTY-ONE

Becca crept back down to the lobby door and opened it a crack. Sure enough, the enormous wall of glass at the front of the building was smashed in, and she could see shapes moving through it in the pre-dawn light. Their eyes didn't glow; they carried flashlights and swore at each other, and in some of their hands Becca saw light gleam off the long, slender barrels of rifles.

"Fuck me," she heard a voice say. "I cut my arm, Steve."

"So wrap it up and shut the fuck up," said the man at the front. He had authority in his voice. He was obviously their leader. "There's definitely someone in here. The door's chained on the inside."

"Fat lot of good it did them," whooped a third voice, high-pitched and excited. "Who locks a glass door? Which way's the fucking bar?"

"Will you shut up!" Steve hissed. "Whoever's in here could come out shooting at any minute, and if they don't, the zombies are going to hear your fucking mouth and swarm all over us. Now keep your mouth shut."

Becca slowly eased the door shut. This was *not* Wendell's

cavalry, and while they might have the best of intentions, the rifles in their hands told her it was best to assume that they didn't.

The door creaked. Steve's flashlight spun around and shone directly in her face.

Shit.

"Over there!" hissed Steve. Becca dropped the door handle and ran up the stairs.

She heard the door open below her and threw herself through the second-story door. She heard feet pounding on the stairs behind her, but Becca was fast and well practiced. Her feet flew down the corridor, but her heart sank when, as she ducked into the other stairwell, she heard a loud voice cry out, "There she is!"

Safety was fourteen floors up, but a deadbolt wouldn't stop a shotgun. Besides, even if she made it there, she would only be leading them to Dylan and Sheila. Becca started downwards instead, heading for the basement. She knew its layout better than they did, and in the darkness, she could hold out until Wendell came back.

She hoped he was bringing a lot of firepower.

Wendell was making better time on the way back than he had heading out, but there were already fingers of light blue caressing the purple sky when he turned onto Richmond Street. He wondered if the kids were still waiting up, and how disappointed they would be when he came back alone. He had succeeded, in a way, and at the very least he had kept his promise to Becca, but none of that made his coming back without Keith or the promised squad of heavily armed men feel less like a failure.

Maybe it was just his mood, thought Wendell as he walked

back up the street in defeat, but it seemed to him that there was a lot more broken glass in the street than he remembered. In fact, he hadn't recalled seeing any smashed windows on Richmond Street as he'd crept up it with Sheila under his arm, a fact he had taken as a good sign when searching for a hiding place.

Now it seemed that every second or third window was shattered. Dark lumps were scattered across the sidewalk, difficult to see in the dim light, but as he neared a smashed television set he realized that the debris were objects that had been yanked from within the broken shop windows. That was definitely new, and Wendell quickened his pace, suddenly worried. Becca had broken into her share of empty stores, but this wasn't her style, he knew. This seemed more like vandalism for the sake of itself, a crude and petty act.

Less than a block from the Sheraton, Wendell saw a body lying in the middle of the street. Richmond Street was more or less clear of vehicles, thanks to two particularly nasty pile-ups at intersections on either side of the hotel, and the empty street was generally a gathering-ground for the dead. Wendell had saved one final Molotov cocktail for this stretch, knowing it would be the hardest part to get through—aside from Union Station, of course. Going back through that darkened pit alone had been a nightmare. He had used up three bottles getting through the station, and it was a wonder he hadn't burned the ancient building down.

But Richmond Street was empty, except for a lone body in the middle of the yellow line. Wendell felt a tickle in the hairs on the back of his neck. He crept up close to the corpse, wondering if it was one he had killed. As soon as he saw the thing's head, he knew it wasn't one of his, or any of the kids. The top half of its head was missing, blown straight away, and it didn't take a CSI detective to know that kind of damage couldn't be caused by one of Becca's little six-shooter bullets.

When he saw the shattered glass of the Sheraton's front entrance, Wendell knew he had come too late. *The heroes find themselves a safe place to hunker down and wait it out,* he heard himself say to Keith, *and the bad guys show up there.*

Wendell resisted the urge to go charging into the building, calling the kids' names. *Lesson One* was still *Wait and Watch.* He knew only two things: that someone had broken into the building, and that at least one of them had a shotgun. He didn't know how many, or what they'd been after. Maybe they only wanted to rob the bar and leave. Maybe Becca and Dylan had the sense to stay put up in the penthouse and never been noticed. Maybe the unknown person or persons had left, undisturbed and undisturbing.

But then again, maybe they were still here.

Becca hoped Dylan had taken her advice and drunk himself to sleep. She hoped he stayed blissfully comatose until long after these men had done what they wanted and left. She dearly hoped those things, because she was about to die, and she didn't want to take him with her.

She knew the layout of the basement better than her pursuers, but the basement was small, and the corridor was circular. It didn't taken them long to fan out and corner her in the gym. She faced them down with her back to the wall and her pistol in her hands, but there were five of them and she had four bullets.

They ranged in age from late teens to early fifties. The youngest was a skinny, bug-eyed youth of about nineteen. He was bleeding from his left arm and twitched a lot. The oldest was the fat man with the crew cut, he of the high, excited voice. He leered at Becca hungrier than any corpse. The two men in their mid-twenties stood back and looked at one another nervously. One of them, the blond man with the glasses, looked Becca in the eye and then looked away just as fast. He turned to his companion, the balding man in the denim jacket, and the other shook his head, once. They were most definitely unhappy with what was about to happen, but they wouldn't stop it.

It was the man in the middle they feared, the man called Steve. He was the one to be reckoned with. Tall and calm, in his late forties and dressed in khakis and a black hunting vest, he was the only one who looked like he knew how to handle his weapon. He watched her with steely eyes and sure confidence; even though she had her pistol pointed directly at his face, he didn't flinch or bring his own rifle to bear.

"Now listen, little girl," he said calmly, even conversationally. "There's no reason to make this worse than it is. You know as well as I do that I could shoot you in the head right now and there's no one in the world going to say whether you were a zombie first or not. So why don't you just put the gun down and relax. You're with friends." He smiled when he said this last, but the smile didn't reach his eyes. They were cold and hard.

Becca wasn't about to just hand over her gun, though. She might be outnumbered, but at the moment it was the only thing keeping these animals at arm's reach.

"Co...come on, baby," stammered the youth. "I'll t...treat you good." He tried to grin seductively at her, but the effect was so pathetic that despite her terror Becca couldn't help but laugh. Her laughter shut the boy down, but the fat man's face turned red. He lunged forward with his shotgun almost in her face.

"Bitch, you shut your mouth or I'll shut it for good!" he shouted. Steve raised a hand for silence, and the fat man backed down.

"Tom, shut up. Billy, you look like a fucking idiot." He fixed his fish eyes on Becca again. "It's nothing personal, girl. It's just that these guys haven't seen a girl in weeks. You understand. Just be quiet, let them do their thing, and then we'll all leave. It's happening one way or the other. You're all alone." His eyes lit up with a sudden bright malice. "Unless there's other people in the building. Are there other people here? Maybe we should go looking for them." He turned to the others. "We could make it a party. What do you say? We could line up all your friends one by one and…" He made a fake gun with one hand and mimed taking aim, firing, and aiming again. "Pop, pop, pop. What do you say?"

"No!" blurted Becca. "No, there's no one else here."

"That's the spirit," chuckled Steve. "Now why don't you put down the gun? Nice and easy."

Becca lowered her pistol to the floor. Her bullets weren't for them anyway. She kicked it away into the darkness. She wasn't letting them have it while she was alive. She had no illusions that they would let her live when they were finished. Why stop at one unspeakable crime, after all? Their jackal grins said everything she needed to know.

They were going to take what they wanted. But she wasn't going to give it without a fight.

CHAPTER TWENTY-TWO

Wendell eased open the stairwell door. He winced as one hinge creaked, but heard no immediate uproar. He stared into the darkness of the stairwell, wondering just how many times he would have to be terrified on these stairs.

He'd found no one in the bar or the restaurant. Rather than reassuring him, it made him fear the worst. There were so many awful things he might find now. He might find them gone, and the children murdered. He might find them still here, and be murdered along with them. He might—

He froze on his way up. There were voices, but they were coming from below.

Quiet as a mouse, he crept down toward the basement. Whoever it was, they were making no effort to keep their voices down; they spoke and swore at full volume, which to Wendell meant they either didn't know there was anybody in the building with them, or that they had already won.

Thank God, the lower door was well oiled. Wendell eased through it on his hands and knees. The sounds were coming from the gym. The basement was black as night, and he could see a pale glow through the open doorway.

No one looked up when he snuck in. All the flashlights pointed toward one corner of the room, where the show was going on. He saw the whole tableau in an instant: Becca, lying on the floor as far into the corner as she could be; the solid figure of a large man standing over her. Four others, in varied states of boredom, spaced around the room, all holding guns, giving the first man some space but awaiting their turn. Wendell felt the bile rise up in his throat. He willed himself to stay still. If he were seen he would undoubtedly be killed, and he'd be no help to Becca then.

A small voice in the back of his head screamed that he would be no help to her anyway, that he was too outnumbered, that it was a lost cause. That voice wanted to slink away, go upstairs and take Dylan and Sheila out of here. Wendell pushed that voice into a corner and told it to shut up. It was not long ago that Becca herself had gone up against impossible odds to pull him out of a closet.

"Hey, can I get a bit of fucking privacy here?" the fat man demanded. "This ain't a public show." Obligingly, the other four flicked off their flashlights and sat in the darkness. Wendell couldn't believe his astonishing luck. He crept up to the nearest of the men, the sallow youth with the bulging eyes.

He rose up onto his knees and raised the Halligan for a two-handed strike, but hesitated. This was only a boy, little older than Jesse, who had so far done nothing to harm or threaten him. Was it right to kill him for being nothing more at this point than a spectator?

"Argh!" roared the fat man. "She fucking bit me." His enormous arm drew back and Wendell winced as he heard the sound of a fist hitting flesh, but Becca made no sound.

"Come on, Tom, be careful!" called the skinny youth.

"Don't kill her before I get a turn!"

That was enough. Wendell buried the pickaxe end of the Halligan directly in the boy's face. The youth gurgled and spat up blood. Wendell yanked the weapon free and shuffled off into the darkness just as the boy's body slumped to the floor with a thump. At once, three flashlights converged on the spot where the boy's body lay sprawled and hemorrhaging blood.

"The fuck?" said one.

Wendell crouched now behind an elliptical machine. He was only a few strides from the nearest of the men, a nervous-looking blond man. The man was staring myopically into the darkness, peering through enormous glasses while whipping the beam of his flashlight around the dark room.

"Steve, there's someone fucking in here with us!" he shouted. His flashlight passed Wendell's head twice, but the giant cartoon eyes, magnified by the lenses, couldn't focus enough to see him.

The man in the center, the man in the hunting vest, the man they called Steve, stood up. He aimed his rifle at the darkness and called out in a confident voice.

"Whoever you are, show yourself. You've murdered that young man, so you probably think you're a hell of a killer, but I'm here to tell you that you're not. You're still outnumbered four to one, and I *am* a killer. You don't have a chance here, and you're going to get your young lady friend killed."

To punctuate his point, the fat man, Tom, gave Becca another solid punch in the gut. This time she did make a sound, an angry groan.

Wendell pulled his hammer from his belt. Thinking, *if it works on zombies, it might work on these assholes,* he hurled the hammer as high and as far as he could. It clattered on the floor in the far corner, and for an instant, all the lights spun in that direction, accompanied by two deafening shots.

"Hold your fire!" shouted Steve, but Wendell was already moving. The nervous man's flashlight snapped back to shine in his face just as he brought the Halligan down onto the blond man's shoulder. The man screamed and collapsed, his neck broken, and Wendell darted back into the darkness. Flashlights trained back in his direction, but now the odds were slightly better. Now there were only three: Steve, Tom, and a man in a denim jacket who looked like he'd rather be anywhere else right now.

Becca lashed out and kicked Tom hard between the legs. He collapsed with a scream.

"You fucking bitch! I'm gonna kill you now for sure!" he groaned, rocking on the floor. He reached for the shotgun he'd left beside him, but it wasn't there.

"Suck on this," said Becca, and Tom's head exploded. His massive body dropped to the floor with a heavy thud.

"Becca, run!" screamed Wendell. He leaped up from his hiding place and tackled the bald man. The man fell on his face, and Wendell threw himself to the left just as Steve's rifle gouged a hole in the floor where his head had been. Jagged shrapnel exploded upwards into the face of the man he'd just tackled. The man screamed and stood up off the floor, but a heavy steel bar met him on the way up and caught him in the throat. He toppled in a heap.

Becca turned her shotgun on Steve. He looked at her coolly, his lip in a sneer. Becca pulled the trigger and the gun clicked, but didn't fire. There were no shells left to fire.

"Run, Becca!" Wendell cried again, and this time she listened. With one last look at Wendell, she turned and ran out the door, into the darkness. Faced with two targets, Steve let her go. The girl could wait. This was personal now.

Flashlights lay strewn across the floor, pointing at nothing. Plaster dust floated in the air, kicked up by multiple gunshots and filling the room with haze. Wendell stood motionless in the darkness, wishing he'd grabbed one of the guns along the way. They were all too far to reach from where he stood, and he didn't dare move.

Steve had both hands on his rifle. To reach for a flashlight was to risk breaking his aim on the spot where he had last heard the other man. It was a standoff that could only work to Steve's advantage in the long run, as the man would have to move eventually, and Steve was the only one with a gun.

"You've done well," he called into the darkness. "You killed three of my friends all by yourself. You did very well. They were all idiots, taken from behind in the dark, but still. Bravo.

"But let me make one thing clear, my mysterious friend. You are not leaving this room alive. I have all the time in the world to find and kill you. And when you're dead, when I've put a bullet between your balls and your eyes, I'm going to find that little girl, and anyone else you've got hiding in this big, empty hotel, and I'm going to kill each and every one of them, too. And why? Because I'm fucking mad, that's why."

He saw movement in the beam of a flashlight to his left. He grinned and fired at the spot, and he heard something clatter to the floor. There was no other sound. Slowly, Steve bent down, picked up the flashlight at his feet, and aimed it at his brave, but stupid, adversary.

The light picked up a long metal bar, covered in his friends' blood, gleaming but idle. There was a hole in the wall behind it, and plaster dust puffed out of it.

Steve spun back around just in time to see the door

swinging shut.

Wendell ran as fast as he could down the short hallway. His last ruse would only last for so long, and the man would be coming. He was out of weapons, out of room, and out of time. He had only one card to play. He shoved open the door just as a loud report echoed behind him, and he felt splinters of wood stab into his hand. He looked behind him and saw nothing. Steve was coming, following Wendell's footsteps, but he was coming blind, without a light. A sharp report and a white light exploded in the hallway before him, and Wendell leaped through the door.

The blast had destroyed both of their night vision, but Wendell knew where he was. He ran into the enormous room and darted immediately left, hugging the wall until he reached a flashlight that lay on the floor. Switching it off and sending the room back into total darkness, he returned to the edge of the doorway.

Silence then. Then a rustling, and the clink, clink, clink as Steve reloaded.

"I know you're in here, my foolish friend," the voice called out from the doorway. Wendell timed his leap with the sound of a scuffing foot. He barreled into Steve from the side, and both men toppled to the floor. Wendell heard a clatter as the rifle went skidding away.

They grappled together on the floor. Wendell couldn't see his enemy or anticipate his punches, but neither could Steve. Arms struggled to push him off, but Wendell held him close with one strong arm while his other hand punched over and over in the space where Steve's head ought to be. The pain in his knuckles and the hard but yielding flesh his fist met again and again told him he was close enough.

Then he felt a searing pain in his side and let go. He scrambled to his feet, feeling blood soak the side of his shirt as he did so. Steve had drawn a knife on him.

The other man would come at him again, so Wendell backed away, in a zigzag pattern so that he wouldn't be in the spot Steve expected. Blind, he circled to the far side of the huge room as quickly and as quietly as he could.

"I give you points for cleverness," called Steve into the abyss before his eyes. "But the fact is we're in the same boat we were in moments ago. You're unarmed, and this time you've got nothing to throw at me. You might as well accept it. You're dead. And so are all your friends.

"Then why don't you come and get me, you prick? Or are you trying to bore me to death?" Wendell rolled to the side, expecting another shot, but none came. Instead, he heard the slow deliberate tapping of careful footsteps.

"Oh, I'll come get you, my friend. You've got nowhere else to go. I'm enjoying this little cat-and-mouse game you're playing, but it's soon going to—" His speech was cut off with a startled "*whoa!*" With a splash, he toppled into the unseen water of the swimming pool. Wendell listened to him splashing for a moment, then slowly got up and picked up the flashlight.

He shone it into the water, just as Steve broke the surface and started swimming back to the ladder.

"Very clever," he said. "You're full of surprises, you are. But don't you think they just keep getting sillier and sillier? A swimming pool? Come on."

"I don't think so," said Wendell grimly. "Steve, I'd like you to meet Michael Phelps." Steve's eyes widened as a viselike hand closed over his kicking ankle, and began pulling him inexorably downwards. Wendell watched as blood began to spread through the water in lazy ripples. Finally, the thrashing of Steve's hands below the surface slowed, and Wendell placed the flashlight where it had been against the far end of the pool, something to keep Michael and his new companion busy until the water eroded them down to bones.

CHAPTER TWENTY-THREE

Becca nearly shot him in the face in the hallway between the pool and the gym. She'd run back and retrieved her pistol from the gym floor. At the last second, she trained her flashlight at his face and recognized him.

"You came back," she said.

"I said I would," he answered. Becca wiped her eyes. Her face was covered in bruises and one eye was rapidly swelling shut, but she had steel in her.

"Did they—" he began.

"No."

"Thank God. Are you—"

"I'm fine. You're bleeding!"

"It's just a scratch. I'll be fine."

"Did you bring the cavalry?"

He sighed. "Not exactly."

"Figures," she said.

They walked back into the gym together in silence. Wendell wanted to put his arm around her and tell her something comforting, but there was nothing he could say to undo what she had just gone through. She had survived, that was the important thing, and Becca being Becca, she would probably just prefer never to speak of this again.

Or so he thought, until they entered the gym. The bodies of her tormentors lay strewn across the floor. Blood soaked the floor and ran up the sides of the exercise machines. Wendell went silently about, gathering up the guns they had left behind when a groan caught his attention. He turned to find Becca crouched over the bald man, who stared up at her with pleading eyes from where he lay with his head at an awkward angle to the rest of his body.

"Please," he said.

"Please what?" demanded Becca.

"Please help me."

"Please *help* you?" she screamed. She kicked him in the gut. He didn't react at all. He couldn't feel it. "Please show you *mercy?* The same mercy you showed me?" She kicked him again. It was like kicking a sack of flour.

"I didn't... I wasn't..."

"Oh, you weren't going to rape me? You were just going to fucking watch, that's all. So you're a fucking hero?"

"I'm...I'm sorry," he groaned.

"You're sorry? You piece of shit!" She kicked him in the face. He screamed. Blood ran from his nose.

"Becca," said Wendell.

"WHAT!" she screamed, whirling on him. She held the gun up, toward his face, but she didn't seem to notice it. Wendell ignored the gun and came in toward her. He took her in his arms and held her.

"It's okay," he said. "It's okay, honey, it's over now."

"It'll never be okay!" she sobbed. "Nothing's ever going to be all right again! It's just going to keep getting worse and worse until we're all dead!" And she collapsed into his arms, sobbing. Wendell sank to the floor, still holding her, and let her fold into him, and she cried until she had no tears left inside. Still he held her, and after long minutes, her exhaustion took hold of her and she fell asleep in his arms. He lifted her up like a little girl and carried her away.

As he pushed open the door, the crippled man on the floor cried out.

"Please, it hurts!"

Wendell looked down at him without pity. "What the fuck do I care?" And he left the room, the door swinging shut with a final thud.

He carried her up all fourteen flights of stairs and kicked at the penthouse door. After a few minutes, Dylan opened it with eyes red and a hand on his head.

Wendell burst through the door. His arms were on fire from carrying Becca so far, but before his strength gave out, he laid her gently on the sofa.

"What happened?" asked Dylan. He looked horrible, and swayed like he was still a little drunk. In other circumstances the sight of a twelve-year-old suffering his first hangover would be either comical or horrifying, depending on the situation. Somewhere between the vodka and his sleepiness, however, he was beginning to register that something was wrong.

"Nothing," said Wendell gruffly. Then he looked at Dylan and his expression softened. "Well, something," he said. "Let's just say that I'm incredibly thankful you slept through it and leave it at that."

Dylan crossed to the sofa. Becca looked horrible, her face was a mass of bruises, but lost in the softness of merciful sleep, she seemed peaceful.

"Is she all right?" he asked.

Wendell smiled. "She's Becca. She's tougher than all of us put together and then some. Now I think you should go back to sleep. You're not looking so good, son."

"No, I think, I think you might be right," Dylan said and began staggering back to Wendell's bed. He paused at the door and turned back to look at Wendell. "You're not leaving again, are you?"

"No, Dylan," said Wendell. "I'm not going anywhere."

Dylan nodded. "That's good. It's not safe out there alone, you know."

Wendell saw Dylan back to bed and covered Becca with a spare blanket. Only the chair was left, and Sheila would be up soon in any case. Wendell sat down, laid his head back, and slept.

"Oh, God! Why do you guys do this?"

Dylan was sitting in the chair by the desk, holding his head in his hands. A steaming mug sat beside him; for his first hangover, Wendell had boiled him his first cup of coffee. He hadn't touched it, and he hadn't more than nibbled at the scrambled eggs and toast Wendell had brought up with it.

Wendell was giving Sheila her second bottle of the day. Bright morning sun shone through the windows. Despite his lack of sleep and the horrors of the night before, Wendell felt good. They were leaving tonight, for good, and the thought energized him.

"How much did you drink?" he asked Dylan. Dylan sniffed at an egg and moaned.

"I only had one glass," he groaned.

"Only *one?*"

"Yeah," he held up a cup. "This much juice, and this

much vodka."

Wendell laughed so hard he startled Sheila into spitting out the bottle.

"You mixed it *half and half?*"

Even Becca chuckled, from where she sat on the couch with her own cup of coffee and a steak over her black eye.

"I guess I should have told him how to mix it," she said. "I figured he'd go easy with his first drink."

"You guys are making fun of me!" Dylan accused.

"Yes," said Becca. "But only because we've both been there before. Welcome to adulthood, Dill." She looked at Wendell now, fixing him with a one-eyed stare.

"Where's Keith?" she asked.

"Keith." Wendell sighed. "Keith…got scared."

Becca nodded, but the look on her face said this was just one final betrayal out of many.

"I guess I'm not surprised. Honestly, I thought it was more than he could take just going with you. Did you make it to the boat?"

He nodded. "One of their people is going to meet us about halfway tonight and take us the rest of the way."

"Well. That's something at least."

"Yeah, but without Keith it puts our numbers at the same as before. And it puts us in a tight spot for the first leg."

"You've been out there, though," said Becca. "You know the route and what we're going to be up against. At least we won't be going blind. Besides, now that I know for a fact you know how to handle yourself, I'm not so worried."

Becca smiled. Wendell smiled back, but he was worried. The girl was smiling and acting as if this were just a normal morning, but he had only to look into her eyes to see that the gym would live on in her memory for a long, long time.

Then again, who among them didn't have horrible memories they'd rather forget?

"That's right!" said Dylan suddenly. "We're unstoppable! We're gonna kick ass!"

"Keggazz!"

Wendell's smile vanished. He looked down at the baby in his arms. Becca and Dylan were both staring at him wearing expressions of mingled shock and amusement.

"Did she just say what I think she said?" said Becca.

"Keggazz!"

"No," said Wendell. "No, no, no. 'Kickass' is not going to be her first word. Mama!" he said to her.

"Keggazz!"

"Mama!"

"Keggazz!"

"Oh, hell," said Wendell.

CHAPTER TWENTY-FOUR

Around noon, Dylan recovered from his private hell enough to take Sheila for a spell. He carried her up to the rooftop, where he was going to let the dogs exercise and do their business, Sheila yelling "Keggazz" the whole way up. Wendell knew they all should be getting some rest before nightfall, but he knew he wouldn't be able to sleep, and he knew the others were feeling it, too. There was an electricity in the air. Tonight they would reach safety or die trying.

It was the die-trying part that had Wendell worried, and that's why he found himself in the bar. He'd emptied five bottles already and was starting on the sixth when he looked up and saw Becca standing in the doorway.

"What are you doing?" she asked.

He gestured toward the empty bottles. "I siphoned some gas out of a few cars outside," he said. "Don't try it if you have the choice. I'll never get the taste out of my mouth. Anyway, I'm pouring it into these liquor bottles to make homemade grenades. Have you seen one before?"

"Yeah," said Becca. "They're Molotov cocktails. I've made them before." She came in the door enough for Wendell to see what she had in her hands. "I bet gas would work a lot better than booze, though."

"What've you got there?" he asked. She was holding Jesse's bunker suit like it was a large, fireproof baby. Inside the helmet was Wendell's photo of Grace.

"This is for you," she said. "It was stupid not to let you have it. It won't fit Dylan and I've got my leathers. It's no good to anybody on the roof, and…well, you might as well have it." She put the suit awkwardly on a barstool. One leg of the pants flopped off and dangled on the floor. She turned to leave.

"Becca," said Wendell. "I've got your answer for you."

"It's okay," she said. "You don't have to. It doesn't matter."

"It matters to me," said Wendell. "And it's important for you to hear it, just so that you can remind me when I start second-guessing myself."

She came back to the bar. "Okay," she said. "Lay it on me."

"I figured it out this morning," he said. "When I shattered that first son-of-a-bitch's skull, it didn't feel wrong—not in the slightest. I realized that right and wrong have nothing to do with the law or the rules we all follow when society's running the way it's supposed to. There's right, and then there are many, many degrees of wrong. Killing those men this morning was…it was the right wrong thing to do. Do you know what I mean?"

Becca nodded. "And when you and Sheila were alone and thought you were going to die, letting her die before the zombies got to you would have been the right wrong thing, too."

"No," said Wendell. "There was never going to be a way

to make that right." He wiped gasoline off his hands with a rag and started stuffing pieces of cloth down the mouths of the bottles he had filled. "My hand was sweating on the door handle. I was losing my grip. When you opened the door, I was at the end. Whoever or whatever grabbed that handle, it was coming open. I had only one choice. I was going to kill that baby, Becca. And then I was going to let that door knob go. I was going to let them tear me apart, and I would have been *glad*."

Becca pulled her gun out of its holster so fast that Wendell drew back, sure for a second—despite all they'd been through—that she was about to shoot him. She took in his reaction with a roll of her one good eye and flipped open the gun's chamber. Two empty holes showed the bullets she had already fired; there were four more still to go.

"This one is for me," she said, pointing at one. "This one is for Dylan. This *was* for Jesse, but it turned out he didn't need it, so now it's for you. There was even one for Keith, though I doubt he'd have appreciated the sentiment." She looked at Wendell with a face both determined and terrified. "If we find ourselves in a place we can't get out of, this gun will be the last resort for all of us."

"So you *do* know what I'm talking about," said Wendell, relieved.

"I know exactly what you mean," she said, sliding the gun back into its holster. "Bullets for my friends, an axe for all the rest."

Wendell nodded. "Let's hope it doesn't come to that."

Dana Campbell, former construction worker and now second in command of the *Thomas Rennie*, stood on a dock in the Ward's Island Yacht Club, pouring gasoline from a red jerry can into her boat's outboard motor. The boats surrounding her dwarfed her small craft in both size and expense, but Dana wasn't interested in status symbols. Hers was a simple wooden fishing boat with a single motor.

"You know, you could probably have your pick of any boat in here," said a voice behind her. She turned. The man standing on the dock was short, portly, and red-faced, and smoking his cigarette dangerously close to her gasoline.

"The fewer doodads on the boat, the less likely it is to break down when you need it most," she said. "Besides, since we'll be rowing in the leg of the journey, I'd think you'd be happy it was something small and light."

"Honestly," said Keith. "I'd be a lot happier to be staying here and not rowing anything."

"Then why are you going?" she asked. Frankly, she was growing sick of the man and his indecision. One minute he was all gung ho for the mission, the next he was waffling.

"Guilt," he shrugged. "I've always done the prudent thing. Kept my head down, did a good job. Didn't make waves. I never did great, but I didn't fall on my face like so many people I knew. I kept to the easy road." He threw his cigarette into the water and immediately lit a new one.

"Don't you think you ought to cut back on those?" Dana said.

"Why? I might die tonight. What's my health matter now? I'd get drunk if I thought I had time." He inhaled deeply. "It seemed like the prudent thing to stay put on the boat with you and your captain, where it was safe. I couldn't figure out why I felt so awful watching the city drift away.

"Well, I've had all day to think about it, and I think I hit the one time when being prudent isn't maybe the best way to go. Maybe this is my last chance to be daring instead, and do something good for a change."

"Listen," said Dana. "I understand you wanting to help your friends, but you're not exactly the person I would pick for this job. So do me a favor. Keep up with me and do *exactly* what I say. I don't want you getting me killed." Reaching into the boat, she retrieved a black police-issue 9mm pistol.

"It's got one bullet," she said, handing it to him. "Don't waste it."

Keith paled visibly, but he took the gun.

"Aye aye, sir," he said, as he lit another cigarette.

Indian summer is waning, and October's chill is just beginning to poke its icy fingers into the shadows, but a hint of golden warmth still lingers where the sun shines as it dips slowly toward the western end of Lake Ontario.

It throws cascades of sparkling fire across the mirrored surfaces of skyscrapers, giving the zeds in the streets a final show for the day. On the leaves of trees turned orange and red, it sets off brilliant waves of color, a final kiss of warmth before the trees release them to the wind and cold.

Over Lake Ontario, the sun dapples the water's surface as the calm water ripples outward beneath a small boat, making a dazzling display on the surface and catching the spray of the boat's wake in a shower of jewels.

Beneath the surface, far, far below in the murky depths, where the sun's fading light is only a hint of brightness far above, a throng of yearning hands reach up to grasp it as hundreds of bloated feet pause in their endless trudge across the garbage-choked mud. In the perpetual murky twilight, nearly four hundred pairs of eyes shine brightly, staring up at the distant sky.

Farther out beyond the city, beyond the island as well, a fleet of ships floats in tiny circles, the barked commands of their crew echoing their growing frustration. For a group of professionals dedicated and sworn by oath to defend their country's people to the death, this waiting and watching feels utterly wrong. Every man aboard those ships, from the captain to the man who sweeps the kitchen floor, yearns to drive forward under full power, sweep the enemy from the city streets, and bring safety to those still struggling. But there are orders from up on high to do no such thing, and having seen what the creatures were capable of and what devastation could befall the entire country if even one slipped through the blockade, who can say for sure that the orders were wrong?

As the sun dips ever closer to sunset and a new night of terror, one captain makes ready to take action. The self-promoted commander, admiral of a fleet of one, walks the decks of his aged, creaky, and poorly armed ferry boat. It is a task he performs every day at this time, and the men and women under him are all well rehearsed at their tasks, but somehow tonight is different. Tonight their people will be taking a more active role than ever before, and they know for certain that there will be people coming to them, under heavy pursuit most likely, people depending on the captain and his crew to bring them safely home.

The sun is at its lowest level now. It is the time that film crews name Magic Hour, the hour when the golden light is at its most diffuse, the best time to film heroes gazing dramatically at horizons while saying, "So it begins," as the wind obligingly whips back their hair. Even on a normal day, this hour is full of potential and charged excitement. Tonight the city trembles like a tuning fork, ready to burst into a crescendo.

Amid this kinetic swirl of potential energy, on a street far from shore, in a tall tower marked with a great red S, in a lobby dusted with shattered glass and blood, four desperate people and two dogs prepare to go out into the night, and the evening holds its breath. For tonight, the entire city revolves around them. Tonight, forces both light and dark will reach out hands to grasp at their lives.

CHAPTER TWENTY-FIVE

There were two shotguns, another pistol, and eight bullets between them. Wendell handed Becca a shotgun and Dylan a pistol.

"Not until there's no other choice," he said. They nodded. They didn't have to be told. Wendell slung his own shotgun across his shoulder and picked up the Halligan. Movement was more difficult in the bulky coat and pants than he had expected, but he felt a great deal more confident. The thick material would not be impossible to bite through, but it would certainly take time, and when a single bite was lethal, time was something he would definitely need. The thick gloves on his hands made holding the Halligan more difficult, but again, the gains more than made up for the losses.

Dylan looked smaller than ever in the second firefighter's coat. He was the worst-protected, and the most precious. Under his coat, in a sling made from a carefully folded hotel blanket, Sheila stared at him with enormous questioning eyes. Over his shoulder, he carried her diaper bag, empty now except for three bottles and a few diapers. They were taking only what they needed. By the time the bottles ran out, they would be on the island or it wouldn't matter.

"Are you sure you're all right?" Wendell asked. Dylan nodded. It had been his idea to carry Sheila. "You and Becca'll need both hands," he'd said.

"You stay in the middle between Becca and me," said Wendell. "Your job is to keep yourself and Sheila safe; our job is to keep you safe. If things get hairy, you run and hide, got it? No matter what you hear or see, you don't stop until you're someplace nothing can reach you."

Dylan smiled bravely and hefted his enormous axe, trying to strike a heroic pose. Wendell immediately realized a problem. Dylan wouldn't be able to swing the axe, which was as long as he was, without whacking the baby at his chest. Wendell wondered if he would even have the strength to use it if he wasn't loaded down with baby and bags.

"Here," he said, sliding his hammer from his belt. "Leave the axe here. You're not going to be doing any fighting anyway, if things go well."

"What if they don't go well?"

"Then this will help keep you alive a lot better than that. It's done well for me."

Dylan took the hammer and slid it into the pocket of his coat.

"Look at you," said Wendell. "Jesse would be proud of you, Dill."

Dylan blushed, but his eyes shone with pride. Wendell turned to Becca.

"Bullets for my friends," he said, lowering the visor of his helmet.

"An axe for the rest," she finished. One by one, he shook all their hands.

"Good luck."

"Keggazz!" cried Sheila.

They went out through the hole in the glass wall.

Campbell tied off the boat at a dock a ways off from Queen's Wharf, and Keith rubbed at his aching arms with relief. He hadn't held a paddle since Boy Scouts, and he'd forgotten just how heavy water could be.

The pair of them crouched in the boat while Dana peeked over the lip of the concrete barrier to the sidewalk to double check that their arrival had gone unnoticed. She turned to Keith and spoke in a whisper.

"Take a sling and follow me." She stood up on the dock, throwing one of the rope slings over her own shoulder. The thick rope had three small jerry cans of gasoline tied to it, and the cans bounced against her back as she crossed to the ramp up to street level.

Keith grabbed his own sling and his breaker bar and followed, wishing once again he'd been content enough with the coward's way out to stay behind. It looked like a long trek through the deadly streets with the red plastic jugs bouncing awkwardly on the small of his back.

Dana stood on the sidewalk at the edge of Queen's Quay Boulevard and Keith worried, not for the first time, that besides the pistol at her belt she appeared to be completely unarmed. He was about to mention this when she lifted up her flak jacket and unfurled a thick six-foot long chain from around her waist. It clinked softly as she held it in her right hand like a whip, and she turned to Keith again.

"Stay on my left," she whispered. "If you get in my way with this thing I'll likely break your neck. If we get into a tight spot, we go back to back and watch out for each other."

Keith nodded and choked up on his tire iron. "This isn't

my first rodeo," he said. The line was supposed to come out dramatic, the sort of thing an action movie star would say, but it sounded reedy and stupid coming out of his mouth, and Dana stifled a laugh.

"Don't do that again," she said, still giggling. "If you make me laugh like that, we'll both be killed." Keith felt his face go redder than normal, but he chuckled, too.

"I'll keep my mouth shut from now on."

"Good thing," Dana said with a smile. The moment of levity passed, and she was moving forward, silent and deadly.

Without another word, they walked east up Queen's Quay. Behind them, the sun disappeared and left the streets in darkness.

Lakeshore Boulevard was a four-lane road that ran directly underneath the hulking Gardiner Expressway from the Don Valley all the way to Bathurst Street. On a normal day, it was a busy street, and a slow-moving one. While the traffic above whizzed by in a semblance of speed, down below Lakeshore was a cavern ground to a halt at every intersection by a conflation of traffic lights. To drive on Lakeshore was to be constantly frustrated. Some would say that to drive anywhere in Toronto was to be constantly frustrated, and yet millions of cars choked the streets, Lakeshore included, every single day.

Tonight, Lakeshore Boulevard was a graveyard. Keith and Dana picked their way in between the cars with Keith peering nervously through every window as he passed. He recalled Wendell's declaration that such traffic jams were likely to be death traps filled with zombies, but Dana was insistent they go this way.

"The zeds can't see very well," she hissed. "Glowing eyes

are creepy, but they have terrible night vision. The darker the area we're moving through, the better chances we won't be noticed." Keith couldn't fault that logic. The overcast skies had blown away, and a bright waxing moon threw silver light across the open streets. In other circumstances, it would be beautiful. Tonight, the light was deadly.

They encountered their first zed in a tight corner next to a stalled school bus. Keith was inching along with his back to the bus, trying not to think about the story that bus could tell, when a figure stumbled around the back of the bus and fixed them with its glittering eyes. Dana, who was in front, had no room to swing her whip-like chain. Instead, she gathered it up into both hands and charged the zed, wrapping the chain around its throat as she drove it to the ground. While it gnashed and drooled on her gloved hands, she wrenched her hands sideways and snapped its neck.

A hiss came from behind her, and she looked up to see another figure looming over her, its unnaturally white teeth gleaming out of the dimness. She had time to think, inexplicably, *dental crowns*, before the creature's jaws began to come down on her.

Halfway down its deadly descent, its head suddenly did a rapid reversal as, with a loud crack, Keith's home-run swing barreled into its mouth and sent thousands of dollars of shattered quality dental work across the street. Keith watched it for a moment to ensure it stayed down, and then reached out with one hand to help Dana stand. She stood on shaky feet. Not for nearly a week had she come so close to death. She had all but forgotten the desperate feeling of being so close to living death, when a single misstep was enough to end your life.

"The ramp's up ahead," said Keith with a small smile. "Can we get this over with, please?"

CHAPTER TWENTY-SIX

They had left the leashes behind; no one had the hands to hold them, and like the rest of them, the dogs would have to make it or not on their own. It was to Wendell's great surprise that Tucker and Asshat took up their usual places to either side of Dylan without being told. Having never owned a dog himself, he had never before seen their fierce loyalty up close.

The group was a tiny solar system, with the dogs orbiting Dylan and Sheila in ever-shifting circles. Wendell and Becca alternated in the lead, one moving back while the other took point, one covering the right while the other went to investigate a sound or a movement on the left. Each held a gas-filled bottle and a Zippo lighter, and Wendell had a dozen more in a satchel on his back. Step by step, moment by moment, they moved forward, terror and excitement mingling in each of their hearts.

A particularly bad snarl of traffic at Yonge and Richmond made them circle to the north, so that they were forced to cross right in front of the looming cave of the Queen Street Subway station's concrete stairs. Both Becca and Dylan kept one eye on that awful hole until they were long past it. From the entrance to that cavern, they heard moans and the sliding of feet, but nothing came out but sounds and the smell of rot.

They were nearing the other side of the snarl when Wendell pulled up short. The others took their lead from him and crouched behind a van. From one corner to another, cars were smashed end to end in a circle. At the center was a streetcar that had plowed into the intersection and only stopped when the half dozen cars in front of it became too heavy to push.

"How many?" whispered Becca. Wendell shook his head and held up three fingers.

"We can take them," she said. Again he shook his head, pointed at himself, her, and then at Dylan who was desperately under-defended. He mimed a bite at Dylan's unprotected face, and shook his head. The message was clear: Not if we can help it.

He lit the rag fuse on the bottle in his hand and tossed it right into the middle of the intersection. It shattered against the side of the streetcar, and liquid flames exploded outward up the trolley and onto the nearest vehicles. Wendell pointed back the way they had come, and the group crawled back up the street, to take shelter behind the smashed window of a burnt-out pizzeria.

"What are we doing here?" Becca whispered. Wendell said nothing, just stared out the window. He seemed to be counting. Suddenly he turned to look at Dylan.

"How's Sheila?" he asked the boy.

Dylan peeked inside his coat. "Out like a light. What did you give her?"

"Benadryl," he said with a shrug. "Not my best moment, but with luck she won't wake up until we're well out of danger. Better get her back, though. This could get loud."

At that moment there was an explosion behind his head and a flaming tire flew north up Yonge Street. The street outside was lit up like day. Wendell's ears were ringing, but for the moment, Sheila didn't stir.

"Out the back," he said. "There are going to be more explosions in the next few minutes. Those gas tanks are all really close together, and the fire's getting hotter."

They had to crawl up the guardrail on the Gardiner's on-ramp, with the line of cars and trucks packed so close together. The good news was that despite their precarious position and the deep drop down one side, the zeds couldn't get onto the ramp either, and Keith and Dana made the slow, dangerous climb undisturbed.

The top of the ramp was a different story. Dozens of zeds were scattered around the graveyard of smashed and stalled vehicles, some drawn there by the previous night's beacon fire and others trapped there from the start after they arose in the seats of their cars. Dana planted herself in a rare wide spot between several vehicles where she could use her whip chain to good advantage, and stood her ground.

"Take the gas," she ordered Keith. "Go as far east as you can, and just start pouring. I'll watch your back."

Keith slung both ropes of jerry cans across his back and picked his way along the line of vehicles. Behind him, he heard Dana shouting oaths at the corpses to draw them to her and away from him.

A pair of eyes appeared directly in front of him. Keith jumped on top of a car's hood and slid down the other side into a new corridor. He passed the zed on the other side, the thing still staring at him with helpless hunger but unable to get to him.

He turned back. Far behind him Dana's whip was flying. A line of glowing eyes stood before her, but she used the chain to good advantage, snaking it around legs and tripping them up, knocking them over and causing the zeds behind to trip and topple into heaps. Over their moans, she still cried curses out at them. Keith watched in wonder for a moment and wondered how long she could hold out. The group was growing by the minute, and only the thick obstacle course of vehicles prevented them from swarming her completely.

He unscrewed the first of the jerry cans' lid and started sloshing gasoline over the nearest car as fast as he could. A hand slapped the inside of the window and he jumped back, but the zombie was trapped by glass and a seatbelt it could not negotiate. He let the last drops drip out and tossed the can, already reaching for the next one.

He had emptied three cans when the sound of drumming footsteps pounded behind him. He looked up in terror, but he saw only Dana, running for her life along the roofs of the vehicles. She leaped a particularly large gap and came to a halt just above him.

"What's taking so long?" she demanded. "Fucking light it already!"

Keith still had three full cans on his back, but he clambered up on the hood of the car next to her, and took out a book of matches. Striking one with his thumb, he allowed the rest to catch and in seconds, he held a fistful of flames. He dropped the matchbook to the ground, where it caught the pooled gas and spread across one full lane of stalled traffic.

Keith and Dana spun around and ran in leaps and bounds over the roofs of cars. When they were some distance away from the growing fire, they stopped to watch the road burn before climbing down the next nearest ramp to the ground. Keith stashed his unused cans of gas in the bed of a pickup truck. "In case one of your people come this way tomorrow night," he said.

Dana gave him an odd look. "I was wrong about you," she said. "I can think of worse people to have at my back."

"Don't change your mind yet," said Keith. "We've still got a long walk up to Bay Street. I've got plenty of time to prove you right after all."

"I think you're kidding," she said. "But you're putting yourself down for no reason. It's a good thing you're doing. Remember that when it all turns to shit."

"Dana, if it all turns to shit, have no doubt, so will I. Now, can we get off this burning deathtrap already?"

Becca got her share of fighting, after all, in the maze of back alleys they had to take to circle around the inferno Wendell had caused. In the narrow gaps between old brick buildings, glowing eyes appeared out of nowhere, often right in front of them. Becca's axe got its exercise.

They emerged onto a street almost empty of the dead. Behind them, the glow of the raging fires could be seen for miles, and the flickering light drew every corpse that could see it like moths to a bug-zapper. Dylan sincerely hoped the moths would fly right into the flames.

The silence and stillness made Wendell and Becca even more cautious as they moved among the cars. They fanned out into ever-wider circles, eyes always on the move.

Becca was in the lead when Dylan saw her glance into the window of an old wood-paneled station wagon and jerk back, with her eyes and mouth wide. The sound that suddenly filled the silent street was so unfamiliar, it took Dylan a moment to realize he was hearing Becca scream. It was a sound he'd never heard her make before.

Wendell leaped over the hoods of two cars and was beside her in an instant. She screamed until she was hoarse and pointed into the wagon. Wendell glanced inside, then spun around and pointed at Dylan, who was coming up fast.

"Not this way!" he shouted, forgetting for the moment to keep his voice down. "Go around!" Dylan followed his order with visible relief as he saw Becca turn and vomit onto the pavement. Whatever was bad enough to make Becca react that way was something he could gladly go his entire life without seeing. Wendell sat Becca down on the hood of a car, and as Dylan passed them by two lanes over, he saw Wendell open the station wagon's door and bring his weapon down once, twice, three times.

He waited for them to catch up. The street was empty of movement and silent as a church when they joined him, both pale and visibly shaken. Dylan looked them each in the eye, and he had never seen such ruined faces on any human being in his life.

"Don't ask," said Becca, and he didn't. Whatever was in that car, he never wanted to know.

CHAPTER TWENTY-SEVEN

The Gardiner was already a red glow on the horizon when the *Thomas Rennie* began the slow braking procedure that would let it drift into the wharf with a gentle thump. Captain Talleck turned to his second mate, a grizzled former mechanic who'd been on board from the moment the *Rennie* had begun its nightly trips.

"We're makin' good time tonight, Hywell," he said.

Hywell rubbed at his thick black beard that was already showing flecks of grey despite his age, and said, "We're going to be early tonight, Captain."

"Aye," said Talleck. "I want to be ready in case anything goes wrong."

"This one's different, isn't it sir?"

"'Course it is. Dana's out there."

"It's more than that, Captain. Every time we come ashore, we find fewer people. Some of the guys are starting to wonder if there's anyone left alive."

"Oh, there are," said Talleck. "But they're not comin' here, b'y. Either they don't know about us or don't think they can manage the risk, the rest of 'em are holing up an building their own little forts.

"No, you're right, me son. This is probably the last time we'll come ashore, for now at least. Kind o' makes it worth pullin' out all the stops to bring these kids out alive, don't it?"

"Aye sir. Should I pass out the extra magazines?"

"Have 'em ready," said Talleck. "We don't want to blow all our ammo 'less we have to, but if we start lookin' like needing to go through the gate, we make sure we got the means to come back."

As they drifted nearer the wharf, Talleck reached for the switch to cut the lights. They would come in dark, to attract fewer zeds.

There was a rippling in the water around and in front of them. To a man born and raised on a Cape Islander plying the waters out of Placentia Bay, it looked like nothing less than a torrent of cod slapping up against the breakwaters. He took his hand away from the light switch. "What the hell is that?" said Hywell.

Talleck stared into the seething black water. Suddenly his eyes widened. "All back full! Full reverse!"

The man in the wheelhouse threw the engine into reverse and the ferry's forward motion slowed, then stopped. As she began to pull backwards away from the wharf, Talleck saw figures rising up from the water, using the latticed tires for handholds as they climbed.

"Dear God," said Hywell. Beneath his beard, his face was pale as a ghost.

Talleck stared in disgust and horror. All along the quay, as far as the lights could pick out, dozens, then hundreds of waterlogged, sagging corpses clambered their way up the breakwaters and onto the Toronto shore.

Talleck killed the lights. The boat went dark. A single pair of lamplight eyes stared out at the boat that had just disappeared, and then turned away, to gaze toward the fire raging in the distance.

"Now what?" said Hywell. Talleck stared at the enormous crowd still surging out of the water, and wished he knew the answer.

PART FIVE
WENDELL JENKINS
VS.
THE ZOMBIES

CHAPTER TWENTY-EIGHT

"Wendell."

"What?"

"The baby's waking up."

"Don't jostle her. We need her quiet for a few more minutes."

Dylan tried to move as slow and steady as he could, but he could feel the infant's body squirm beneath his jacket. She was making tiny "ah" sounds and waving her hands around. She wasn't awake yet, but it would not be long.

They were across the street from the Scotia Bank, and a crowd had gathered out front and spilled through the doors.

"She must have been chased here," whispered Wendell to Becca. Becca rolled her eyes. It would be only fitting if they had to rescue their rescuer.

"Throw a bottle at them," she said.

"What, and burn the building down? No, we're going to have to be cleverer than that."

"So what?" growled Becca. She felt terribly exposed. They were crouched behind a Lexus in the middle of the financial district, where the signs of wealth were clean streets with no cover. The zombies that she could see outnumbered them ten to one, and that didn't account for the ones crammed inside the building. And now Dylan said that the baby was waking up, and she had seen what the cries of a startled and confused baby could do to a pack of zombies.

"That's it," she whispered. "I have an idea."

"What is it?" said Wendell, but she was already standing up. "Becca!" he hissed. "Don't do anything stupid!"

She turned back, gave him a *who-me?* look, and went in a crouching run down the street toward Saint Andrew Station.

She pulled her iPhone out of her pocket and checked the battery level. Half a charge. It would do. Scrolling across to Music, she selected the loudest, most irritating song on her play list, a song she had once loved so much she felt she could listen to it for hours. She set the phone down on the sidewalk far from the bank, turned up the volume and pressed PLAY.

Then she ran. The song was like a grenade. If she was too close when it went off…

She heard the opening warble, electronic music rising to a crescendo, and dove behind a car before the robot voice of the singer could utter the first fatal line of the song.

She had to bite her tongue to keep from screaming. The song threatened to obliterate her carefully maintained sanity and leave her curled up on the dirty concrete. She peered over the trunk of the car. The song was doing its work; a crowd began to gravitate down the street from the bank to the phone. She duck-walked back to the others.

"Is that 'Scream and Shout'?" said Dylan. "God, I'm so sick of that song."

He stood up to follow Wendell, who was already halfway across the street, headed for the bank. She glared at his back and followed Asshat's wagging tail.

Wendell stood just outside the doors, peering in. "Good job," he whispered. "But there's still quite a few of them inside. I can't see just how many, but if we move carefully..."

Becca was already moving. Rage and Britney Spears were in her head, and if she didn't slaughter something fast, she would lose her mind. She hefted her axe in one hand, her shotgun in the other, and strode into the darkened bank.

"Becca, *wait!*"

Becca held the axe handle right up at the top, below the curved blade. When a pair of eyes turned to her, she punched at them, smashing with the axe head. She came through with her fist flying, lashing out at every face she saw. They were men and women, some tall and some wide, but all of them fell in front of her. Dimly behind her, she heard someone whisper her name, but she ignored it. Then she felt a sickening pressure on her leg.

A zombie with a shattered, bloody face—he had dropped but not died. She hadn't bothered with that base of the skull bullshit. He had her ankle in his mouth and was biting down. His teeth couldn't break through the leather, though, and Becca pointed the barrel of her shotgun at his face and pulled the trigger.

Suddenly she wasn't the only one in the fight. Wendell was there, but so were two strangers who'd come charging out of the rear of the building when her shotgun went off. Dimly beneath the ringing in her ears, she heard the wail of the baby.

Then strong arms had her by the waist and dragged her backwards. She kicked and punched and tried to bring her gun around, but the shotgun was wrenched from her hands. She was set down in a small room full of tiny metal doors amid a flurry of activity. A flashlight flicked on.

"Shut it! No, shut it now! Turn that crank!"

"I'm trying!"

"Would you all shut up?" Dylan shouted. He had Sheila in his arms and was trying to rock her gently as she screamed in fear and confusion.

Wendell crouched in front of Becca. His eyes were sad, worried, angry. He looked like so many teachers who'd given her detention over the years, like her father when she'd pissed him off. She fully expected him to say, "Rebecca, I'm very disappointed in you."

"What was that about?" he said instead. "I thought we were a team, Becca."

"Very well done," said an unknown voice from behind him. "It was good of you to show up when you did, guys, but now we all get to suffocate in here together. Good one."

"We'll get out of here, Dana," Wendell said calmly. "We just need a breather first, that's all. Dylan, how's Sheila?"

"Cranky," reported Dylan. The baby was wriggling around so much he could hardly keep her still.

"She needs a diaper change and a fresh bottle," said Wendell. "Can you handle that?"

"A diaper change?" said the fourth voice. "Can't that wait 'til we're somewhere safe?"

"Not if you don't want to die before we get there," said Wendell. "Everyone settle down and take a rest. We'll get Sheila settled, and then we'll figure out a way out of here."

"Goddammit," muttered the man in a voice that was eerily familiar.

"Keith?" said Becca.

Everyone spun around. Sure enough, the big man with the red face stood in the shadows next to Dana. He gave a surly smile and a wave.

"Um," said Dylan, looking around the cramped vault. "Where can I, um. There's no, uh, no table."

"Here," said Wendell, and he bent forward with his head nearly to the floor. "Will that do?" Dylan looked at him in confusion for a second before realizing Wendell wanted him to use his back as a changing table.

"Please hurry," said Wendell as Dylan worked. "This is more uncomfortable then it looks."

Dana stood in one corner of the vault by the massive steel door and rolled her eyes. Becca looked down to see Wendell's face turned up to hers. She grimaced and looked away.

"Becca, come on," Wendell said. "What happened back there? I thought we were finished with this video game hero crap."

"That wasn't it." What it was, even *she* couldn't explain. In her head, it was all red. But Wendell nodded a knowing look on his upside-down face.

"Sweetheart, you have been through so much, I can't even imagine. Both of you have. I don't even know half of what you've gone through, but the half I know about is enough on its own to break a person." He smiled at her. She didn't even realize how scared she was of him being angry with her until she saw him smile. Relief washed over her so quickly she thought she might faint. From his awkward position on the floor, he scrabbled his hand over to hers and she took it and squeezed.

"You don't know," she said in a voice so small it couldn't be called a whisper. "You don't know."

"I *don't* know," he said. "I can never know. It would kill me to go through what you've been through. I'm not nearly as strong as you are. But the strongest of us run out of strength at some point. Becca, we're so *close* now, so close to being able to stop looking behind us forever. You just need to keep being strong a little longer."

Dylan wrestled the snaps shut on Sheila's jumper. "Done!" he said. Wendell gratefully stood up and pressed two hands into the small of his back.

"Oh, that hurts!" he exclaimed. With the immediate diaper problem out of the way, Sheila's cries dropped off. Wendell turned to Keith.

"You came back," he said. Keith shrugged and smiled.

"I ran out of smokes. I figured you might have some." Wendell laughed and shook his hand. "It's good to have you. And you, too, Dana. Thank you for coming all this way for us."

"Thank me when we're on the boat," she said. "Now how do you suggest we get out of here?"

It surprised Becca to see everybody automatically deferring to Wendell. It was like she'd said in the beginning—the suit. They all looked up to the suit. But that wasn't all of it, was it? For firefighter's uniform or no firefighter's uniform, Wendell Jenkins appeared to stand taller than all the rest. He was the calm in the center of the storm. The frightened man she had pulled out of a linen closet had become that man they all looked to when they were frightened—even her.

"Well," said Wendell, taking Sheila from Dylan. "First we're going to make sure baby gets her bottle. Then, we're going to walk out the front door."

"We are?" said Dana.

"Oh yeah," grinned Wendell. He sat on the floor next to Becca. "We've been through way worse than this, haven't we, Becks?"

She grinned back at him. "Don't call me Becks," she said.

"First of all," said Wendell. "Every lesson is always Lesson Number One. You know why?" He looked around the cramped bank vault at four blank faces. "Because you might not live to learn Lesson Number Two. So Lesson Number One is: Hide when you have to, run when you can, and fight when you have no other choice. And how do you know which one to do?" he asked. More blank looks.

"It's simple," Wendell smiled. "After the fact, whatever you lived through was the right choice. Whatever got you killed was a mistake."

"So you're just making this all up as you go along?" accused Dana.

"Of course," he replied. "But I'm doing it with *confidence*." He turned to Dylan. "How's Sheila?"

"Calm for now."

"How are the dogs?"

"They need to pee," said Becca.

"And how are you?"

"Claustrophobic," admitted Dana.

"Then let's get the hell out of here. Weapons up, Dylan in the middle, everyone else in a circle. Keith, the door."

Keith spun the handle and flung the door open to reveal a sea of glowing eyes. Wendell threw the flashlight through the door, over the zombies' heads. Some turned to follow it; darkness rushed back in on the rest. Wendell charged forward with his Halligan swinging, and the rest followed as best they could.

He felt hands on his arms and the press of bodies in the dark, but the only two things he worried about was the continuous swinging of his weapon and the rectangle of moonlight ahead that was their way out. Swing, smash, jab. Something wet splattered on the faceplate of his helmet. Bodies fell like wheat before a thresher. Slowly, he shoved through the press. Slowly, the door loomed closer. He heard the barking of the dogs and the grunting of his companions beside and behind him. He felt the ache in his arms go from a dull afterthought to a burning agony, but still he swung, shoved, and moved forward. Somewhere behind him, he heard a bark and a whine.

Suddenly he was in the moonlight. The others were coming through the door, one by one. The last to arrive was Dana, using her chain two-handed across the doorway to hold back their pursuers. Wendell yanked a liquor bottle from his bag and lit the fuse.

"Is everybody out?" he called. He looked around. Keith, Dylan, Becca, Dana… "Where are the—"

From within the building there was a whimper, and then a growl. In the dim moonlight, he saw Tucker lying on the floor, a terrible gash in his side. Above him stood Asshat, growling. The cowardly mutt stood over his companion's prone form, snarling and snapping at the hands that reached down toward them. Wendell watched the scene with a sinking in his heart. With one hand, he threw the cocktail through the door, over Dana's shoulder. With the other, he yanked her back out of the blast.

The others started running, but Wendell stood a moment longer. As the flames licked the walls and the zombies turned back inwards, he got one more look at the two dogs, the one defending the other to the death. It was the choice of teeth, fire, or a bullet. It was no choice at all.

He drew his shotgun and fired two rounds through the door. Then he, too, ran like hell.

CHAPTER TWENTY-NINE

"Absolutely not," said Dana.

"It worked for me and Keith," argued Wendell. "The traffic is too thick down there. Union Station is the best bet. We know our way through."

"Union Station is a slaughterhouse," Dana said. "You two might have made it by the skin of your teeth, but there's no way you're coming back out with that baby still alive."

Wendell rubbed his temple with two fingers. He was getting tired. They were so close, but had so far to go.

"I'm not going into another subway station," said Dylan, and his trembling lip belied the terror the idea held for him. Becca put her arm around him and reaffirmed the decision. Union Station was out.

"Then what do we do?" he asked.

"We go straight down Bay Street. The wharf is a straight shot at the bottom of the street. We skirt the traffic as best we can, and make for the ferry by the straightest route."

"And you've done this already?"

"Like you said, it worked for me and Keith." Keith ducked his head and backed away from the argument, feeling like the small boy caught between two squabbling parents. Wendell looked dubiously down the traffic-choked street. The lake seemed very far away. But should Dana have risked her life to come all this way only to have him ignore her advice?

"All right," he said. "We'll do it your way."

He had two gas-bomb bottles left. They had four bullets left between the five of them, not counting the final insurance policy of Becca's pistol. Wendell's arms burned with fatigue. Sheila was still awake.

"Should we give her more Benadryl?" asked Dylan. Wendell shook his head.

"It's not safe to keep her drugged for so long. I shouldn't even have done it the first time. We'll just have to go as well as we can."

"What if she starts crying?" demanded Dana.

"Then we run as fast as we can until we get somewhere safe where we can calm her down." He snapped. He shouldered his bag and choked up on the Halligan. "Let's get this over with."

They set off down Bay Street. As far as he could tell, the only difference between the affluent section of town and the poor neighborhood he had started in was that nicer vehicles choked the streets, and more of the zombies wore suits. Wendell kept his eyes constantly moving. Now and then, he saw the silhouette of a zombie against the silver moonlight, but either it didn't see them or it couldn't find them in the maze of cars. He looked to his left and saw Becca stalking along in the same careful fashion, eyes watching everywhere at once. He caught her eye and gave her a reassuring smile. She returned it quickly and then looked away, her expression intent on what she could not see.

Wendell had to admit that Dana had been right. This way

was shorter and much less terrifying than the darkness of Union Station. Rather than being trapped like rats in the maze of stalled cars, they moved easily through them, while the dead could find no easy way into the traffic, and so avoided it entirely. Above him and off to his left, he could vaguely see the orange glow of the still-burning Gardiner fire, and he knew that Dana and Keith's efforts there were largely responsible for the empty streets.

Bay Street dipped down into a pitch-dark tunnel as it ran beneath six lines of elevated railway track, and it was Dylan's turn to insist they find another way around. He dreaded to go inside that pitch-black space.

"Fine," said Dana. "Who's up for climbing?"

She used a pair of wire snips to cut a hole in the chain-link fence around the rail yard, and they all squeezed through and climbed up the grassy hillock that sloped up to the top of the bridge. At the top, it was clear and moonlit, and though he was at the lowest point of the city, Wendell felt he could see for miles. Lake Ontario had never looked so tantalizingly close.

"This is kind of pretty," said Dylan. "Almost like a—ow!" He stumbled over a railway tie and fell. He caught himself in time to avoid the hard steel track, but from inside his coat came a thin, exhausted wail.

Wendell stripped off his gloves and held his arms out for Sheila. Dylan placed her in his hands gratefully, and Wendell said, "Fan out and kill anything that moves. I need a few minutes to calm her down." As the others began moving in an outward circle around the yard, he began to rock the baby gently, crooning, "There is a young maiden, she lives all alone…"

The bridge and the adjacent yard were empty but for a few

scattered boxcars left behind on side rails. Since these were the only possible hiding places, the rest of the group moved toward them in pairs to make certain they were empty. One by one, Wendell heard the hushed calls of "Clear here!" and "Nothing!" as he gently rocked Sheila back to sleep. He felt almost peaceful in the still air and the moonlight. He watched Dylan give hand signals to Keith as he pressed his back against a boxcar door and wondered at how much the boy had grown in such a short time. He wondered if this was a ghostly shadow of the pride he might have felt as a father, watching his son grow up into a man.

The thing that fell from the boxcar's roof onto Dylan must have been there for weeks. It must have fought its way through terror and blood and climbed the ladder to apparent safety, never realizing the small bite on its arm already spelled death. Wendell saw it fall in slow motion, with a bemused and helpless horror. He didn't even have time to shout a warning to Dylan, and the thing was on top of him, biting and tearing.

Keith came charging in and dealt the creature a two-handed blow that threw it back juddering onto the rails, where it lay still. Wendell was already moving, as quickly as the sleeping child would let him, but his heart sank when he heard the horrible words, "I'm bit!"

Now the entire group was gathered around the boy who lay on the ground, sobbing, "I'm bit, I'm bit!" To get so close, thought Wendell, and to lose one of them now. Sure enough, there was a huge gash down the side of Dylan's arm, pieces of his thick coat hanging in tatters from it, and coated with black slime.

Becca stripped off his coat and examined his arm. She searched up and down the length of his arm and then dropped it with a curse and picked up the sleeve of the coat.

"Dummy!" she said. "He bit you all right. Almost right through your coat."

Dylan looked at his unmarked arm in confusion. "I'm okay?" he asked, daring to hope.

"Didn't break the skin. Didn't even get through the sleeve."

Dylan looked about to faint. The others laughed with relief. Keith poured a bottle of water over the black slime on the sleeve and rubbed it clean of ooze.

"Don't get bit in the same spot and you'll be alright," he said, handing the coat back to Dylan. He was grinning like the rest, but Wendell could see the glint of something at the corner of his eye. In that moment, he knew Keith cared for the kids more than he was willing to let on.

Becca saw it, too. "Thanks," she said gruffly. "I can't believe I'm saying this, but I'm glad you came back."

"Yeah, well," Keith looked unsure whether to feel pissed or praised. "Don't get too worked up over it."

"Don't worry, I won't."

Wendell shook his head. Some things never changed.

"All right," whispered Dana as they climbed down the other side. "This is the home stretch. There's four lanes of Lakeshore traffic to get through, and then it's a straight shot to the ferry. No cars, no zeds. They're all enjoying the bonfire about a klick away."

"We're gonna make it," sighed Dylan, and to Wendell he looked about to cry. They were all exhausted, but they still had a long leg to go.

"Don't relax yet, son," he said. "We're not home free until the boat's away from the dock. It looks easy, but that's when people make mistakes, when they think they're already in the clear."

"Yeah," said Dylan with his shoulders slumped. "You're right."

They moved slowly, returning to the shifting circle they had adopted before. They came to the beginning of Lakeshore Boulevard without incident. Directly above their heads spanned the massive edifice of the Gardiner Expressway, extending for miles as far as they could see. Not far away at all now was the waning glow of the still burning fire, but it seemed lower now, to Wendell. It was burning out.

Beyond the four lanes, they could see the clear road straight to the wharf, just as Dana had said. Either the masses of desperate evacuees had been unwilling to be bottled up against the lake itself or Talleck's men had risked life and limb to do a massive road-clearing job, Wendell didn't know. It was something he could ask Dana about after they were safe aboard the ferry.

"Okay," he said. "Let's go."

They negotiated the packed cars slowly. Wendell gave a yellow school bus a particularly wide berth. It was bad enough to imagine what had happened to all the refugees trapped in their cars without delving into the silent horror story of the trapped school bus. He could only hope that the driver had been alone on the bus, having either dropped off all of his charges or not yet picked them up.

This time Dana reached the other side first, and stopped, staring to the south. Wendell clambered over the hood of the last car and dropped to her side, relief washing over him. They had made it.

Then he looked in the direction Dana was staring with frozen fear.

The last jaunt to the wharf was *not* clear; they lined the street from one side to the other, hundreds strong. Their skin was bloated and puffed out, and to a man, regardless of race they had the pale complexion of albinos, and the wrinkled consistency of soap. They looked as if they had just walked across the bottom of a lake, which of course they had.

Thronged together and pressed into the cattle gate of Bay Street by the lure of the guttering fire, they sloshed forward with their waterlogged feet and gazed directly at Wendell with the eyes of lantern fish.

CHAPTER THIRTY

"**B**ack!" screamed Wendell. "Get back!"

Wendell and his companions clambered back over the hoods of cars they had just crossed. Behind them, the dead came in their hundreds, slowly and inexorably. Wendell looked back the way they had come; between the street and the rail yard, there was no cover at all, no place to hide. The rail yard would be a killing field, with nowhere to run and all the time in the world for four hundred hungry corpses to find and dismember them.

"The bus!" he shouted. "Get on the bus!" They turned and made for the derelict school bus. Wendell came last, standing at the door and watching the approaching horde, not zombies now but ghouls, until the last straggler, Dana, was aboard, then he turned and ran up the short stairs, slamming the door shut behind him.

He was relieved to see that the bus was empty and showed no sign of the bloodbath he had imagined. In fact, aside from a layer of dust from weeks sitting idle, the bus looked fresh from the wash bay.

"Get down and don't make a sound," he whispered. "If

we're quiet enough, they'll forget we're here and move on toward the beacon fire."

He crouched on the ground between two seats, and the others followed suit. For an eternity of seconds, the bus was deadly silent, with the only sound the movement of the dead outside. He jumped whenever a fist thumped uselessly against the locked door of the bus, but the entire group did their part and kept silent. The pounding on the walls grew less frequent; the shaking of hundreds of bodies pushing on either side grew gentler. He dared a peek up over the window ledge. The dead were moving away, toward the fire.

Then Sheila began to cry.

"Dylan," Wendell hissed. "What's wrong with her?"

"I don't know!" Dylan cried. "Maybe she needs another diaper?"

"Well, try it! Change her diaper, give her a bottle, try everything. We need her quiet for a few more minutes!"

The thumping on the side of the bus started up again. The ghouls had heard the cry and were drawn to the sound, just like in the storage closet so many lifetimes ago. He closed his eyes and prayed.

"Uh, Wendell?" came the frantic-sounding voice of the boy two seats back.

"What, Dylan?"

"I, um, I don't have her diaper bag."

"What?"

"I, um, I think I dropped it outside."

"What!" exploded Keith. "Are you that fucking stupid?"

"I'm sorry!" cried Dylan, "We were all running away. I don't remember."

"Will you shut up, Keith?" Wendell hissed. "You're not helping. Dylan, try singing to her."

"It's definitely her diaper, Wendell. It's really soggy. I think she did a Two."

His heart sank. Sheila wouldn't calm down from a full diaper. Not unless they could change her somehow.

"Just change her into something else! Use your sweater!"

"For God's sake, we don't have time for this!" Keith cried. He was right. The bus was shaking back and forth. Some of the ghouls had climbed to the roofs of adjacent cars; Wendell jerked back as a pale hand slapped at the window above him, leaving a wet smear and a layer of goopy skin behind.

"Becca?" called Dylan, his voice small and scared. "This is exactly what you said would happen, isn't it?"

"Yeah, buddy," said Becca, drawing her gun. "I'm sorry."

"Look," said Keith. "It's decision time. In a few minutes, those things are going to turn this bus upside down or smash that door, and then we're all going to die. Wendell, you know what has to happen here."

Wendell felt his blood run cold. "No. Absolutely not."

"Look, I get it. You're attached to the kid. But she's not your baby, man. You willing to die for someone else's kid? You did all you could, Wendell."

"I'm not doing it."

"Keith, fuck you!" shouted Becca. "She's a baby."

"It's simple math," insisted Keith. "One death or six. I know it sucks, but one of us has to make a tough decision here. I'll do it myself if it'll make you feel better. I don't want to, but I will if I have to. We have to survive."

Wendell felt dizzy. It was all a dream, he thought. He could still feel Sheila's body under his hand, still hear the crinkle the plastic shopping bag had made in his fist. From somewhere far away he heard, *You're a coward who hides while people die.*

It was all coming true again.

"Bullshit!" sobbed Becca. "You're just a fucking coward, you always were, you fu—" Her rant was cut off in a scream as the bus lifted up on two tires, and came crashing back down, making Sheila scream all the harder.

The jolt knocked Wendell back into the moment. He was not alone in the storage closet. He was only minutes from safety, with people counting on him for their lives.

He knew what he had to do.

"You're right, Keith," he said. Becca gasped, and Dylan sobbed.

"No," he cried.

"One of us has to make the tough decision here, right? One life for six. The numbers speak for themselves."

"Great, Wendell, I'm glad you came around. Look, I'll be honest, I'd rather you did it, but if you want me to—"

"Keith, if you even touch that baby I'll snap your back and use you for zombie bait." Wendell snapped. He stood up and pulled his last two Molotov cocktails from his bag.

He handed one to Becca. "Wait five minutes, then throw this as far as you can and run in the other direction. Dylan, you hold Sheila tight and run. Don't stop for anything. Not Becca, not Keith, not fucking Santa Claus, got it? You don't stop running until you're sitting on board the ferry." Dylan nodded mutely. "The rest of you, the drill is the same. Go in a circle, surround the children, and get them there alive, or I swear I will come back and haunt you for the rest of your lives."

The bus lurched again. Wendell nearly toppled, but grabbed onto the drivers' seat and held on tight. The windshield shattered from the impact, showering him with pebbles of glass.

"What are you going to do?" asked Becca. He grinned at her and flipped down his visor.

"The right wrong thing," he said. He crossed the narrow corridor to the emergency exit at the back of the bus. He lit the fuse of the cocktail and threw open the door onto the sea of grasping hands.

"Five minutes," he said, and hurled the cocktail into the crowd below him. Then he leapt through the flames and ran screaming.

He screamed curses, movie quotes, inane gibberish, anything just to be louder than the squalling baby. Without stopping to see if they were following him, he barreled through the surging crowd, using the Halligan as a battering ram rather than a weapon, clearing a path ahead of him. He sang a snatch of dirty limerick, and laughed maniacally at his own stupidity. They fell in front of him like snow to a plow, but formed up behind, trampling to mush those that didn't rise fast enough. When he reached the edge of the line of traffic, he turned around to see if they were behind him.

A massive horde advanced on him, but above and beyond them he could still see a large group congregating around the beleaguered bus, shaking it back and forth.

"Hey, you guuuyyyysss!!" he screamed. His voice cracked at the end. "Come and get it! Sooeee! Soooeeee!" He leaped up onto the concrete berm of the Gardiner's on ramp and drove his Halligan smashing down into the skull of a corpse who was reaching for his leg.

The gang surrounding the bus turned to the sound of his voice, and he laughed out loud again and turned and ran headlong up the ramp, leaping over hoods and bounding across shiny metal roofs. His legs burned inside his thick pants, and his arms were on fire and heavy, but he needed only expend them a little longer, and then he could rest.

His followers were not following. They stared from the bottom of the ramp. He bounded back down, nearly stumbling and falling face first to the street below. He stopped and shouted, "Come on! The fuck are you waiting for, Christmas?"

The first of them started clambering over the bumpers toward him. He laughed and climbed higher.

He was nearly to the top of the Gardiner when he realized his mistake. Over the lip of the guardrail, he could see bobbing heads coming his way. There was already a massive group on top of the overpass, lured there so obligingly by Dana and Keith's massive fire. Now two groups converged on him, each of them enough to rip through the layers of his protective clothing, or simply hold him down and use enough force to tear his limbs off. He was out of chances. But of course, that had been the intent all along. To give the others a chance by giving up his.

He paused on the roof of a pickup truck while death scrabbled up to meet him and agony awaited above him.

"I'm sorry, Grace," he said. "I never did find you."

At that moment, a shaft of moonlight caught the face of one of the corpses at the top of the ramp. It was a young man, the floppy remains of a careful Mohawk lying greasy against the side of his head. In that instant, he did not look deadly or hungry, but mournful. A being trapped in a hellish half-life he had never chosen. Suddenly he realized they were all Grace. Every single one of them had been a human being who had loved and hoped. Every one of them had died in agony and terror, only to be yanked from sleep to prowl the earth as a monster.

Every one of them deserved to be released, to be allowed

to rest. They deserved what only he could give them.

Wendell smiled a smile of pure joy and rightness, and with no doubt in his mind he clambered up the rest of the way, to deliver the mercy that only he could give, for as long as his strength held out.

CHAPTER THIRTY-ONE

They were not in the clear, not by a long shot. Becca drove her axe through the skull of a ghoul who was trying to climb through the shattered windshield and hurled her burning bottle as far as she could. Without waiting to see what it hit, she charged out the open door just as Wendell had, swinging her axe with all her strength as the others followed her out. Dylan clutched the screaming Sheila in his arms, but looked around frantically, mindful of Wendell's last words but unsure which way to run.

"This way," cried Becca and took him by the arm, half-dragging him across the lanes of vehicles and over to the sidewalk. Dana and Keith were not far behind, but Becca didn't stop to wait for them. At this moment, it was everyone for themselves, and Becca owed more to Dylan than to Keith.

She raced around the corner, back onto the straight stretch of Bay Street that led directly to the harbor. She heard the watery moans of the ghouls behind her and jumped four feet in the air when a hand grabbed her shoulder. It was only Keith, however, trying to reassure her that he had made it.

"Get the fuck away from me," she snapped and ran on ahead. Dana had passed them both and was leading the way to the ferry when a new wave of corpses appeared from the harbor road. The stragglers were smaller in number than the enormous group they had escaped from, but they still blocked the way from one sidewalk to another.

Becca came to a halt beside Dana. "We have to punch a hole!" Dana cried, snaking her whip out before her. Becca dug in her heels beside her, and they stood their ground against the advancing ghouls.

Dylan was lagging behind. Despite Wendell's orders to "Run, and don't stop running," Dylan was past the point of exhaustion, and the new wave of zombies in front of him sent him spiraling into despair. He slumped and staggered, but a hand grabbed his elbow and pulled him to his feet.

"Come on," said Keith. "You heard the man. Last dash."

Suddenly, a weight hit him in the side and he toppled over, knocking Dylan down with him. The two zombies had come from the warehouse yard opposite them, completely unnoticed by either of them. Keith found a weight pressing on his chest and looked up to see a pair of slavering jaws inches from his face. He shoved its head back with one hand while the other hand patted on the ground for his weapon. He couldn't feel it anywhere. It had rolled out of his reach. Out of the corner of his eye, he saw Dylan desperately holding back a second creature with both hands. His hammer lay useless on the sidewalk, out of reach. Sheila screamed on the pavement between them, a bundle of fear and noise.

Keith felt foul air on his face as the teeth snapped shut just above his nose. His own strength was failing fast, but he remembered his pistol.

"You've got one bullet," Dana had said. "Don't waste it."

Keith used the last of his strength to push the body upwards long enough to reach for his belt and pull the gun. With seconds to spare, he pressed the barrel into hard flesh, and squeezed the trigger.

With an explosion of black blood, the zombie on top of Dylan slumped to the ground.

"Dylan," Keith cried. "Run!" Then he screamed as iron jaws sank into the flesh of his cheek.

Dylan shoved the corpse off his chest with the last of his strength and grabbed Sheila around the waist. He scooped the screaming baby up into his arms and, weeping with terror and exhaustion, he ran.

"Okay," shouted Dana. "This is it. One last push." She lashed out with her chain, looped it around the pale neck of the ghoul, and yanked hard. The zombie's neck snapped; it flopped to the street. Becca drove her axe deep into her zombie's skull, and it twitched and was still.

"Now," she panted. "Run."

Before she could move, Dylan raced through the gap and was gone up the wharf. Becca followed as fast as she could. Ahead of her, she could see the lights of the ferry. They were almost there.

She turned back. Dana was holding the line at bay with the last of her strength, forcing the ghouls to keep their attention on her and not turn back toward the lights. She was sagging with exhaustion, but still she snaked her chain back and hurled it out. Becca didn't know how long she could hold out.

"Go, Dylan!" Becca shouted, then turned back to the dwindling, but still deadly throng. She unslung her shotgun from across her back. It still had two shots in it. She chose her targets carefully—they hadn't seen her yet. Dana's left side was flagging. A zombie darted in close and she didn't have time to defend. Becca raced in, rested the shotgun against the side of its head, and fired. Its head exploded, and it dropped to the ground, the top of its neck nothing but a bloody stump.

One more shell left, and now they were coming for her too. She didn't aim, just pointed the shotgun at the center of the growing crowd and fired. The spray of the blast carved holes in half a dozen corpses, but only two fell to the ground, permanently disabled. She dropped her shotgun and readied her axe.

Footsteps pounded behind her, and now there were a dozen shouting men surrounding her and Dana. Gunshots peppered the air, and the dead dropped, one by one. Becca felt herself being pulled backwards, toward the dock. When she saw Dana running beside her, she gave in and let them lead her to the safety of the boat.

Wendell Jenkins advanced up the Expressway, killing as he went. The dead were easy pickings, separated as they were by the barriers of the stalled traffic, but for every one he felled before him, two more gathered up behind him. He was the Pied Piper, but the road led not to the sea, but to the fire.

He killed his wife a dozen, three dozen times over, sending a body to the ground and willing her soul to Heaven, but he was out of strength. Exhaustion was creeping up behind him as fast as the gathering dead, and when it overcame him, it would be the end.

He fought all the way to the edge of the fire, a massive graveyard of twisted, red-hot metal and melted foam, but to his dismay, the flames were all but burned out. They had decimated four lanes of vehicles and incinerated who knew how many corpses, but the fire had been Wendell's last hope of escape. Now, with the dead bearing down on him and nowhere to go...

He leaped to the top of the roadway's crash barrier. The molten concrete melted the soles of his boots, and he felt the heat under his feet as he walked, balance-beam style, above the spent inferno. If he had hoped it would stop the zombies, he was sadly mistaken; they crawled atop the wreckage, blackening their skin and burning away the remains of their tattered clothing, but still they came. They followed him without pain, without fear.

Wendell jumped off the barrier onto the hood of a pickup truck, the first in the line that was undamaged. His boots were a wreck of melted rubber, but he had survived with both feet intact. The slow press of the dead continued, their journey from water into fire still not complete, their final reward helpless in front of them.

Wendell heard, in the distance, the tiny pops of far-off gunfire. He paused and counted the shots. There were dozens of pops, a great deal more than the ammunition left to his friends. He hoped that meant they had found rescue, that they were safe. He supposed he would never know.

The first of the ghouls had reached his truck. It stood naked, clothes burned away, charred black skin covering most of its body. It was no longer distinguishable from male or female. Lips, nose, hair had been melted away. All that remained were its ravenous jaws, its searching eyes. It was no longer human, a being escaped from Hell. Wendell shattered its skull and clambered up over the truck's roof and into the bed.

He nearly cheered when he saw the red cans. Three of

them, tied to a loop of course rope. Hope, in the form of gasoline.

He cast about him for an ideal spot to use this unexpected gift. Across the four lanes, just outside the radius of the spent fire, sat an enormous tanker truck, full of pressurized, explosive fuel, he hoped. Just as likely, it was sewage. In the dark, he couldn't tell.

There wasn't time to do things right. The creatures were lined up all along the edge of the truck, reaching for him with hands burned down to the bones. He unscrewed the lid of the first can, turned around its yellow spout, and lit the yellow plastic with his Zippo.

The can caught fire immediately, and he didn't wait. He threw it up against the tanker, where it splashed flaming gas across the side. He quickly lit the next one and threw it. The third can guttered and went out in midair, but the gas caught anyway when it splashed down into the puddle he'd created.

His new small fire was nothing like the inferno that had consumed the road from one end to the other in front of him; it didn't even take the attention off of him that he'd hoped. He aimed a savage kick at the head of the nearest zombie and leaped off the truck onto the guardrail.

Balanced precariously above the zombies on the one side and the drop on the other, Wendell took up his shotgun. He had one shell left, and he wasn't sure that it would be powerful enough at the distance. He didn't know if it would work at all. He had seen it in a movie once, but that meant less than nothing in the real world.

It made no difference. He was at the edge. The shot would work, or it wouldn't. He looked down below him. He had always admired the elegance of it. It was a surefire strategy. A fall from a height, and it would be over, one way or the other.

He fired at the truck, and even as he did, he jumped over the ledge. *Goodnight, Gracie,* he thought.

He didn't even see the propane truck explode behind him, incinerating every unliving thing left on the bridge and sending flame jetting in every direction.

CHAPTER THIRTY-TWO

"What do you think you're doing?" demanded Dana.

"I told you," said Becca. "I'm going back for him." She shrugged off the wool blanket Hywell had tried to drape over her shoulders and drew her silver revolver.

"Little girl, after all we risked to get you here, you're going to take off and go after a dead man?"

"He came back for me," said Becca, as if that explained everything. "Besides, I've been saving a bullet for him."

"Becca, it isn't safe," said Dana. "You don't know what's out there."

"Yes I do," she said. "The streets are empty. You saw the explosion. There's nothing out there but my friend, and he's dying. I won't be long, I promise."

Hywell looked to Dana. Dana looked to Talleck. Talleck shrugged his shoulders. "I'd want someone to do for me if it came to it, b'ys."

"Oh, fine," said Dana. "I'll go with you."

"No," said Becca. "I have to do this alone. I'll be back, and if you leave without me, I'll swim to the island and make your lives a living hell."

Talleck chuckled. "I believe you, girl. But if you don't mind, the b'ys and me'll come along, too. If not to keep you safe, the man at least deserves an honor guard for what he did."

Becca nodded. Without another word, she walked off the ferry. Talleck and his people followed at a respectable distance.

It didn't take long to find him. There were mangled corpses scattered all along the street, but he still lay, staring up at the moon, alive for the moment.

He was in bad shape. He was bleeding from dozens of bites and the black tinge to his wounds said that he was already infected.

"You…came back," he rasped. He looked a combination of annoyed and relieved. "After all I…did to get you on…that boat, you fucking came back."

"I had to," she said. "I owe you one." She held up her revolver. He looked puzzled for a second, then nodded.

"That's…the nicest thing…anyone's done for me in years. You always were an…honorable sort of girl." he said. "I always liked that about you."

She knelt down beside him and put the gun against his neck, at the base of the skull.

"I'm so sorry, Keith." Her eyes filled with tears and she couldn't understand why. She had hated him so much, and he had let her know the feeling was mutual. Why was this so hard?

"Come on," said Keith. His breathing was becoming labored. Flecks of black spittle stained his lips. "Don't make this harder than it has to be."

Becca looked into his fading eyes and pulled the trigger.

His body jumped and a spray of black slime shot out the back of his neck as the thing that was taking him over died. Keith lay still, staring up at the moon.

"If it matters," she whispered. "I think you ended up on the right side of the line."

She couldn't see a thing as she staggered back down the empty street. She didn't even notice the figure standing in front of her until she ran straight into it. It reached around her and took hold of her.

"Are you all done?" asked Dana.

"Yeah," she sniffed. "I'm good now."

EPILOGUE

When the ferry first began its nightly run, it had gathered crowds on its return. Every person single-handedly rescued by Captain Talleck and his growing crew of volunteers would turn out night after night to see who arrived with the boat, to shower them with welcome and watch the faces for those they knew. The ferry runs were a nightly influx of hope. People still survived in the city. Maybe their loved ones did, too.

After a while, the number of arrivals slowed to a trickle, then when the power went out across the lake, to a halt. One by one, the gathered masses began to decide that they were it, that the hundred and twenty of them were alone and it was time to start moving forward. Tonight all that was left was Mark, and the woman.

He had seen her around the island once or twice, a vibrant, smiling woman. She carried her swelling belly around in her hands and waved to friends and strangers alike. She had spotted Mark walking the paths at Hanlon's Point one afternoon and waved. He'd waved back, but they never spoke. They met every night at the ferry terminal, and left disappointed after each new arrival, but they never said a word to one another. They were together in hope, but alone in their grief.

The ferry was late tonight. They seemed to be waiting longer every trip, waiting for just one person to walk aboard, but Mark was beginning to think no one was left. The trips across the lake would soon come to an end, and with them, his last hope.

He and his crew were among Talleck's first retrievals. Holed up in a half-constructed building he'd been running the wires through, they had all cheered when they heard the voice on the radio, promising rescue. Only Mark hadn't been happy. He'd tried to convince them to come with him, to help him find Christine, but they wouldn't hear of it. She's all the way on the other side of the city, they'd said, it's too dangerous, she's probably dead anyway, I'm sorry, buddy, I feel your pain.

Mark was never a fighter. His world was one of books and schematics and the ways that the world all fit together to make a light bulb turn on. Faced with the awful choice—go together to the island or go alone into the city—he had come to the island.

Every day that passed since then deepened his despair. He was hanging on a very thin thread of hope that he would see Christine walk off the ferry with their daughter in her arms. He knew that when that hope was gone, there would be nothing left to do but walk into the lake like the zombies had, let the water flow over his head and drown out the light.

He heard the distant rumble of engines that heralded the ferry's return. Off in the murky night the floodlights drew closer and closer. Finally, the huge white boat bumped up against the dock and the ramp slid down.

Slim pickings indeed, thought Mark as he watched a pair of children walk off the ramp. The girl looked older, maybe seventeen, but her eyes were haunted and her face was marred by a mass of angry bruises. The boy was no older than twelve, with the gangly arms and boyish face of the pubescent. They came off the ramp with no family to greet them, no one to help them home. All they had were each other.

At a sudden cry, the boy reached inside his coat and cooed a little song, and a tiny hand reached out to grasp his finger. On hearing the cry, instinct drove him forward; before he knew it he was in front of the kids, staring at the bundle in the boy's arms.

"Hello," said the boy nervously. The girl put an arm in front of him and drew him back behind the protective wall of her body.

"Can I help you?" she demanded. Her eyes were like ice.

"I'm sorry," he stammered, "Is...is that your baby?"

"It is now," said Becca. "She's an orphan. Or are you Child Services?"

"No, I'm...can I ask, what's her name?"

The baby's head swiveled to the sound of his voice. She locked eyes with his and let out a joyful, "Da!"

Don't ever tell a father that all babies look the same. He recognized her in an instant. His voice choked and he dropped to his knees. "Sheila!" he sobbed. "Oh God, I thought I'd never see her again."

The boy and the girl looked at each other. He was convinced, but she looked skeptical.

"What's Sheila's favorite toy?" she asked warily.

"I bought her all kinds of dolls," Mark said. "But all she wanted to play with was a stupid purple octopus."

"He's the real deal, Becks," said the boy.

"Don't call me that," snapped the girl. "Don't just stand there, hand her over." To Mark she said, "She may have learned some new words while you were away. It's not *my* fault."

"Please," said Mark. "Come home with me, both of you. They'll find you a house tomorrow, but for tonight, I'd...I'd be overjoyed if you would stay with us."

The girl looked askance at the woman who waited alone. The expression on her face was puzzled, as if the woman was familiar to her somehow. Throughout the entire reunion, the silent woman had watched with a small, sad smile on her face. She looked back at the ferry, as if Mark's daughter was proof that miracles do occur, and she was waiting patiently for hers. Slowly, almost apologetically, the crewman shook his head and began to close the ramp.

The woman nodded, gave him a sad little smile, and turned to walk away from the dock, into the night, alone.

There was a new sound rising over the water. From far away came the mosquito whine of a small motor boat coming closer. The two youths looked up excitedly, and the woman stopped to listen.

Dana Campbell's tiny boat bumped up against the dock, scraping along the hull of the ferry to come to rest alongside it.

Wendell Jenkins needed the crewman's help to climb out of the boat. He had misjudged the distance from the Expressway's guardrail to the off-ramp below and had landed wrong, turning his ankle on the pavement. After about ten minutes of rolling around clutching his leg and groaning, the heat from the raging fire above had become dangerously intense, and Wendell had been forced to hobble down the ramp, using his Halligan as a cane.

Halfway down, he'd reached up to brush away something that was tickling the back of his neck and flicked away a glob of melted, dangling plastic. Unclipping his firefighter's helmet, he had taken it off to find that it had melted into a twisted mass of red glop. He had come a hat's thickness away from blowing off the top of his head.

He struggled to the top of the dock and nearly sagged with relief when he saw Dylan and Becca standing in the path next to a mousy-looking man with thinning hair. He had feared the worst when he'd seen Keith's body lying on the street.

"Wendell!" shouted Dylan and the kids rushed up to greet him. He gathered them up in a three-way hug, nearly stumbling on his bad leg. Looking up, he saw the thin, awkward man shift uncomfortably and noticed for the first time that he was holding Sheila. Wendell frowned and was about to say something, but then he saw the other figure standing on the dock. Suddenly, all other thoughts were forgotten.

He let go of Dylan and Becca and limped across the dock. There were no words to speak. He took her in his arms and she folded into him like she belonged there.

He drank her in with his eyes. Then he smiled.

"Well," said Wendell. "Aren't you going to say hello, Gracie?"

She gave him *that* smile.

"Hello, Gracie," she said.

###

ACKNOWLEDGMENTS

There are so many people whose care and support were instrumental in the completion of this novel. Luckily, nobody is going to strike up the band to usher me off the stage. I have all the time in the world.

Thanks to the volunteers who read my first draft and offered their feedback and enthusiasm: Jen, Rob and Melissa.

Thanks also to the volunteers who showed up in full zombie makeup to help shoot my YouTube videos and made them look incredible: Darlene Holloway-Sawchuk, Nathan Mackenzie, Nancy Sutton, Kim Broten, Ryan Wheeler, Florie May Ajunan and Allan Phinn.

Thanks to two people I've never met, Max Brooks and David Wong of Cracked.com. Brooks' Zombie Survival Guide and Wong's various and well-researched zombie-themed articles comprised the bulk of the research that I did before beginning this book.

Deborah Riley-Magnus, dean of Assent Academy, whose knowledge of marketing strategies knows no bounds.

Les Denton, my editor at Bad Day Books, who made herself available 24/7 for even the smallest of problems and the stupidest of questions.

And of course, to my wife, Jennifer, whose support, encouragement and love have kept me going through this and so much more, who was willing to read the book despite an uncompromising hatred of zombies (and like it anyway), thank you and thank you and thank you again. There's no one I'd rather have at my side at the end of the world.

ABOUT THE AUTHOR

Born in Ontario, Canada, Brian Malbon has been all across Canada as a professional driver – from bus to truck to heavy mining equipment. He is a former volunteer firefighter, video editor, and film student (with a single credit on imdb.com), a husband and a father of two.

Brian has always had a passion for writing and creating new worlds, and a morbid fascination with horror movies. His particular terror of zombies coupled with his new found worry for his baby daughter led to the creation of *Sheila: Baby's First Zombie Apocalypse*, his first novel.

Brian lives in Northern Alberta with his family.

If you enjoyed reading this, I would appreciate it if you would support my work by posting a review online where you purchased this book.

Thank you,
Brian

www.brianmalbon.com
www.sheilasurvivesthedead.com
www.brianmalbon.com/blog
Twitter: @MalbonBrian
www.facebook.com/Brian-Malbon

CPSIA information can be obtained at www.ICGtesting.com
Printed in the USA
LVOW01s0137180915

454496LV00013B/128/P